BETRAYING

THE

CROWN

T0017841

ALSO BY TP FIELDEN

The Miss Dimont Mysteries

The Riviera Express

Resort to Murder

A Quarter Past Dead

Died and Gone to Devon

The Guy Harford Mysteries

Stealing the Crown

Burying the Crown

BETRAYING THE CROWN

— A —
GUY HARFORD
MYSTERY

TP FIELDEN

THOMAS & MERCER

This is a work of fiction. Names, characters, organizations, places, events, and incidents are either products of the author's imagination or are used fictitiously. Any resemblance to actual persons, living or dead, or actual events is purely coincidental.

Text copyright © 2022 by TP Fielden
All rights reserved.

No part of this book may be reproduced, or stored in a retrieval system, or transmitted in any form or by any means, electronic, mechanical, photocopying, recording, or otherwise, without express written permission of the publisher.

Published by Thomas & Mercer, Seattle

www.apub.com

Amazon, the Amazon logo, and Thomas & Mercer are trademarks of Amazon.com, Inc., or its affiliates.

ISBN-13: 9781542017428
ISBN-10: 1542017424

Cover design by Ghost Design

Printed in the United States of America

For
Charles Thornberry

CAST OF CHARACTERS

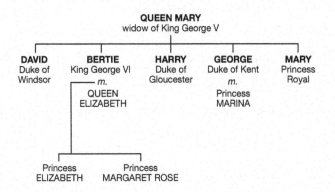

GUY HARFORD – Artist, Palace courtier, reluctant spy

RODIE CARR – Burglar

RUPERT HARDACRE – MI6 officer

ALAN 'TOMMY' LASCELLES – The King's Private Secretary

EARL of BLACKWATER – Former aide to Prince of Wales/King Edward VIII

LAURA, COUNTESS of BLACKWATER – Estranged wife of Lord Blackwater

TED ROCHESTER – Journalist

OSBERT LOTHIAN – Acting deputy to Tommy Lascelles

JOSEPHINE (FOXY), COUNTESS OF SEFTON – Guy's former girlfriend, now married to Lord Sefton

FANNY GOLDINGTON – Courtesan

KING ZOG – King of Albania

ELENA HOFFMAN – Dancer, Vic-Wells Ballet

SIMON GREEN – Dancer, Vic-Wells Ballet

MICK (MIKHA) – Dancer, Vic-Wells Ballet

PETE (PYOTR) – Dancer, Vic-Wells Ballet

RONNIE MORGAN – King George V's valet

ARTHUR SCABBARD – King's Messenger

JOE CARSTAIRS – Island-owning eccentric

CAREY FAIRFAX – Equerry to the Duke of Windsor

AGGIE – Lady clerk, Buckingham Palace

CHAPTER ONE

Summer, 1943

The old Austin rounded a bend and nearly went into the ditch. A powerful motorbike in the centre of the narrow road was aiming straight at them at high speed, the driver not seeming to care whether he hit them or not.

'You stupid idiot!' shouted Guy Harford, the words choking in the back of his throat as they missed each other by inches. But the man on the bike, a ghoul-like face hidden behind oversized goggles, just flashed them an evil grin and flicked a contemptuous gesture with his hand.

'You OK?' Guy said to his passenger.

'Dunno why you brought me up 'ere anyway,' replied Rodie Carr. 'I thought you were takin' me down the pub. I don' like all this fresh air.'

The canvas top was down, the better to enjoy the sunshine, but without its protection, if the bike had hit them, they'd all be dead.

'I just wanted to take a quick look . . . but if you don't feel . . .' He could see she was shaken – or maybe it was just the wide open spaces around Windsor Castle that were making her feel queasy. Burglars tended to be city dwellers. 'Go back then?'

'Go on. But let's not 'ang about.'

The Austin trundled up the hill and turned a corner to be confronted by an odd-looking castellated building, its tall tower pinkly blushing in the late afternoon sunlight. But though chirpy in appearance, Fort Belvedere seemed deflated in spirit as they approached.

'Nobody about,' said Rodie, looking round. 'Quiet as the grave.'

'That's because it's out of bounds. We're not supposed to be up here.'

'Oh good,' she said, brightening. 'I never do what I'm told!'

'Seriously. Nobody comes here any more. The lady clerks say it's cursed.'

The car came to a halt in the circular gravel driveway and they got out.

'That view! Amazin'!' she said, skipping to the edge of the terrace and looking out over Virginia Water to the hills beyond.

He came to join her. 'Isn't it. Now turn around and look at this – to me, the most important building in royal history,' he said. 'The reason I had to come up here and take a look.

'Forget Buckingham Palace, Windsor Castle, the Tower of London, all the rest. *This* is the place where monarchy fell to its knees. The abdication, Rodie!'

A pair of rooks high in the yew trees barked their disapproval of this reminder of an inglorious past – but Rodie wasn't listening. 'C'mon, let's go and take a look around!' she said joyously. 'At this *important* old pile.'

'Oh no! No, no!' Guy grabbed at her arm. 'Not a chance! The Fort's off-limits. It's not to be mentioned, not spoken of. It doesn't exist.'

'In that case nobody'll mind us going in to take a non-existent look around, darlin'.' She skipped away.

'No!' barked Guy. 'No! Come away!' But he was talking to a disappearing back. 'It's all locked up!'

She turned, a slight and balletic figure standing for a moment on tiptoe, her eyes stretched wide at the prospect of doing something illegal. 'Since when did that ever bovver me?' she teased, flashing him her glorious smile. 'Trouble with you, mate, is you take yourself too seriously.'

She darted through the arched brick entrance towards the front door. 'Look at this,' she replied disapprovingly, her elbows busy. 'Shockin'. It wasn't even properly shut.'

'No, you can't . . . !' But Rodie had already pulled the large casement window open and was stepping through into the room beyond.

'Come *out* of there!' he ordered, grabbing at her sleeve.

'Bit of a pong in 'ere,' said her muffled voice. 'But nice. Comfy.'

'OK, OK, I'm following you in – but only to make sure you don't pinch anything,' Guy called, irritated.

'Oi! I'm a reformed character. A civil servant! No more burglin' for me.'

'You just did!'

'This is different, darlin, this is *'istory*. You just tole me.'

Rodie led the way through a wide empty space with painted oak panelling into the domed entrance hall. The place seemed much larger inside, with high ceilings and leaded-light windows casting diamond-shaped patterns on the floor. Ahead of them lay a hexagonal room of immense proportions, its bay windows looking out on to the terrace and to the collection of brass cannons which, in an earlier reign, had shone in the sunlight and heralded kings' birthdays with their fusillades.

'This must be it,' said Guy, pushing open the door, his voice echoing in the empty air. 'Where King Edward VIII signed the instrument of abdication. Where monarchy was nearly smashed to smithereens.' Despite the room's nakedness and its odour of abandonment, he found himself overawed. Was it really nearly smashed? Wasn't monarchy supposed to be immune to the caprice of a mere individual – king or not?

'Could do wiv a feather duster. Look at them spiders chasin' each other!' She went over, inspected the glasswork in the window, then ostentatiously drew a heart on the dusty windowpane.

'Stop that!' he said, his irritation growing – this was no place to play games. 'We've had a good look round. Time to go.'

'No fear, I'm going to have the full guided tour now we're 'ere!'

On the walls where once Canalettos had hung there were now brown patches. The paintwork had faded, the elaborate plasterwork in the ceiling appeared shrouded in dust. A damp stain was spreading from one corner high above, and there was a musty smell in the air.

'Depressing,' said Guy. 'A house of the dead. No royal will ever live here again.'

Indeed, once it may have been a magical hideaway for the Prince of Wales, but stripped of the trappings of royalty, it seemed just another old building – big, grand, imposing, but nothing more. It was as if when he hurried away that night in December six years ago, the ex-king packed the magic into his suitcase and took it with him.

Rodie grasped the handle to the ante-room door and gave it a twist. It turned easily and she stepped into the space beyond. A moment later Guy heard an agonised cry and saw her back quickly out of the room, hand at her throat, her face white and pinched, as if she'd suddenly been hit.

'What?' said Guy, striding over. 'What is it?'

'I'm goin' outside,' she said shakily. 'If you're goin' in there be . . . careful.'

Guy pulled the door back. There, on its side in the middle of the floor, lay a body.

The man was unquestionably dead, the legs splayed out and an arm flung up as if trying to catch a cricket ball or hail a cab.

His first thought was to follow Rodie out through the window, jump into the Austin, get away. Things had gone well at the Palace since his mission to North Africa last year, but Guy was still regarded with suspicion by the old guard. Employing an artist, of all people, to do the King's work was a chancy decision and, to be fair, they weren't entirely wrong in their prejudice – things hadn't gone altogether smoothly since he first arrived.

He stood quite still in the doorway, taking in the air, attuning himself to its stillness. He looked round the room, a paler imitation of the one next door – a place where a man might retire with his papers, perhaps, while his wife entertained.

Though otherwise empty, a pair of faded yellow chairs stood like sentries either side of an elaborate fireplace. One had a raincoat thrown over it, the other a leather attaché case.

This is the moment to go, he said to himself. Don't get sucked in.

Rodie came up behind him and put her arm through his. 'I couldn't leave you 'ere,' she said. 'I had to come back. What are you going to do?'

'We should go,' he said in a low voice. 'For a start I shouldn't be here – if it's discovered that His Majesty's factotum bends the rules just for the hell of it and goes for a joyride with his girl-friend to break into Fort Belvedere, that'll be the end. As for you, the police could start asking awkward questions – what with your background . . .'

'What background!'

'Do I have to spell it out, Rodie? You just broke in. You're a burglar – a criminal!'

'Not any more, darlin'; not since your friend employed me as a special civil servant.'

'To burgle on behalf of the government.'

'Why are we standin' here arguing? Come on!'

Outside the rooks set up a mocking chant as if accusing Guy of sedition, or worse. He started to retreat to the car but in that moment suddenly changed his mind.

'I ought at least to find out who it is. Let somebody know. We can't just leave a dead body lying around – who knows when someone else may come by and discover him? It could be weeks.'

'I wonder how he got in,' said Rodie, ever the professional when it came to matters of forced entry. 'Front door's locked – I tried it.'

'Sure to be a back way in,' replied Guy vaguely, advancing across the room to where the body lay. 'He looks vaguely recognisable, but I'm pretty certain he's not one of the Palace crowd.'

'A gennelman,' said Rodie, drawing this conclusion from the state of the man's well-kept shoes. 'Has he been shot?'

'Not that I can see. It could be a heart attack, something like that, but what the devil's he doing here?' He looked down, his artist's eye taking in the detail of the corpse dressed in a tweed suit with a thin gold watch-chain suspended across the waistcoat. The man wore a striped tie – his old school or regiment, Guy estimated – and on the little finger of his left hand there was a small signet ring.

The man's iron-grey hair was cut neatly and everything seemed to point to his being a gentleman of the kind who might socialise in royal circles, but with one exception – the shirt he was wearing had seen better days and looked drab, if not to say dirty. The head was on one side, the eyes shut, and his cheeks had a blueish tinge about them. But there appeared to be no signs of violence, no blood and, given that he looked as if he was approaching sixty, it could be that he'd just died of natural causes. The body was still warm.

'What the hell is he doing here in this place?' he repeated.

Rodie tugged at his sleeve. 'Come on,' she urged. 'You don't want trouble, Guy – let's get out of here.'

'Hang on, I'm just going to see if I . . .' He bent over, his hand feeling inside the man's coat.

'Come ON! Don't dig yourself into a hole you'll never get out of!'

But Guy had the man's wallet in his hand, reaching for the identity card within.

'Oh,' he said.

'What? Who is it?'

'It's Lord Blackwater.'

'Who?'

'Blackwater. A very famous man. One of the close circle round the Prince of Wales. He was the one who helped Mrs Simpson escape to France.'

'What's he doin' here?'

'Good question. And now I know who it is, I'm going to have to report it.'

'Oh *'ell*,' said Rodie. 'I smell trouble.'

The streets around Cambridge Circus were dirty, cramped, and filled with people stepping with care – bomb sites had a habit of throwing their debris back on the pavement in the dead of night just to trip you up. The Luftwaffe, determined to destroy Trafalgar Square, had failed despite their many attempts, and Nelson still stood proudly atop his column, the slumbering lions at his feet untouched.

It was the streets nearest this great metropolitan hub that took the brunt of the bombers' rage and, up here in Cambridge Circus, just a few hundred yards away, the horror of war came as a reminder with every corner you turned. Houses, flats, shops and offices had their innards exposed, with a bath hanging perilously from a first-floor wall, an armchair upside down in the rubble beneath.

But the people marched on – to work, to the pub, to the Tube station, in search of their loved one. Hats were worn at a jaunty angle, workmen whistled, policemen directed the traffic with unnecessary vigour. And through a tiny archway in Moor Street an energetic, cosmopolitan bunch of men and women crowded four times daily, eager to shut the door on the demoralising effects of the conflict and to live again.

Many were refugees, from Poland and Russia, Norway and France – the lucky ones who'd escaped. Once inside they cast off their outer garments and filed into a large first-floor room with a barre attached at waist height around the walls.

'Now *plié*, if you please,' commanded a firm feminine voice from the back. 'Second. First. Fifth. Fourth. Rise . . . and balance!'

In unison they followed her orders, moving on to work their way through *battements tendus* and *ronds de jambe à terre*.

'Lean back against a cloud – and enjoy it!' she ordered, as if this were actually possible. But the dancers did her bidding, quickly lost in the world of dance and a million miles from the death and destruction outside those walls.

These were the ones who'd managed to persuade Madam Vera Volkova they deserved a place in her class, the ones who hoped some unexpected injury or absence at Sadler's Wells might allow them to dance professionally once again soon.

Volkova they called her, apart from the select few, like the fabled Margot Fonteyn, who were allowed to address her as 'Vereshka' – but most of the dancers in this class had only heard Volkova's name whispered with awe in corridors and backstage dressing rooms. Now, here she was, the great Russian prima ballerina, giving classes in London, and here they were too, in with a chance – who said war was all bad?

She clapped her hands. 'Now! Let me see sixteen *grands changements* and then we finish with the *révérence.*'

The feet moved as if tied by invisible string to the hand of a puppet master, before finally the men bowed and the women curtsied, a courtesy not to each other but to their great teacher.

'*Do svidaniya,*' Volkova said, flipping her hand, sending them on their way.

And off they went. In the changing room next door a blond-haired young man was listening to the girl sitting next to him on a bench. 'She asks too much,' she sobbed, her thin shoulders shaking. 'This Volkova is a slave driver.'

'You should eat more,' he said, looking at her thinness. 'When did you last have something?'

'Oh . . .' she said, shaking her head and drying her eyes. 'I . . .'

'Come on,' he said, putting on his shoes. 'There's a little place near here.'

Her name was Elena Hoffman, a refugee from the Anschluss, the theft of Austria's independence by its bully-boy neighbour Germany. She'd been a dancer in the Vienna Ballet at the Staatsoper, but with no more dancing in Nazi Austria, what does a ballerina do?

'I had to leave. I came to Britain, I wanted to dance – I'm *good* enough to dance here,' she said, as they drank disappointing coffee and ate egg rolls in Romilly Street. 'But where is my chance? Where are the productions? So few!'

'So what do you do meanwhile? To make ends meet?'

She pushed her straggly hair away from her face and eyed the man. 'Do you really want to know?'

He paused and looked round the café. 'Look,' he said, 'we meet after class, then we go our separate ways – I don't know anything about you, and you don't know anything about me. Tell me what you like, and leave the rest – we're here to support each other. Would you like another roll?'

Her eyes fell to the crumbs on her plate. 'Yes. I only know you're called Simon – I don't know your last name.'

'Greenleigh. Only I call myself Green in class – the real name may be familiar to some of the boys and they don't always like to be reminded about the war.'

'Because?'

'My father's a general. Quite a famous one.'

She drank the remains of her coffee, a slight twist of the mouth as she put the cup back on its saucer. 'A general? What does he think of you dancing? Shouldn't you be . . . ?' The question always arose in class, unspoken and unanswered – what were these able-bodied boys, muscular enough to lift a ballerina over their heads, doing here in Soho when men were losing their lives in Tripoli and North Africa?

Simon shook his head. 'When we know each other better,' he said. 'Tell me about escaping from Vienna – the Nazis were rounding up Jews in Austria even in '38?'

'My uncle put me on a train to Milan, then I caught a ship from Genoa. It was chaos. There were over two thousand people on a vessel meant for eight hundred, and for the first time in my life I understood the word "panic".'

'And then?'

'I got to Southampton, made my way to London. I'd been given an address in Kilburn. I have a room there. And now I have freedom. I live to dance – there's nothing else for me!'

'Me too. Come on, let's go and get a drink somewhere.'

She looked at him. 'When I said I live only to dance, Simon, I mean it. No romance, I don't have it in me.'

He smiled at her. 'Oh,' he said, 'you needn't worry about me when it comes to that.'

10

CHAPTER TWO

No matter that the war was far from won, a parade was always good for morale – and to celebrate Britain's victory in the Battle of Britain three years before, Air Force chiefs dreamt up a glamorous show of strength in front of Buckingham Palace.

That so many men could be torn from their duties while the nation still needed their fighting skills seemed remarkable, but here they came, squadron after squadron of men in their light-blue uniforms, marching from right to left, from The Mall round the Victoria Memorial and across the face of the Palace.

At the main gate, the King and Queen took the salute while onlookers in St James's Park and on the steps of the memorial watched with approval. It was magnificent, a show of military splendour quite the equal of the Changing of the Guard. From his special vantage point the *News Chronicle* man sketched words into his notebook, knowing that his glowing prose would be read in Berlin the following morning. He was writing not to comfort the British public, but to impress the hell out of Hitler.

'Is there much more of this?' he tiredly asked the Air Ministry man by his side.

'What's that?' the man snapped disapprovingly – it had taken him three months to pull this show together and he didn't care for Rochester's tone.

'It's boring.'

'I just saw you write down the word "uplifting". What's the matter with you!'

'I want my lunch,' said Ted Rochester sourly. Once upon a time he'd have been invited inside the Palace for a drink along with other favoured pressmen once the day's business was concluded – but no longer. Since the discovery of his plan to write a tell-all book about the foibles and frailties lurking in the closets of Britain's ruling house, Rochester was on the outs. The Ministry man had even ensured the chair he sat on had a wonky leg.

'Percy here will take you off to the pub,' he said grimly. 'Buy you a drink. You like The Pig and Whistle, I think.'

'Are you coming?'

'Sorry, old chap, lunch with Their Majesties.' He said it slowly to let it sink in.

'I'm off,' said Rochester angrily.

'Here's a list of the units and squadrons taking part today. Make sure you get 'em all in, or someone will be having a word with your editor.'

Rochester took the roneoed sheet and stuffed it crossly in his pocket. Shaking Percy off, he wandered down The Mall away from the Palace, pushing his way through the crowd hoping for a bit more pageantry before lunch. They were going to be disappointed – there was a war on and the military had to get back to work.

As he reached the foot of St James's Street he saw a familiar figure walking towards him, an intense expression on his face.

'Guy! What a surprise! Haven't seen much of you since you came back from Tangier! What an adventure that was!'

'Oh,' said the courtier, not bothering to hide his displeasure. 'Ted.'

'I've missed our little chats.' In time-honoured tradition the journalist placed himself in front of his prey in a determinedly obstructive manner, certain that Harford's good manners would not allow him to brush past. 'Isn't it time we resumed normal service? The war isn't over yet, and frankly your royal master and mistress are looking a trifle boring at the moment. Need a bit of spice put into their act.'

Since his arrival at the Palace it had been part of Guy's duties to feed titbits to Rochester to keep up public interest in a monarch and wife who could, occasionally, seem a trifle dull. To start with the plan had worked – Rochester was a prolific writer who not only filled the pages of his Fleet Street newspaper but also wrote, under a pseudonym, a column in the New York papers. But he'd come unstuck when the offer of riches to write a tell-all tome about some of the House of Windsor's less reputable habits was discovered, and the information supply was cut off.

'Really, Ted, you're a terrible rogue. Do you honestly think we're ever going to do business again? After what you did? That disgraceful book?'

'Look,' said Rochester, his habitual oily smile on his face, 'I'm a journalist. What d'you expect? I'm not some whited sepulchre – you have to take the rough with the smooth. Never made a secret of it.'

'Well, good luck, is all I can say,' said Guy, stepping around Rochester. 'Now if you'll excuse me, I have to get back to the Palace.'

'Come and have a drink.'

'No thanks.'

'Go on. On expenses.'

'What's the point? I've nothing to tell you.' Guy was backing away now in a half-turn, making his escape, when suddenly he came to a standstill.

'On the other hand,' he said slowly, 'where were you thinking of?'

'Pig and Whistle. The private bar – we've chatted there before, it's safe enough.'

'OK. If we must.'

The two men made their way up a side alley on the north side of Pall Mall, then turned a corner into a small passageway where The Whistle stood, almost invisible, a gloriously hidden secret.

'Sudden change of heart then, is it?' said the journalist as he brought the pint jugs over to their table in the corner. The private bar was deserted, though it was almost lunchtime. 'You suddenly saw the truth of what I was saying? That Ma and Pa' – his names for Their Imperial Majesties – 'are looking a shade dusty these days?'

'No,' said Guy. 'This is going to be a private exchange of information, OK? I'm going to ask you some questions, then in return I'll tell you something you'll want to hear. House rules – absolute privacy on the source of this.'

Rochester's lips were working. Was he finally being allowed to climb out of the professional hole he'd dug himself? Life had been a nightmare since the book incident, with precious few exclusives from his usual sources as they put distance between themselves and this marked man.

'Of course, of course!' he jabbered. 'Another?'

'No thanks, I've hardly started this one.'

'A whisky, maybe?'

'Look,' said Guy, 'don't take this as a resumption of normal service. It's a one-off. You help me, and I help you.'

'Go on, then.'

'Lord Blackwater. What do you know?'

Rochester looked at him sideways. 'What d'you *want* to know?'

'Anything. Pretend I know nothing. He was one of the old king's closest friends. In the days when he was still Prince of Wales, HRH would stay at Castle Blackwater when he was hunting up that way. During the abdication crisis, Archy Blackwater became invaluable to Mrs Simpson – ferried her away to the South of France, and for a moment he became almost famous. But that was six years ago, Ted. What happened to him after that?'

Rochester leant forward over the table. 'Why are you asking?'

'If you're lucky I'll tell you. But only if you give me something I don't know.'

'My goodness, Guy, you've come on a long way since I first met you – suddenly you're ver9y hard-bitten!'

'It's dealing with rats like you, Ted. My Palace work is supposed to be about more important things, but unfortunately I got landed with talking to you lot. Now go on, tell me what you know.'

Rochester lit a cigarette, enjoying the fact that Guy would have to wait while he teased out the moment.

'Well,' he said finally, 'it's an interesting story. You know, of course, that when he came back from Mrs Simpson in the South of France he was *persona non grata* with your boss. Anybody who'd had anything to do with the outgoing king was blacklisted from court, and Archy was one of the figureheads of the Fort Belvedere crowd.'

At the mention of this Guy winced slightly, but nodded quickly to Rochester to carry on.

'It was Blackwater's bad luck that the Duke of Windsor then took against him as well. Blackwater was so determined to get back in with the Palace crowd – after all, his family have served the royals for centuries – that he turned down the invitation to go to the Duke's wedding at Chateau Candé in '37.

'So now he was out with both lots, the King and the ex-king, and he took it badly. At the same time his wife – d'you know Lally Blackwater? A really tough old coot – finally decided she'd had enough and kicked him out. He had, let's say, a *varied* private life and I think she finally saw through him. A bit of a coup, marrying a five-hundred-year-old title with enough money to drown in, plus

15

a moated castle and Lord knows what else, but he wasn't exactly a *husband*, d'you see?'

'Chaps?'

'Lots of 'em.'

'Not unknown,' said Guy, brushing this aside. 'So what happened?'

Rochester took a swig of beer. 'He was always a pretty feeble sort – looked the part, of course, Old Etonian and all that – but it was Lally who wore the trousers. She ran the estate, did the books, kept the show on the road. He just mooched about Blackwater Abbey playing ducks and drakes when he wasn't down here in town. She's the real power.'

'So what happened?'

'Well, he rather fell apart after the abdication – a lot of his friends wanted to stay onside with the new management at the Palace, so they didn't want to be seen with *him*. Somehow, Lally managed to stay in with Ma and Pa – she's big chums with the Princess Royal – so that created a rift in the marriage. And then something happened, I don't know what, and she just kicked him out.'

'What, kicked him out of his own stately home?'

'Well, yes.'

'Let me get you another,' said Guy, and a watery smile slowly spread over Ted Rochester's face. He could smell a scoop a mile away, and Mr Courtier Harford was a lot closer than that. He had only to sit back and wait.

But at the bar, Guy was asking himself whether this was going to work – whether he'd get enough out of Rochester to make the gamble worthwhile – but now he'd started, there was no other choice but to go on. He returned to the table with two more pint mugs.

'And?' he said as he sat down.

16

'It was the right decision. His son will inherit everything in time, but Lally Blackwater will keep the estate intact until then. Lord B started gambling – big sums, not the chicken feed they play for in White's. Bezique, chemmy, blackjack – he was draining the family fortune. And of course he had expensive tastes when it came to his love life. Liked to give handsome tokens of appreciation, let's put it like that.'

'But she kept her hands on the main money.'

'What she could. He had a swanky apartment on Piccadilly, but that had to go. He sold it for absolute peanuts. I wish I'd known, I would have bought it. He ended up renting a house just up the street here from some kids whose parents were killed in the Blitz, so he was paying virtually nothing for it. That gave him the money to gamble more, and play more.'

'Did – does – he drink?' said Guy, hurriedly correcting himself. He still wasn't sure he was going to give Rochester what he wanted.

'It's not that. I think he just lost control of his destiny when he was dropped by the Palace, and you can see their point – they didn't want old chums of the Duke of Windsor drip-feeding information back about how the new management was doing at Buck House. He realised he'd wrong-footed it but there was nothing he could do. He felt he'd somehow disgraced the family name and so he just disappeared inside his own shell.'

Guy looked at him. 'How d'you know all this?'

'I'm a journalist. We may seem like rats to you, but even rats have their uses. Now tell me what you were going to tell me.'

'Wait a minute, wait a minute. Let's just go back – so he was estranged from his wife . . .'

'His son Lord Waterbeach too. Who sided with Mother.'

'. . . and running out of money. Was he the type, d'you think, to take his own life?'

Rochester joyfully leant back in his chair. 'Ah!' He smirked. 'So the poor old blighter's dead, eh? What was it – a pistol? Pills? Hanging from the chandelier by his braces?'

'Don't be so disgusting!' said Guy. 'It's a man's life we're talking about!'

'So he's dead.'

'Yes.'

'And you're asking me all this because . . . ?'

Because like Lord Blackwater I've been frozen out, thought Guy bitterly. Because when I reported his death to my bosses, there was all hell to pay – a colossal row about breaking the rules by going up to Fort Belvedere when it was out of bounds. And further breaking the rules by burgling the place. Further still, doing it with the help of a known criminal. And even further still, it being discovered that you're having a relationship with the woman who occupies your bed in your so-called artist's studio down by the Chelsea riverfront. And all this after we have leant over backwards to make you welcome at the Palace!

'Go on, then,' said Rochester, a gleam in his eye. 'Spill the beans.'

I can't tell you that I've probably been fired, and the only way out of it is to find what Blackwater was doing at the Fort. To quickly solve the mystery before some further scandal emerges that might damage the King and Queen. And to keep the truth away from the police – if they get to hear the details of Blackwater's passing they'll be all over it with their hobnail boots and the stories will start to leak out. The only way is to, how shall we say, manage the news.

'Tell me this,' said Guy, delaying the moment. 'Did he have a . . . friend? A special friend?'

'Not that I know of. He used to go around with a few hangers-on, but nobody special, I don't think.'

'Nobody who might want to cause him harm?'

18

'Oh! Don't tell me he was *murdered?*' Rochester had to restrain his hands from reaching for notebook and pencil. Damn and drat the RAF and their snooty minder from the Air Ministry – they won't even make a paragraph on page six if this story is what I think it is!

'No note-taking. Here's the story. Lord Blackwater, as you guessed, is dead. He was found in a car in Windsor Great Park, some long distance from the castle. No foul play, he appears to have had a heart attack but we won't know until the post-mortem.'

Rochester sat quite still. 'Are you giving this to me as an exclusive?'

'On two conditions. The story's embargoed until I've had a chance to let the family know. Second, you agree to help me with any further questions I've got. They may come thick and fast in the next few days and I want to be certain you'll be around to help when I need it.'

'On my word of honour.'

'Honour?' laughed Guy scornfully. 'You're a journalist!'

Half a mile away in Quaglino's, two women with jaded expressions and empty coffee cups sat lingering over a last cigarette while gazing at the fat, chain-smoking figure at a nearby table.

'Why they call him a king I don't know,' said Esme Ferguson-Fergusson dismissively. 'Look at him!'

'Zog? Because he's stinking rich – richer than our King, that's for sure,' replied her companion, who answered to Lady Sutch. 'All those bars of gold he took with him when he fled Albania. Enough to pay off our war debt *and* have enough left over for a party at The Ritz!' The King, engrossed in entertaining a lady with an impressive bosom, did not notice their interest. 'And what's he's doing fooling around with Fanny Goldington I really don't know,' Esme went on, 'when Queen Geraldine is so gorgeous.'

'Guess.'

'Well, that's pretty obvious. But Fanny's tricky, always causing trouble. Men get their fingers burnt.'

'Well, Queen Geraldine's mother better not get to hear about it. She's a dreadful old dragon. Thrilled, of course, that her daughter is a queen.'

'You would be, if you come from Noo Yawk. I gather that she's living with them out in the country somewhere.'

'Her and about fifty others – the Zogs come from a bankrupt country but they've got more household staff than the rest of London put together.'

Caroline Sutch took a last sip from her cup and shuddered. 'That lunch was awful. I shall be remembering the lentil soup for the rest of the day.'

Her friend wasn't listening. 'There's a war on,' she said absently, the excuse for everything. 'Fanny's going to get very rich very soon if she goes on lunching like that. But think of *that* bouncing on top of you.'

'And think of his breath, dear. He never stops smoking.'

They drifted up the stairs and out into Bury Street, adjusting their tiny hats as they went; not everyone had urgent war work to go to.

Esme nudged Caroline. 'Isn't that Guy Harford walking up the street?'

'Haven't seen him in years. We used to dance together in the Café de Paris but then he disappeared. Went to art school in Paris, then inherited a house in Morocco and never came back.'

'Still handsome.'

'Mm. He was going to paint my portrait, or so he said. But you know what that is – just a ruse, like singers saying they've written a song about you.'

Esme was jealous of this since nobody had ever offered to paint her or sing her name, but then she was haughty, which maybe explained it.

'What's he doing back here?'

'I heard he was some high-up at Buck House.'

'*Guy*? Some sort of joke, surely?'

'Gerald told me. Bit of a jack-of-all-trades but apparently highly regarded.'

Oblivious to their scrutiny, Guy made his way slowly up Bury Street, his head filled with the information Ted Rochester had given him – was it enough to prise open the door on Archy Blackwater's death, to find the truth, and deter the palace backstabbers from doing their worst?

The scene he'd had in the Private Secretary's office that morning had been particularly unpleasant. Tommy Lascelles, now elevated to a position that made him effectively managing director of the royal family, had handed the problem to a new sidekick, Major Osbert Lothian, a vicious Scotsman who, it was plain to see, didn't believe the silver dirk stuck in the top of his sock was purely ceremonial.

'Seems to me you've shot your bolt, Harford,' he said with a supercilious smile. 'We've had problems with you before, I hear. Not sure what a chap like you is doing in a place like this anyway.'

'I often wonder that myself,' replied Guy, smoothing his hair back. If he was about to walk the plank he certainly had no intention of showing any fear.

'We expect certain . . . standards. Even from chaps who are artists. You were trespassing at Fort Belvedere!'

'Yes, I've already told Tommy how sorry I am.'

'*He* won't save you,' said Lothian, waving his head in the direction of the next-door office. 'He's got bigger fish to fry. You're my pigeon now.'

Lucky me, thought Guy. Not a brain in the man's head even if his turnout is immaculate – though why he insists on wearing his kilt south of the border I have no idea.

'To add to the trespass there's the breaking and entering. Then there's the matter of the very questionable woman accompanying you. A security risk, I think you must agree, in a highly sensitive area.'

'She's a civil servant. Highly regarded, I'm told. As for security, she's signed the Official Secrets Act so she's as secure as you are. Sir.'

The Scotsman's eyes contracted. 'Your career's in the balance, Harford. I'd watch my P's and Q's if I were you.'

'What do you want me to do, Major Lothian?'

'Find out what Lord Blackwater was ruddy well *doing* at the Fort, of course! Why the hell was he there? And how did he come to die? If this gets out, there'll be a terrible stink. The King's doing awfully well just at the moment – the people are behind him. The last thing we want is the whole ruddy abdication business being hauled out and dusted down!

'Blackwater's a controversial character, a Vicar of Bray – supporting one side, then the other. No wonder in the end he fell between two stools. But again I say – what the hell was he doing there? How did he die?'

Unbidden, Guy lit a cigarette. Lothian looked down his nose and stiffened visibly but said nothing.

'The post-mortem will tell us how he died,' he replied. 'Obviously I'll make inquiries and see what's known about Blackwater and see if I can talk to his friends – unofficially, of course. See what's known about his final movements. I take it you want to keep the police out of this.'

'Too risky to have them in.'

'We'll have to let the family know . . .'

'That'll be your job. Do it personally.'

'. . . and put out something to the press.'

'The *press*? What are you dragging them into this for?'

'Better to get our version of events out first. Feed the hand that bites us, ha ha.'

'Very funny,' said Lothian, stony-faced. 'But if you can't sort this out satisfactorily I have something else in mind for you.'

'Oh?' Guy didn't like the way he said it.

'Assistant Keeper at Holyroodhouse. There's a vacancy. Might be just up your street, what with lots of paintings on the walls and all that.'

'Well, that's very kind, but I fear I must decline in advance – I've a new exhibition of my own paintings coming up in the autumn and, when I'm not here, I am working to a deadline,' said Guy, alarmed. 'An important exhibition.' The man needed to know he had another life outside the palace railings.

'*You'll go where you're sent!*' bellowed Lothian. 'So you can forget that exhibition right now!'

It was this exchange that was uppermost in Guy's thoughts as he headed up Bury Street towards Piccadilly. He saw two women on the pavement and stepped automatically into the gutter to allow them room to pass.

'Guy!' said one of them. 'Guy *Harford*!'

Automatically he raised his hat. 'I . . .'

'You don't remember us, do you?' they chorused. 'Esme Carter, only now I'm Mrs Ferguson-Fergusson.'

'Oh, hello.'

The other woman leant forward and kissed his cheek. 'Guy!' she breathed; he could smell her perfume. 'Surely you remember those nights dancing to Bert Ambrose in the Café de Paris?'

'Oh, hello, Caroline,' Guy said distractedly. 'How nice. Must be ten years.'

'I'm Lady Sutch now.'

'How grand. What sort of lady – countess, marchioness? I don't know the name, I'm sorry to say.'

'Only a baronet, I'm afraid. *Sir* Hywel Sutch to you.'

'Ah yes. Old castle in Merionethshire?'

'Reduced to rubble these days, and not by the Luftwaffe. Even the Tudors had gerry-builders, darling. It's a sort of bungalow now. I tend to keep away. Hew has his sheep to keep him warm.'

'Well, this is lovely, but I have to get along. These days I'm—'

'We know what you do, darling. It's *you* who's the grand one.'

Then they told him about King Zog and his popsy – because a man who works for a king might need to be kept informed about what other kings are doing on his patch – and what an absolute nightmare Queen Geraldine was.

Guy expressed interest before raising his hat once more and making his excuses.

Viewing his retreating back, Lady Sutch said to her companion, 'What do you think?'

'Oh *yes*,' said the other, digging her in the ribs. '*Very* much so, darling!'

CHAPTER THREE

It was a sketch no more than the size of a foolscap envelope, but Guy had had it framed and hung on a wall where it caught the light from the long window where he painted.

The head was turned away as if in disapproval, the neck stretched taut, the profile sharp and commanding, the angular cut of the hair falling to the jawline. An experimental splash of colour had been added but this was not a whole painting; merely a preliminary work by Augustus John, their neighbour.

It showed Rodie Carr as she was – proud, brave, agile, funny. Not a cockney burglar, but somehow more like an important figure from history.

They'd had a row about it. The bottom-pinching genius had spotted Rodie in Tite Street, the Chelsea avenue stretching back from the river where their studios were housed, and chased her into The Surprise, the local pub. From then on he would not let her go until she agreed to sit for him. Rodie never knew what particular brand of jealousy had caused Guy to lose his temper – was it because John was by far the better painter? Or because, as Tommy Lascelles had said, he had 'farmyard morals'?

Either way there'd been a stinking row, the consequence of which was that Rodie finally moved in with Guy. And Guy rescued John's sketch and had it framed.

'Ain'tcha going to buy the finished article?' she'd scolded, but Guy pointed out she could afford a small house in Elephant and Castle, where she came from, for the price the old goat charged for his pictures. So all that remained was the sketch. It had in many respects become his inspiration.

The object of John's lust was leaning over the balcony looking at the river when Rupert Hardacre came up behind her.

''Lo,' she said, looking over her shoulder. 'Are you dancin' tonight? There's Billy Cotton on at the Lyceum. Guy can't go.'

'Sorry,' he said, 'work to do. And we need to talk, Rodie, so can you come inside?'

'I'm watchin' a boy and girl on a bench down there. He wants to kiss her.'

'This is quite important.'

''E's shy. She wouldn't mind, but I can see she's not that keen. Sometimes it's nice to be kissed by someone you're not interested in.'

'If you mean . . .'

'Not *you*, Rupe!' She laughed her jagged laugh. 'You don't kiss, do yer?'

'I've got to talk to you about Lord Blackwater.'

She turned and eyed his dandified suit, silk tie, polished shoes. 'It's Saturday,' she complained. 'Can't we leave the work till Monday?'

He shook his head and unfastened a battered old attaché case. There was a stillness in the vast cavern of the artist's studio, sunlight pouring on a rag covering an unfinished oil that stood on an easel in the corner. Since Guy Harford's heart ailment prevented him from fighting, he gave all his energies to oil and canvas – when not protecting the royal family from their foes, at home and abroad.

Rupert sat on a sofa and patted the space next to him. 'Come on. Sit down and look at these,' he said, drawing out a handful of photographs. 'Is that him? The man you found dead at the Fort?'

26

'Why don't you do this with Guy? He was there, you don't need me.'

'On the contrary, Rodie, I do. Is that him?'

The first picture gave very little away. It was of a peer of the realm dressed in ermine and scarlet robes, his tiaraed wife by his side, standing in a queue outside Westminster Abbey.

'The 1937 coronation,' encouraged Rupert.

'Can't see 'is face,' said Rodie. 'Ruddy great crown on 'is 'ead.'

'Coronet.'

''E looks a bloomin' fool. Show me another.'

Rupert laid out three more pictures of a man with a slender figure, a boyish smile, a mop of blond hair falling over his forehead, and dark rings under his eyes.

'That him?'

'He looked older.'

'You do, when you're dead.'

Rodie got up and strode back to the window. 'OK,' she said, 'what's this all about?'

'There's a problem over Lord Blackwater's death. I need you to fix it.'

She shook her head. 'That's Guy's department. Royal, an' all that.'

'Yes and no. He probably told you he's in a spot of bother himself.'

'No, 'e didn't! 'E never tells me anything!'

'Apart from how beautiful you are. I've heard him do that.'

'Butterin' parsnips! 'E told me when we finally got together, an' 'e certainly took 'is time about *that*.' She said it *thett*, emphasising the word with a hefty inbuilt irony. ''E told me 'e wouldn't talk shop when 'e came 'ome. And that suits me fine. A complete caper what goes on there at the Palace, if you ask me.'

'Well, I'm going to ask you to do a bit of capering yourself.'

She walked back towards him as if on tiptoe, eyeing him suspiciously as she came. 'Oh yes?'

'I want you to hop back to Fort Belvedere and take a good look round. I gather you only went into a couple of rooms – I need you to do the full works.'

'No!'

'Yes.'

'No! What would Guy say? If 'e's in trouble like you say he is, how's that going to make him look if I get me collar felt?'

'Look,' said Rupert, 'this isn't about Guy. It's about Lord Blackwater. We've got a problem.'

'You said that.'

'Then let me explain. And give me a glass of beer.'

She went over to the kitchen area and opened a brown screw-top bottle. 'Stout. That's all there is.'

'Excellent.' He put his feet up on the sofa. 'This is how the story goes, Rodie – please pay attention because it's complicated. What Guy doesn't know – and doesn't need to know – is that my department had their eye on Lord Blackwater long before the abdication and his famous drive through France with Mrs Simpson.

'Blackwater has – had – a wealth of important contacts, including a man called Charles Bedaux. French–American. It was through Blackwater that the Duke and Duchess of Windsor ended up getting married in Bedaux's chateau, not far from Paris.

'The man's pro-Nazi. He's been arrested by the Americans but they refuse to tell us how he comes to be connected to Blackwater and, through Blackwater, to the Windsors.'

'None of our business, then,' said Rodie firmly. 'Let the Yanks get on with it. What d'you say to Billy Cotton? Say yes, Rupe!' Clearly the prospect of going back to the Fort bored her rigid.

Rupe took a sip of stout and shuddered. 'That's horrible! Now listen – Bedaux has been dealing with the Nazis since I don't know when. It was through him that the Duke and Duchess went to Germany in 1938, and shook hands with Hitler. The man ultimately responsible for this shameful hook-up was Blackwater – and now he's dead.'

'Are you saying that somehow the Nazis killed him, just because this Beddowes has been arrested?'

Rupert shook his head wearily. 'Bedaux, Rodie, not Beddowes! I have no idea. All I know is this: Bedaux will try to talk his way out of it by laying the blame elsewhere; anybody in that situation would do the same. So when he starts singing to the US authorities about the Duke of Windsor and Hitler – d'you see? We could be put in a very embarrassing situation.

'All the more embarrassing because the Duke is now Governor of the Bahamas, whose nearest landfall is . . . the United States. Anything that comes out when Bedaux sings is likely to smash Anglo–American relations, just at a moment when together we can win the war.'

'What d'you want, then?'

'Go back to Fort Belvedere. You didn't have any difficulty getting in there first time round – get inside and see if anything's been left behind.'

'What sort of thing?'

'Anything that shows what the hell Blackwater was doing there. He must have got in there somehow – I don't see a peer of the realm having quite your skills in housebreaking – so why and how did he get in? Did he leave anything in any of the other rooms?'

'Surely the cops will have done that when they went to get the body?'

'Not necessarily – they're royal cops, their job is protecting, not detecting. Just anything you can find. We need to know about the Blackwater–Windsor–Bedaux connection before it blows wide open in the US press. Then, if necessary, we can get the Duke and

Duchess out of Nassau and bring them home before the damage is done. And, of course, construct a plausible cover story to handle whatever the Duke was doing with the Nazis, both during his time in Germany and after.'

Rodie looked at him shrewdly. 'Am I doing this for the royal family, or because Guy's deep in the doo-doo?'

Rupert shrugged.

'If the cap fits,' he said offhandedly, tossing away his cigarette.

◆ ◆ ◆

Blackwater Abbey lay at the end of a mile-long drive through flat golden fields scattered with yew trees. Occasionally a bouncing squirrel brought the landscape to life, but otherwise the walk to the entrance gates went undisturbed. Guy had a hole developing in the sole of one shoe, and the sharp gravel underfoot made the walk in the rising heat seem twice as long.

The odd army vehicle swung by, but nobody seemed in a hurry to give a lift to a mere civilian. Ahead a grey stone building, tinged with butter-coloured splashes, rose in eminence, stretching endlessly to left and right. Three hundred years of one family's occupation was reinforced by the shape, weight and sheer number of pillars, windows and flagpoles adorning the frontage.

He trudged on, finally arriving at the side entrance where a military policeman checked his name against a list on his millboard.

'Fambly?' he asked gruffly.

'Well, no, I'm not actually a member of the—'

'I can tell that, sonny. You've come to see the fambly?'

'Yes.'

'West wing. The rest of the house is off-limits to . . . civilians.' He seemed to spit the word, as if nobody had the right not to wear a uniform.

'How do I . . . ?'

'Out-the-door-walk-across-front-of-building-go-right-down-to-other-end-turn-left-turn-left-again,' came the rat-a-tat reply. Guy expected him to add, 'And at the double!' but did as he was instructed and ambled the length of the abbey's frontage past its ornate entrance, shut for the duration, and round to a side door.

The servants must need roller skates to get around this place, he thought, wincing as a grain of gravel finally pierced what remained of his shoe sole.

'Mr Harford?' said a middle-aged lady, hair tied up with a floral scarf. 'Come this way. Lady Blackwater has been waiting for you and the coffee's getting cold.'

He was taken into a tall, mirrored room with gilded pillars, painted panels and long casement windows looking out over parkland. A woman dressed in black rose as he entered and stuck her head on one side.

'We'd given you up.'

'I had to walk from the station. No transport. I'm sorry for the delay.'

She offered no sympathy but waited for him to introduce himself.

'Harford,' he said.

She nodded. 'Laura Blackwater. I had a word with Princess Mary on the phone this morning. Up till then I was disinclined to meet someone who'd been fooling around on royal property but she says you used to be highly regarded at the Palace, so here we are. Gwendolyn will bring coffee.' She was tight-lipped, tense, but not apparently particularly upset that her husband had been found dead barely forty-eight hours ago.

'It was felt I should come and personally let you know the circumstances,' said Guy. 'May I sit?'

The chatelaine nodded slightly, but it was hardly an invitation. I wonder if she's ever had to trek from the station, Guy thought, irritated – forty-five minutes, and in these ruddy shoes too. No wonder her husband spent his time in London, boys or no boys. She's a horror.

'Tommy Lascelles called and gave me the news of Archy's death. He said you broke into the Fort with your girlfriend.'

'Well, it wasn't quite like that, I—'

'Tommy described it as "conduct unbecoming".'

'It's a long story, Lady Blackwater.'

'Make it a short story, Mr Harford. I have a meeting of the War Bonds committee any moment. If you'd managed to arrive on time . . .'

The lady secretary brought coffee, laying it on a side table. There may be a war on, but here at Blackwater Abbey you'd never know it – the silver, the china, the linen napkins and lump sugar lifted by heavy monogrammed tongs, all brought to assist the consumption of reheated black water with barely any taste.

Guy offered his condolences at the sad loss. He described his discovery of the corpse of Lord Blackwater and asked gently if the widow knew what the hell he was doing in the abandoned building.

'How should I know?' she snapped. 'Archy led a separate life, as I'm sure Tommy will have told you. He found the responsibility of running this place too enormous. He ran away. I have no idea where he went, or with whom, and it's a struggle, I can tell you, keeping this place shipshape until my son gets back from the army and can take over.'

I wonder if he ever will, thought Guy. This woman looks like she's finally got what she wants – power, a title, land, the friendship of royalty – and now, her very own stately home to do with as she sees fit. Will she find it easy to relinquish all that once the war's over?

'Look,' he said, 'I don't want to keep you from other business but I'm afraid there are a few questions I must ask.'

'Questions?' she said sharply. '*Questions?* I don't expect to be quizzed by a junior courtier. As Princess Mary said to me only this morning—'

Guy plunged on. 'Lord Blackwater had a – let's say – unusual group of friends in London.'

'The pansies, you mean.'

'That's not a word I'd—'

'Well, I *do*. My husband was stolen from me – *abducted!* – by young men who . . . who . . .'

'Yes, Lady Blackwater, I understand. I just need to discover what on earth Lord Blackwater was doing at Fort Belvedere. There are, let's just say, disturbing ramifications. To do that I need to find out who was closest to him at the time of his death.'

She gave a shuddering laugh. 'Closest? You mean who was the last one in his bed? Which of those . . . catamites . . . had most recently helped themselves to his cufflinks and his wallet? They did that, you know, time after time.'

'Can you give me a name?'

'Who? *Why?*'

'Well, let me put it this way, then – do you know the name Charles Bedaux?'

'Of course. One of the Duke of Windsor's less fortunate choices of friends.'

'I understand your husband also knew him well.'

'No idea,' said Lady Blackwater, her eyes narrowing. 'What exactly is this about?'

I haven't a clue, thought Guy. I'm completely in the dark myself but my job hangs on finding out.

'Did Lord Blackwater know Bedaux before the Duke met him?'

'I think I've told you all I know. If you see Princess Mary when you get back to the Palace, please remind her we are doing the Red Cross annual meeting next week.' And with that she got up and walked to the door.

'You've come a long way, Mr Harford. Gwendolyn will see you have a sandwich in the servants' quarters. Good day.'

Well, thought Guy, she's lost a husband but gained her freedom. Naturally she'll wear black until the funeral, but I don't think things could have turned out better for her – so why the icy response to his questions? Was she ashamed of her husband's activities?

Hardly – she talked openly about his boyfriends, the squandering of his cash. But she shut down all questions that referred to Archy Blackwater's Nazi connections, so she must know more. Or . . . the thought slowly formed like mist over a mountain river . . . does she know more about her husband's death than she lets on? It couldn't be, could it, that she had him liquidated so as to grab control of the Blackwater estate?

As Lady Blackwater marched out, the private secretary gave him a sympathetic smile and, beckoning, led him down a long corridor peopled with marble busts of previous residents of the Abbey. 'I expect you'd like a glass of wine,' she said encouragingly. 'We don't get many visitors these days, not since Lordy left. If you like I can join you for lunch – we'll sit on the back terrace in the sunshine.'

'Thank you,' said Guy, relieved – the tension in the drawing room had been almost unbearable. 'Have you worked here long?'

'Ten years. And before you ask, yes, she's a very tough taskmaster. But she's had to be, what with all the hoo-ha over the abdication and all that. Come and sit.'

The sun splashed down on the terrace and in the distance it lingered on the dome of a classical temple, now a fashionable ruin. Gwendolyn poured wine and offered sandwiches.

'Been at the Palace long?'

'A couple of years.'

'Milady's great chum is Princess Mary – d'you see much of her?'

'From time to time but mostly HRH is up at Harewood. They call her the Queen of the North for some reason; I think because no king bothered to go there for two hundred and fifty years. Yorkshire's grateful to have the King's sister paying attention to them.'

She took off her glasses and patted her hair. 'Is there anything I can help you with?' she asked, leaning forward. 'Lady B's not exactly the most communicative person in the world and, just at the moment, with the funeral to arrange and all that . . .'

Guy smiled and nodded. 'Thank you,' he said, 'that's kind. I've heard all about Lord Blackwater's love life. Not so very different from many others I know.'

'But illegal,' she said.

'Let that pass. I'm desperate to find out who he was closest to in the weeks before he died. There's a really quite important consequence to all this which I can't go into, but if there's anything – anybody . . .'

'Drink your wine,' said Gwendolyn, lowering her voice. 'And listen to what I have to say.

'Lordy was hopeless. Good at wearing the ermine, if you know what I mean, not a bad shot, and a fair ballroom dancer, I'll grant you – but that's about it. He made a good choice in marrying Lady B because she wanted to wear the trousers and he let her. She's a formidable horsewoman, you know, strong as an ox. They had just the one son – he's a prisoner of war just now – but there were never going to be any more children.'

'Because of his preferences.'

'Yes. Lady B got all she wanted, and as long as he behaved himself up here that was fine – they'd come to their arrangement and that was that. Things only started going wrong in the run-up to the abdication. Lordy was spending huge quantities of time down at the Fort, presumably helping plot the King's next move. He helped design the swimming pool, recommended the wine, and acted as a kind of social host for the Windsors, bringing down all sorts of people they'd never met.'

'So a very close friend.'

'I don't think you can ever say that about the royals – you should know that. Lady B loves Princess Mary, but does Princess Mary love her back? I doubt it. She's just a useful chum, no more than that. The same with Lordy and the Prince of Wales.'

'Anyway, go on.'

'On his increasingly rare visits up here, he'd occasionally drop an indiscretion which made us all sit up and take notice.'

'Such as?'

'The King planned from the start to marry Wallis and for her to be his queen.'

'Really?' said Guy, startled. 'I thought he wanted to give it all up – the throne, the empire, the whole bag of tricks – "for the woman I love". That well-worn phrase.'

'Not according to Lordy. The plan was definitely that Edward VIII would stay on the throne *and* marry Mrs Simpson – and he talked about it so often she began to want it herself. And he bullied that Ernest Simpson out of his marriage, always begging or telling him it was over. He even followed him into the bathroom one day to order him to give Wallis up. The two of them had it all planned and quite honestly if he hadn't backed off, I fully anticipated that Mr Simpson would find himself run over by a steamroller.'

'So all that "I will give him up" stuff she said when she fled to France was just eyewash?'

'Just that. Have your sandwich. Now, in answer to your question, Lordy *was* a close chum of Charles Bedaux, and it was he who fixed up the Windsors' wedding venue at Candé, the Bedaux family home. It was all done through him.'

'And did Lord Blackwater also fix up for the Duke and Duchess to make that dreadful trip to Germany where they met Hitler?'

She looked at him over heavy horn-rimmed glasses. 'Yes,' she sighed, shaking her head. 'One of his playmates in London was a chap at the German Embassy who helped smooth the path.'

'Nazi?'

'Aren't they all?'

Guy stood up. 'Look,' he said, 'we barely know each other and I'm taking a risk in telling you this, but you've been refreshingly frank with me, and I can tell from your years of service here in this, er, difficult household that you believe in the utmost discretion. I urgently need help in finding Lord Blackwater's last boyfriend – that way I might be able to discover what he was doing at the Fort.'

He explained the Palace fears that Bedaux might spill the beans about the Duke and Duchess's Nazi leanings in return for his release from an American jail. 'The Duke is no longer his friend, despite all the good things Bedaux did for him. It makes the Duke vulnerable, and . . .' His voice tailed off. He couldn't talk about the plan to airlift the Windsors out of their Bahamas exile.

'The situation's desperate. So anything you know, Miss . . .'

'Gwen. This much I know, Mr Harford. Archy Blackwater had become involved in something – I don't know what – that terrified him. The last time he came up to the Abbey he was in a dreadful state, and it wasn't his rackety life – he didn't drink much and he didn't take drugs. Yes, he had a gambling habit, but he only had a certain amount of money to play with . . . No, it was something else, something far worse. He was frightened. One morning I walked into his study with some papers and it was as if I'd come at him with an axe; and him so happy and jolly in the early days when I first worked here.'

'He was being threatened, d'you think?'

'I don't know by whom but yes. Of course all his chums at the German embassy – Ribbentrop and all that lot – pushed off long ago when war broke out, so it can't have been them. Please tell me, do we know how he died?'

'Post-mortem's this evening.'

'Well, if he didn't die of a heart attack I would not be surprised to learn he'd been murdered.'

Guy looked at her for a moment, then got up.

'I really wouldn't repeat that if I were you,' he said, and made his way out.

CHAPTER FOUR

Ted Rochester was scribbling random words in his notebook as the man in front of him distractedly chain-smoked and gave anxious looks to left and right, as if trying to catch the eye of a barman.

'Care for another, Mr Lambert?'

'Let me do this,' said the other, wandering down to the end of the room and opening negotiations with an aproned old soak.

Formidable, wrote Rochester. *Damaged*. He just managed to add *Starved of inspiration* before the famous composer and conductor came back, sploshing two overfull glasses in his hands. They joined the two equally full glasses from which they'd only just begun drinking – clearly being a musician was thirsty work.

'We'll get on to the new show in a moment. First, can we just recap, for the readers, what happened to you and the ballet troupe when you bumped into the Germans back in Holland? And how the hell you escaped with your lives?'

Constant Lambert took a long pull at his glass and banged it down hard on the bar. 'Those idiots at the British Council,' he said savagely. 'A man called Lloyd. We could all have been killed!'

'What happened?'

'Their grandiose idea of taking the dance to Europe. Like taking coals to Newcastle,' spat Lambert, pulling out a crumpled cigarette packet and fruitlessly fumbling inside. 'And long before we got there the tanks were already rolling – fat chance we had of enlightening the masses, they were too busy digging their bomb shelters.'

'Have one of these.'

'Great heavens,' said Lambert, eyeing the gold-banded Sobranie cigarettes Rochester produced. 'How much do they pay you at the *News Chronicle*?'

Obviously a darn sight more than they pay the musical director of the Vic-Wells Ballet, thought Rochester but said, 'Go on.'

'They were just about to go onstage in Arnhem when the Germans invaded – *The Rake's Progress*, since you ask. We were only six miles from the German frontier, only nobody told us that. But you could hear the explosions and the planes and the air raid warnings and people shouting – *not* the time to be dancing! So we got in the bus and scarpered – had to leave the scenery and props behind, half the girls were still in their tutus. The Germans were blowing up the bridges behind us as we went, and by the time we reached our hotel in The Hague, the bombers were right overhead.

'We saw parachutists dropping all round the place, and – you can hardly believe this – the German civilians who lived in the town were leaning out of their windows and taking pot-shots at anybody who was fool enough to be out on the street. Then a bomb dropped on a children's hospital. It was chaos. We were stuck in the hotel and we counted twenty-six air raid warnings that day alone.'

Rochester's pencil slid smoothly over the notebook page. 'Shocking,' he said, shaking his head.

'We were sitting in a café. Frederick Ashton, Robert Helpmann, Margot Fonteyn, Ninette de Valois – all of us! – when a bullet came through the window and fighting broke out in the square. Then when we finally managed to get to the ship to bring us home, a German plane machine-gunned the gangway.'

'But nobody was injured?'

'Mercifully not. By a curious coincidence the ship already had a bunch of dancers aboard who'd been trying to escape Europe for weeks – they seem to have come from all over the place, and what's rather lovely is they've attached themselves to us now, a kind of cadet company. They go to Volkova's dance class every morning and we're never going to be short of substitutes.'

Rochester had almost got what he needed for his column, but not quite. 'I gather things are faring so well with the Vic-Wells that the King and Queen are going to rename it the Royal Ballet,' he said as he rose. This was to be his introductory paragraph, and his headline, but he employed the old trick of making it a statement, not a question. That way it appeared as if he already knew it for a fact, whereas he'd heard only the merest whisper of a rumour.

Lambert's eyes narrowed as he looked over the brim of his glass. 'I wonder how you would know that,' he growled. 'It's supposed to be top secret.'

'As they say on the posters,' rejoined Rochester with a gleeful smile as he picked up his hat and started to walk away. 'Walls have ears.'

◆ ◆ ◆

The composer wandered down the bar in search of less irksome company, a glass in each hand and a vague tune in his head which in earlier days would have sent him scurrying for his manuscript book. He let it linger, hoping it would still be there in the morning.

His unsteady progress caused him to bump into a table where two young people sat, heads together. 'Ah, Simon!' He beamed. 'The most covetable boy in the company! Arnhem, eh?'

'Arnhem,' replied Simon Green, his head twisting oddly. A memory that would last a lifetime.

'G'night.' It was only eight o'clock but the maestro had had a long hard day of rehearsal followed by an hour or two of equally arduous drinking. Maybe Margot, the prima ballerina, would be waiting for him in his bed, though these days more likely not . . . He wandered off, wreathed in dreams.

'You wouldn't think it, but he is quite the most astonishing genius I've ever come across,' Simon said to Elena.

'He looks like a drunk.'

'He is, quite a lot of the time. But the way he holds the whole lot of us together – the music, the dance – in the most commanding way . . . It's incredible.'

She reached over and took his hand. 'You've been so kind,' she said. 'I wish there was something I could . . . but . . .'

Simon smoothed back his sleek blond hair and smiled. 'Better times ahead, Elena,' he said. 'I think your moment may come soon. To step up into the company.'

She started forward. 'Why do you say that? Are you trying to humour me?'

'It's like this,' he said. 'The main company's back from their latest tour and they're exhausted. Coventry, Aberdeen, Leeds, Blackpool – they're fed up being pushed about from pillar to post. They're supposed to be based at the Sadler's Wells Theatre but the powers that be have other ideas for the building – so off they go again on the circuit, round and round they go!'

'Dancing, though – at least they're dancing!'

'Margot . . .' He articulated the name as if it carried some special kind of magic. 'Margot was telling me after class what it's been like these past few weeks. They're all on five pounds a week; they're half-starved because they have to hand over their ration books to their landladies when they get to a town, and the landladies don't care and rob them blind. Their rooms are damp, the loos are usually outside, they're dancing on concrete floors and when they travel

42

it's in the dead of night, crawling through the blackout on trains without heating.

'Some of the girls can't take it any more. I don't know what it is about Margot but she's . . . *untouched* by it all. She's a miracle. But some of the others say they've had it. So there are going to be vacancies in the corps de ballet, Elena, and you're perfectly placed to step up.'

A hungry light shone in the dancer's eye. 'In the repertoire, there are small parts I could dance? Not just stuck in the back row?'

Simon was about to reply when the table was jolted by the bulky figure of Constant Lambert who half-fell into a chair between them, each hand grasping a glass. 'The most covetable boy,' he repeated vaguely, looking at Elena. 'You don't know how lucky you are to have him. Most of the company want him – boys *and* girls, young *and* not-so-young – but here he is with you!'

She thought of the way Simon mentioned Margot Fonteyn's name. Had he . . . They . . . ?

'Well, he . . . I . . .' she answered, shaking her head and leaning back as the musician lolled forward across the table. He smelt, and not just of booze.

'I don't know you, do I?' Lambert said, his florid fleshy face pushed close to hers. 'Where did you spring from?'

'This is Elena Hoffman,' said Simon protectively. There was no need, given the way she sat, her taut figure erect and still, to add that she was a ballerina. 'She was in Vienna, at the Staatsoper . . . but then the—'

'Don't tell me,' blathered Lambert, genial and noisy. 'With a name like that you had to get out. Welcome to the free world! Are you dancing at Volkova's?'

'Every morning,' she replied, nodding fiercely.

'Hoping for a place in the company?'

'Well, I . . .'

Lambert poured the contents of one glass into the other and swallowed the mixture at a gulp, taking out his handkerchief and waving it in a circular motion over his head. 'Alphonse will come,' he said with a genial smile. 'His name's not Alphonse at all, but he knows how to pour a drink – what will you have?'

The young couple looked at one another. The man was a basket case but his company was not unpleasant. There was something about the bulbous untidy figure that marked him down as a genius, even if it was clear he couldn't find his way out of the pub.

'Shouldn't you be . . . ?' said Simon. 'Should I call you a taxi? Won't somebody be expecting you?'

Everyone in the company knew that somebody was Margot, but nobody said.

'I daresay she'll have found someone else to keep her toes warm,' said Lambert, waving his handkerchief again. 'They do get awfully cold. She's always complaining.'

Alphonse, cheeky East Ender with a floppy hairdo, sidled over and took their orders.

'You'll find life a lot different,' Lambert said to Elena, 'if you come and join us. Wolverhampton isn't exactly the City of Dreams, you know. And have you ever seen Luton?'

'That's OK, Mr Lambert – I left my dreams behind in Vienna. There, I was a solo artist – now I'm struggling to get a place in the line. But please don't get me wrong, I live for the dance. Anything, anything!'

'Well,' said the musician, absently looking round to see if there was someone more interesting he could bore, 'all I can say to you both is keep your little romance a secret. Too many jealous eyes and vicious tongues in this company. You never know what trouble you could get in – especially you, Simon.'

The boy blushed slightly, all too aware of the effect he had on the libido of exhausted, hungry, anxious, punctilious dancers. All his adult life he'd been cursed by what Byron called the fatal gift of beauty.

◆ ◆ ◆

With a sinking feeling, Guy climbed the familiar red plush steps up to the Private Secretary's floor at the side of the building. Since his initial rancorous exchange with Osbert Lothian, he'd kept well away, hunkered down in his office in the Royal Mews with his lady clerk Aggie, completing paperwork, planning future events and hoping the dust would settle and palace life would soon resume a more moderate pace. In court circles, things had a habit of smoothing themselves over if you kept out of the way for a bit.

But he remained concerned that the threat to send him to Holyroodhouse was a very real one – at stake, his forthcoming exhibition at the Gardner Galleries. He hadn't been able to seek out Tommy Lascelles to gauge how much of Lothian's threat was bluff, how much a calculated plan.

'Ah! The Tanja Man!' barked Lothian as Guy stepped warily into the office. 'Been doin' any breakin' and enterin' recently? Made off with the Crown Jewels yet?' His tone was cold, old-school and disparaging.

'Is Tommy around?' replied Guy, refusing to be bullied. 'A few things he should know about.'

'He and the King have gone off somewhere hush-hush. Tell me.'

'No, it's fine, I'll leave it till he—'

'Until he gets back, I'm in charge. Tell me. Then I have something to tell you.'

Guy thought about it. So far he was no closer to providing an answer to Lord Blackwater's bizarre death at the Fort, and was not inclined to show his hand as to how far his inquiries had taken him.

'King Zog,' he replied, as the thought suddenly struck him.

Lothian groaned. 'I thought we'd successfully put him out to grass. We've got enough displaced heads of state eating us out of house and home without Zog. What about him – he doesn't want to see the King again? Because if he does, tell him there's nothing His Majesty can do about getting the Rolls Royces out of Ankara. He should never have sent them there in the first place. We're not here to fix his transport arrangements, there's a ruddy war going on.'

'Zog's got himself a new friend,' said Guy. 'Fanny Goldington.'

Lothian's hand slammed against his forehead 'That's all we need!' he exclaimed. 'How d'you know that?'

Guy described his encounter with the chattering ladies who lunch and their eyewitness account of the moustachioed majesty dropping sugar lumps into the mouth of London's most notorious courtesan. She'd seduced her way up the ranks, starting with a viscount, an earl, then a marquess. Her long legs and wicked ways invariably left her lovers in a state of delirious exhaustion as she engineered her ruthless climb through the pages of the peerage until she'd ended in the bed of a royal prince.

The courtiers looked at each other.

'You know what this means,' said Lothian, his face drawn and anxious.

Guy nodded.

'Just when we thought we'd put the Harry Gloucester problem out of the way.'

'He seems to be behaving himself reasonably well these days,' said Guy, nodding and recalling the time when, newly arrived at the Palace, he was put in charge of arranging anonymous cars to transport the King's brother off to see his popsies.

'Don't you see?' snapped Lothian. 'All Fanny Goldington ever wanted to do is end up in bed with a king – and now she's done it.'

'One has to admire her tenacity. Can you imagine the number of frogs she's had to kiss to get where she is today?'

'No, no, don't you see?' said Lothian, getting angrily up from his desk, 'The pillow talk! The secrets! The—'

'You mean she'll tell Zog about what a great lover Harry Gloucester is?'

'No, you fool! The duke's thoroughly indiscreet – who knows what he may have told that tart about the King, about the progress of the war, about the Prime Minister – the whole bag of tricks. Gloucester may appear a bit dim but he has an extraordinarily retentive memory – he remembers things. Lots of things.'

'And then blabs to all the wrong people?'

'Just so. What's horrifying is how Zog could use whatever Lady Goldington revealed to him to lean on His Majesty. Get concessions out of him. HM will go mad when he hears about it.'

'And I thought we'd got rid of him,' said Guy, shaking his head. 'He was told he wasn't expected at Court, in fact he was decidedly discouraged from entering the Palace. And why not – for heaven's sake, he's the leader of a population of no more than a million people. That's one-tenth the size of London – he counts for nothing, surely?'

'You don't get it, do you?' barked Lothian. 'He's a *king*. That's enough for our senior management.' He tossed his head back to the ceiling. 'Kings stick together, because if they don't they go down like dominoes, one after the other. So though we've managed to persuade him to stay away from the Palace, he doesn't like it and desperately wants more recognition.'

'I should've thought he'd be too busy counting all that gold he smuggled out when he escaped Albania. That and Lady Goldington – I expect she keeps him pretty busy too.'

'I have no doubt of that. But if there's one thing more important than sex to kings, it's recognition. Status. If she's given him the dirt on our royal family, he'll use it to get himself invited to every damn party and reception there is going.'

'How can he?'

'*You* ask *me* that, when you're tête-á-tête with that broken-down old hack Rochester!'

Once again Guy asked himself whether he was being watched: it wasn't the first time senior courtiers had let slip that they knew his movements outside palace walls.

'You mean he'll drip-feed royal secrets into Rochester's ear? What would be the point? No newspaper proprietor would run anything anti-House-of-Windsor during the current conflict.'

Lothian was pacing around the elegant, pillared room. A sharp blue light fell in from the summer sky, casting a sheen on the ancient oil paintings lining the walls. 'We don't want trouble from the press,' he said. 'It's barely six years since the abdication. At the time the whole of Fleet Street was persuaded to keep its trap shut for months on end. Many of them regret having done that – they were made to look fools by their American counterparts – and you of all people, Harford, should know there are more ways than one of skinning the cat. Fleet Street doesn't seem particularly fond of our King at the moment, and they'll find a way of letting it show.

'On top of that, as you know, Rochester has his American publications where he writes all the stuff he can't get in the papers here. The last thing we want is revelations about the bedroom activities of the King's brother – or worse.'

'Better send old Zog a few invitations then, let him come up to the Palace. That should shut him up.'

'The King detests him. Doesn't want him in the place.'

'I can't see what else can be done.'

Lothian ceased his perambulation and leant over his desk, fixing Guy with a cold stare. 'Go and see Fanny Goldington. Appeal to her better nature, and if not that, then apply some pressure. There must be something we know about her that she'd rather didn't get out.'

'Blackmail?'

'You can hardly call it that when it's preserving the reputation of the King and his family.'

'If she's blabbed already, what would be the point? From the sound of it, she and Zog have been at it for weeks. She'll have told him all she knows by now.'

Lothian looked Guy up and down. 'You're a handsome chap,' he said slowly. 'At any rate, a darn sight more handsome than that disgusting Albanian. Go and work your magic on her, get her to tell Zog that she's prone to exaggeration, that actually all the things she told him about our royal family are taradiddles and inventions.'

'What? You mean . . . ?'

'Lie back and think of England.'

'I don't believe what I'm hearing! And anyway, I can't see that working – I don't even know the woman.'

'You'll find a way. Get to work on it without further delay.'

Guy spied his moment. 'What about Holyroodhouse, Osbert?' he said wickedly. 'Don't you want me to go up there?'

The other man's cheeks twitched. 'Apparently you're too valuable here, according to Tommy. He used the word "indispensable", though frankly after your behaviour at the Fort, I can't see it.'

Guy rose and made for the door. As he reached it, a thought occurred. 'Wasn't there something else you wanted to mention?'

Osbert Lothian was staring out of the tall window down on to the parade square beneath. A small platoon of guardsmen, shorn of their customary scarlet brilliance and encased in khaki, stamped and turned and turned again.

Lothian picked up a file on his desk and waved it vaguely in Guy's direction.

'The police report on Lord Blackwater's death,' he said. 'Since you're in charge of the case you'd better take a look.'

Guy walked back across the thick carpet and took the buff folder, which seemed to contain very little.

'I don't understand it,' he said after a minute or two. 'This seems to state quite clearly that Blackwater was killed.'

'Does it?' said Lothian, still looking out of the window.

'Surely you've read it,' said Guy sharply. 'A punch to the throat. There's an unsigned report, presumably from a doctor, which talks of a crushed trachea, the result of a single blow. It caused Blackwater to choke to death, yet left little or no outward evidence.'

'Couldn't have happened to a nicer chap,' said Lothian dreamily. 'Hadn't you better be getting on your way?'

'Wait a minute,' said Guy, confused. 'You gave me the task of finding out what Blackwater was doing in the Fort. I uncovered quite a lot of his background story – do you still want to know? Or are you bored with it all now?'

'Look,' said Lothian stonily, turning to face him. 'The man was a disgrace – a turncoat who backed King Edward, and a man who made all the plans for that awful woman's flight to the South of France. Then came home and tried to wheedle his way back into King George's court, presumably so he could spy on the new king for the old king. Well, we saw to that!'

'Do you *know* that? Isn't it more likely that he realised the truth of that old adage, "the king is dead, long live the king" – and, having seen the Duchess into safety in France, wanted to come back and carry on his work at court? The Blackwaters have served the royal family for two hundred years, you know!'

'And his reprehensible private life. D'you know that he tried it on with one of the footmen here?'

He wouldn't be the first, thought Guy. 'To be honest, Osbert, nobody's private life bears too close a scrutiny.'

'You would say that, wouldn't you? Shacked up as you are with a common criminal!'

Guy bit his lip. 'So what do you want me to do? Carry on my investigations to discover what the hell he was doing at the Fort, or just bury the whole thing?'

'If you could be bothered to read to the end of the report, it suggests that Blackwater may have suffered a heart attack. Forget the rest. An unfortunate accident.'

'But—'

'That's what you go and tell Lady Blackwater. An accident. Case closed.'

Guy lit a cigarette. 'A couple of years ago,' he said slowly, 'a hugely likeable fellow called Edgar Brampton died here in the Palace. Gunshot. No post-mortem, no inquest. Because of some bizarre ancient rule, I had to arrange for his body to be shifted to non-royal premises. The whole thing was to be brushed under the carpet.'

'Don't know anything about that,' said Lothian unconvincingly.

'This time it's a different story but the same result – a man's murdered in the ex-king's home and the old machine whirs into action again: bury the evidence along with the man. Is that what you want?'

The man opposite looked down his nose. '*I* don't make the rules. Blackwater was an embarrassment to the royal family from the moment he shot off to France to find a little love-nest for that ghastly American. If any of this came out – if his love of nancy boys came out – what good would it do? More to the point, what *harm* would it do?'

Guy shook his head in disbelief. 'Lord Blackwater had a wife, a son, an estate with its workers – aren't they entitled to know what happened?'

'No. Now buzz off, shut your investigation down, and forget all about it. Go and use that fertile brain of yours to sort out King Zog and his piece of stuff. And come back to me tomorrow morning with a progress report.'

51

CHAPTER FIVE

The walk home did little to clear Guy's state of confusion, though in the early evening light the Chelsea streets still exuded their old charm, despite the bomb damage. People clustered in small groups outside The Markham Arms and The Surprise, basking in the sunshine at the end of a day's work and perching their glasses on top of the sandbags. Most by now had discarded the gas masks, which a year ago had been obligatory, but their clothes were more muted, hats looking their age and even the uniforms looking tired and scruffy. People talked of victory but there was scant evidence of it and spirits remained at a low ebb.

Guy made his way down Tite Street, pausing outside his front door to breathe in the sweet-sour odour of the Thames before letting himself into the studio, his home for two years, a safe haven and, in its small way, a creative crucible. Rodie shared the vast space with him now, though their relationship remained peppery and unpredictable. In the first hour of meeting him she'd urgently insisted that she marry him, but still it hadn't happened – who knew where it would all go?

He let himself in with his latchkey to find Rupert Hardacre making himself a cup of tea.

'Just the man,' said Guy, grimly nodding a welcome. 'But get out the whisky, Rupe.'

'Problems?'

'Nothing but. When this war started I pictured myself doing heroic deeds, serving the country, maybe winning a medal or two. Making a difference. Instead . . .'

'Instead?' Rupert plonked a tumbler in his hand.

'Here's my to-do list. One, find out just what the hell Archy Blackwater was doing in the Fort. Two, find out about his private life and who could possibly want to kill him.'

'You don't say.'

'Now I don't have to do either of those. But three, go and tell Lady Blackwater her husband died of a heart attack, even though he didn't. And four, while you're about it, go and seduce Fanny Goldington.'

Rupert spluttered into his whisky. 'Seduce . . . Fanny *Goldington*? In the name of the King? I've heard of some awesome tasks handed out in this war, but that isn't one of them, Guy – what on earth are you complaining about?'

'She needs to be coaxed into untelling all the bedroom secrets she learnt from the Duke of Gloucester.'

'Because she's now blabbed them to . . . ?'

'King Zog.'

Rupert roared with laughter. 'So what are you doing here then, Guy? Get to it! Go and do your duty. She's a fine-looking woman!'

'Ha ha, very funny,' he said bitterly. He repeated his orders from Osbert Lothian, and the consequences of failing in his mission.

'But no Holyroodhouse now. And Fanny shouldn't cost you more than the price of a dinner at The Ritz, from what I hear.'

'You're an idiot. She's the nation's number one social climber – she started with a viscount and now she's with a king. What's a lower-ranking courtier got to offer that's going to convince her to shut her trap?'

'Wakey-wakey, old chap – you won't be Guy Harford, the lowly assistant private secretary, taking her out on the town, you'll be Guy Harford, the celebrated portrait artist. No woman can resist the offer of having their picture done.'

'Hadn't thought of that.'

'Bring her back here, say you heard she has the most beautiful shoulders in Mayfair and you'd like to capture them in moonlight – and hey presto.'

'You're forgetting one thing.'

'What's that?'

'Rodie.'

Rupert smilingly shook his head. 'Remember, Guy, all's fair in love and war, and you've got a job of work to do. Besides, what about Augustus John painting her portrait in return for a pinch of her bottom?' He nodded towards the sketch on the wall, which didn't show the bruises.

'Not the same,' replied Guy awkwardly. 'Anyway, leave me to take care of that. I wanted to ask your advice about Archy Blackwater because I'm in a quandary. I was given one set of instructions – find out about his death – but now another: we know how he died, off you go and lie to his widow.'

'That sounds easy enough.'

'Up to a point it is. But there's obviously far more to the Blackwater death than we currently know. I can't just leave it there.'

Rupert poured more whisky. 'What d'you mean?'

'It was all too neat, the way he was lying there. Almost as if he'd laid down for a snooze. The briefcase, but no hat. No apparent sign of violence. The whole thing is frankly very odd. What was he doing inside the Fort anyway? And how on earth did he get there? There was no car, and it's a ruddy long walk from Windsor Castle.'

'Sounds like you've got enough on your plate. I'd leave the whys and wherefores alone, get on with Lady B and brushing up your Casanova technique.'

Guy shook his head. 'Have you seen Rodie?'

Hardcastle crossed his legs and looked away. 'She's off on a job.'

'She didn't tell me.'

'She's gone back to the Fort.'

'*What?*'

'Knows her way in, thanks to you – shouldn't be too difficult a job. She'll be back in the morning.'

Guy got up, walked over to the kitchen area, picked up a saucepan and threw it on the floor. 'Are you mad?' he shouted. 'This could finish me at the Palace!'

'You're not that keen on working there, you're always going on about it.'

Guy walked back across the studio floor, face flushed with anger. 'If I ever want to stop working there, it'll be me taking the decision,' he said. 'Nobody else. I don't want to be kicked out because Rodie broke into the Fort again – don't you know the stink that caused the first time round?'

Rupert shook his head and smiled. 'She knows what she's doing,' he said quietly. 'She's probably the best burglar in London – that's why we took her on. The trouble with you, Guy, is you look at her first as an artist's model, second as a woman. You don't take into account the colossal skills she's acquired in her lifetime. In her way, she's a genius.'

'I'd like to hear that read out in her defence when she ends up back in court,' said Guy bitterly, remembering her appearance in the Bow Street dock after a failed safe blag. 'I managed to get her off once – it won't work a second time. So that'll be two people you've put out of work – two people who are supposed to be your friends!'

Rupert shrugged. 'Relax,' he replied. 'You said yourself that the Fort's abandoned. There's nobody guarding the place – it's surplus to requirement. It's almost as if they'd welcome a stray bomb dropping on it and knocking it flat.'

'You can never tell. There are sure to be random security patrols. And anyway, what the hell has she gone back there for? I told you what Osbert Lothian said – forget about it, Blackwater died of a heart attack. End of story.'

'You work for your lot, Guy, I work for mine.'

Guy snorted. 'The *Post Office*? Hah! Pull the other one! Despite the fact we've known each other all this time, I still don't have the first clue who actually employs you, what you do. Couldn't you give me a job description, some clue as to why you've sent Rodie somewhere where there's a great chance she'll get arrested?'

'Defence of the realm,' replied Rupert roughly. 'And on a need-to-know basis. You don't need to know.'

'Between these four walls.'

'OK,' said Rupert slowly. 'Blackwater may have been a chum of the former king, he may have fixed up the departure of Mrs Simpson to the South of France. He may have once been a regular at Buck House and Windsor and he may have been found dead at Fort Belvedere, but the death of Lord Blackwater is no longer a palace matter, Guy. That's why you've been told to cease your investigations.'

'Well, thanks for letting me know!'

'But you can do me a favour.'

'No chance. At least not till Rodie's back safe and sound with both our reputations still intact.'

Rupert ignored this. 'When you see Lady Blackwater there are a couple of things I'd like you to ask her. Casually, almost as an afterthought.'

'You can forget that, chum. And now I'm going to paint, so let yourself out.'

The old fellow slowly filled his pipe and looked out at the rolling countryside. Once, a thousand years ago, a man in his position might be surrounded by outriders, his progress marked by doffed caps, open doors, townsfolk agog at his arrival, and crowds round his horse anxious to learn the purpose of his visit.

Nowadays it was a pasteboard ticket on a train to King's Lynn, a Thermos of tea, and the *Daily Telegraph* crossword. A well-brushed bowler hat sat four-square in the luggage rack above his head, pinning down a neatly folded mackintosh, and though everything in his demeanour and appearance spoke of anonymity, nevertheless he was something special. In his pocket he carried a rare, heavily embossed passport, and hanging from the watch chain across his waistcoat, hidden from view, a silver greyhound.

Once this man might have been the transporter of a priceless royal jewel, or tasked to eat the document he carried should it be in danger of falling into enemy hands – and be prepared to sacrifice his life immediately after. But though the world was in turmoil, the job of King's Messenger was, these days, a peaceful backwater for a faithful old soldier approaching his seventieth birthday.

The lights dimmed as the train entered a tunnel, but he could still see the compartment door slide open. When they emerged into the light, the smell of soot and burning coal and sulphurous smoke squeezing its way in the door, the man found himself sitting opposite an elegantly clad gentleman in a striped suit and foulard tie. He was wearing coloured socks.

'Hope you don't mind,' said Guy Harford lightly. 'The couple in my compartment have clearly only just got married and I felt a little *de trop*. All right if I join you?'

The man grunted and rattled his newspaper. He was obviously not the type for chit-chat.

'Sorry,' said Guy after a moment, 'but I'm sure I know you. Don't you work at . . . ?'

The man eyed him uneasily. On the road to Walsingham, eight hundred years ago, hadn't a King's Messenger lost his head after engaging in casual banter with a seemingly friendly baron?

'Don't talk much,' he said. 'Not in my nature.'

'Guy Harford,' said Guy, ignoring this. 'I work for Tommy Lascelles. You're something to do with the Lord Chamberlain's department, surely?'

'Mm,' said the man, turning away and doing his best to hide inside the newspaper.

'Let me think. Could you be a—'

The King's Messenger put down his newspaper in exasperation and glanced quickly out through the compartment's glass door into the corridor. 'Show me your pass,' he said, not kindly.

Guy felt for his wallet and, as if by way of acknowledgement, the man got up and drew down the door blind. Once having inspected the proffered card he sat down again with a heavy thud in the seat opposite Guy.

'Scabbard,' he murmured. 'King's Messenger.' The way he intoned this piece of information carried with it a warning that nothing further should be said between them, except perhaps a brief exchange on the weather and the prospects for Somerset's cricketers in the county championships.

'Going far?' persisted Guy. It had become a game. Scabbard was determined to say nothing, Guy was equally determined to get him to drop this ridiculous guard. King's Messengers, such as they existed today, were part of a dying industry. They did little more than carry billets-doux from the Sovereign to his relatives and there was no need, in this enclosed compartment, to fear eavesdroppers.

'Got about another hour to go,' said Scabbard, almost rudely evasive. He glanced down pointedly at Guy's socks. 'And you are . . . ?'

'An Assistant Private Secretary. Dogsbody really. Just off to give a lady the sad news her husband died of a heart attack. Not the sort of thing you can do over the phone. And you?'

Scabbard thought of his secret mission to Sandringham. He compared it in his mind to the glory days of the Silver Greyhounds – the bad roads, the highwaymen, the long distances at furious speed. Taking a package to His Majesty from Her Majesty, which for all he knew contained no more than a slice of HM's favourite seed cake, seemed a worthless task in war.

But then was it so very different from Queen Victoria's man, bidden to take a cage of eight canaries from Windsor to the Sultan of Turkey? Or the Greyhound stuck with the job of keeping a consignment of rare moth eggs alive on his journey from London to Belgrade?

'Must be a challenging job,' said Guy disingenuously. He wanted desperately not to have to think about what he would say to Lally Blackwater about her husband's murder. 'Dangerous. I seem to recall that you Greyhounds also have the reputation of being particularly accomplished lovers. All part of the job description. Wasn't there a story about the Orient Express en route for Vienna and a lady of Spain who—'

'Don't know anything about that,' snorted Scabbard dismissively, his Presbyterianism welling up from the soles of his shoes. Though no human action could prevent his salvation, he didn't want to tamper with his private arrangement with the Lord by talking about sex on trains.

'Been at it long?'

Scabbard gestured at Guy's socks, which clearly bothered him. 'Being a bit sporty, are we, sir? Seeing as we're off to the country?' He said it *awf*.

Guy followed his gaze and sensed the old chap's disapproval. 'A bit of light relief away from the Palace. You know, the trouble is—'

'Because His Majesty is a stickler – a *stickler* – for the right dress, sir. Why, many's the time I've seen him give a right rollicking to a man whose cap badge was a tiny bit skew-whiff, or whose medals needed a bit more shine. He's a terror that way.'

I wonder, in the overall scheme of things, thought Guy, quite how important a man's turnout is at this juncture in the war. But he sensed this was not a debate he could engage in with Scabbard, dressed precisely as he was in navy-blue suit, regimental tie and freshly laundered handkerchief billowing from his jacket cuff. The man may have retired from the army but he wore his civilian clothes like a uniform.

'I'm getting off at Waterbeach,' Guy said, changing the subject. 'You'll be going on to King's Lynn.'

Scabbard didn't like being rumbled. 'Lord Blackwater's place, is it?' he said aggressively, turning the tables. 'The Abbey? Ruddy nuisance that chap turned out to be!'

'Oh?' said Guy idly. 'You know he's dead?'

'We Messengers hear all the news,' said Scabbard with a nod. 'We keep our ears to the ground. Strange he should want to go back to Windsor after all he put us through with that blessed Mrs Simpson.'

'At the time he probably thought what he was doing was for the best. Getting her out of the country when they started throwing bricks through her windows. Good idea, wouldn't you say?'

'Nasty piece o' work that woman. Anyone who sided with her deserved what was coming.'

'Which was?'

'Being kicked out from the court. Blackwater, Lord Brownlow *and* the rest. They may've thought themselves gentlemen but you could just as easily call them traitors. Should ha' run them out of the country.'

If only you knew just what a traitor Archy Blackwater turned out to be, and I daresay he had the temerity to wear coloured socks too, thought Guy. This man is like so many who cuddle up to the crown – blindly loyal, excluding all alternatives, creating a myth they seek to spread abroad sometimes in the face of the facts. Haven't you just described one of the sovereign's more tiresome traits, upbraiding men who didn't have the luxury of a valet for not being smart enough in his presence? You see that as a virtue, whereas in the real world wouldn't it just be considered plain bad manners?

'My stop coming up,' said Guy, rising and gathering his hat and briefcase. 'Are you on a day trip? If so we might meet on the down train.'

The man scowled. Anybody who was chums with a traitor and his family hardly merited the company of a King's Messenger.

'I'll probably stay the night,' he said. 'York Cottage.'

'Goodbye, then.'

Mercifully there was a taxi this time. The ride to Blackwater Abbey took only a few minutes and he arrived in the gold drawing room at the appointed hour. His greeting from Lady Blackwater was no less icy but, on this second encounter, he had the chance to study her more closely. The lines in her handsome face etched deeper, it seemed, than when they'd first met. Had she learnt something of her husband's last days? Was she going to share what she knew with him?

'I won't keep you.' No offer of hospitality, no invitation to sit down. 'Tell me what you have to say and I won't detain you further.'

He could see over her shoulder the smiling face of Gwendolyn, eyebrows raised in amusement at the chilly reception he was getting.

'It's very simple, Lady Blackwater. Your husband died of a heart attack. I've brought a letter from Tommy with a fuller explanation which also offers the King's sympathies – you'll understand, I feel certain, why HM won't be writing personally. Also the various arrangements for the memorial service – the funeral, I gather, is being handled up here.'

'That's all?'

'I'm sure you're very busy but if there's anything I can—'

Lady Blackwater turned towards the massive fireplace with its heraldic achievements carved deep in the stonework. She appeared to be studying a bear, improbably supporting a shield with its front paws. It did not look best pleased.

Over her shoulder, she said, 'You asked me some questions last time. I was probably a bit rude.'

'No, I quite understand, Lady Blackwater. You—'

'Don't *presume*, Mr Harford. I wouldn't expect you to understand how we live here, any more than I could picture how you live *your* life. A painter – living with someone who I gather is a burglar – working for Their Majesties?'

'It's not quite like that. I—'

'Princess Mary told me about you, that you're a bit of a detective. I wasn't sure why you were asking the questions before, but now I am, I want to know what happened to my husband. I have to write to my son to let him know he's inherited the titles and the estate. I must have some idea when I write whether Archy's death was an honourable one or . . .'

'Won't your son's commanding officer be making contact?'

'My son is in a prison camp, Mr Harford. The only communication is by letter. Tell me what I'm to say to him.' Her shoulders trembled slightly.

'May we sit down?' said Guy, waiting till she turned and gestured him to take a seat. Her eyes were full of tears.

'Look,' he went on, 'the official verdict is that Lord Blackwater died of a heart attack. There appears to be no reason why he should want to break into Fort Belvedere, or how he got there, or if anyone was with him. But the powers that be feel his is a controversial name, and therefore they want to play down any scandal – if,' he added hastily, 'there were to be any scandal. We don't know that. In fact, since I last saw you, Lady Blackwater, there has been very little new information to explain your husband's death. Except this.'

'Yes?'

'I'm not supposed to tell you, but it seems inhuman that the facts should be kept from you merely to avoid a scandal. On the other hand, what I'm about to tell you may seem equally inhuman. It would appear your husband was murdered, Lady Blackwater. Killed by a single strike to the throat.'

She did not move.

'We can only assume that he was driven to the Fort by his assailant and, because he knows the place well, he was able to find a way in. The purpose of that visit remains unclear, and the reason for his murder.'

'But the Crown wants it hushed up.'

'Of course. You can imagine the ramifications otherwise. Also, this way, the history of the Blackwater family remains unsullied. You can tell your son what you like, but he inherits the title without any shame.'

'If he survives. People are dying in that camp.'

'I'm sorry. If there's anything—'

She rose, her back ramrod stiff, her chin up and jutting out. 'There is something you *can* do, Mr Harford. Find who killed my husband, find out why he was killed. It doesn't matter now, but it may matter later when – if – William comes home. It doesn't need to be made public, but I do profoundly need to know.'

Guy got up too. 'Lady Blackwater, I work for the Palace. I'm expected to do what I'm told. And what I've been told is that the investigation into your husband's death is over. The war goes on, there are tough times ahead, the King needs no distractions now – no murky scandals that bring up the whole abdication business over again. He's arm in arm with President Roosevelt now, a leader of the nation.

'I was . . . let's say *disappointed* when I was told to stand down my inquiries because, as with other cases I've handled, I think that truth is a very important element when someone loses their life. It's all too easy to wipe the slate clean, say there's a war on, people die, let's move on. But in this case I can see the damage that could be caused by opening up the whole abdication can of worms right now, and why that decision was taken.

'So I'd like to help, I really would, but I've been ordered otherwise. I just don't think that in the circumstances . . .'

She got up and strode across the Aubusson carpet, grabbing at his sleeve. 'Just . . . you . . . listen,' she snarled, her blue eyes blazing and her hand shaking. 'Do this for me and I will be eternally grateful.'

'I really don't think I can . . .'

She came up close to his face and pushed herself roughly against him.

'I'll give you a name,' she hissed.

CHAPTER SIX

No surprise that the *News Chronicle* was the first with it:

DEATH OF FAMOUS PEER
The EARL of BLACKWATER
– PLAYED CRUCIAL PART IN
ABDICATION CRISIS

Exclusive from our Special Correspondent

The death has been announced of Lord Blackwater, the courtier made famous during the short reign of King Edward VIII for his part in the abdication crisis.

Blackwater, 59, was found dead in his car in a Berkshire lane on Monday. Police say there are no suspicious circumstances and the family has been informed.

Humphrey Archibald Willoughby Wilsby-Tenby, the 11th earl, rose to prominence as part of the 'Belvedere Set', that international

coterie with which the former king surrounded himself at his private residence, Fort Belvedere, on the Windsor Castle estate.

Together with Lord Brownlow, he was responsible for the escape of Mrs Simpson to the South of France in the days leading up to the abdication. Blackwater formed the advance party that prepared the Villa Lou Viei near Cannes as a temporary residence for Mrs Simpson, now Duchess of Windsor.

On their return to London, Brownlow, a lord-in-waiting to the ex-king, and Blackwater, who held an unofficial position at court, were not invited to become part of the new king's circle and, it is rumoured, found themselves distanced from their former circle of friends.

Lord Blackwater, a considerable landowner in East Anglia, was married to the former Lady Laura Crust, by whom he had a son and heir, Lord Waterbeach. It is understood that the new peer, a captain in the Royal Dragoon Guards, is currently held as a prisoner of war in Germany.

'What a load of old rubbish,' spat Ted Rochester's editor, tossing the paper to the floor and wiping the Special Correspondent's grin of self-congratulation off his face.

'Really?' replied the reporter tetchily. 'It's not in any other newspaper, Sid, not that I've seen. It's why they put "exclusive" on it. It's what you pay me a king's ransom to deliver – exclusives. And lo and behold, here is *an exclusive*, on page one of your newspaper!'

The editor growled. 'You have a single fact here, Ted. Just one. Famous chap is dead. Everything else in your story is dredged up from the cuttings library. Isn't there anything else to say? I trust you've got something better on this for tomorrow.'

'Don't be like that. Of course there's more – but do you really want it? Blackwater was in debt. His wife had kicked him out – bad with money, worse with boys.'

'We can't print any of that. What the hell was he doing in that car "in a Berkshire lane"?'

Rochester readjusted the small cornflower in his buttonhole and smirked. 'It was parked near Windsor Castle, actually.'

'*Really?*' squawked the editor, unbelieving. 'This is a man who's been ostracised by the new king, the entire royal family, the court and most of London society – and he's hanging around Windsor Castle? A place where he's – what d'you fops call it – *persona non grata*? Don't you think there's a story in that somewhere, Rochester?'

'If you think so why don't you get one of your news hounds on it?' came the sniffy reply. 'My job is talking to the big boys, getting *exclusives* like this – not chasing police cars, getting my fingers grubby. I've no idea what Blackwater was doing at Windsor and neither does my contact, or he'd have told me.'

'I want to know what Blackwater was doing there – that's the story, man! Was he trying to creep back into favour? Trying to snoop on the current management so he could report back to the ex-king? Rogering one of the pantry boys? Stealing the family silver? Tell me, man!'

'Well,' said Rochester huffily, 'I can only ask my contact. But I know what the answer will be. And with Buckingham Palace officials, you don't go to the well too often.'

'The well seems pretty dry to me, Rochester.'

'Oh, come on, Sid!'

'Off you go. And send in the news editor. Maybe he can get someone with a bit of pep to find out what the hell's going on. There's a story there, Rochester, but you don't see it – either you're getting too big for your boots, or too old for them. Bring me something new on this, or don't come back!'

Rochester swung angrily out of the room but in his heart he knew the editor was right. He'd been blindsided by Guy Harford, who in return for Rochester telling all he knew about Archy Blackwater's private life, had given him a single fact – the peer was dead.

This broke every journalistic rule – that you only exchange information on an uneven basis, gathering more than you give out. It was how Rochester had risen to such heights but now, he asked himself as he walked to the wages office to collect his expenses, was he getting too old for the game?

One thing was for sure – Harford had landed him in it, and nobody did that to Ted Rochester and lived to tell the tale!

'Sorry, Mr Rochester,' said a blinkered old fellow through the grille, 'can't give you no money. A bit of a question mark over your expenses. The managing editor wants to see you.'

'Well, just give me a couple of tenners, Walter. Tide me over. I've—'

'I've been told to say, "No more golden eggs for Mr Rochester." Sorry, chum.'

The reporter stalked angrily out of the building, wondering how he would pay for his lunch at The Savoy. He was still fuming when he arrived in the American Bar ten minutes later.

'Ted! Long time no see!'

'Foxy, lovely to see you again.'

The Countess of Sefton, sitting by a window, the light catching her to best advantage, looked what she was – a former Paris model, redhaired, with the gloss of America still upon her, now married into one of the oldest families in England.

'How's Hugh?'

'Being the brave soldier. On exercise somewhere, under canvas.'

Rochester thought of the vast family pile and rambling estates in the north. 'He can't like that.'

'On the contrary. It's boy scout stuff for him. He'd like to see some action though.'

'Shall I write something?'

'He wouldn't want to be singled out when there are so many enduring far worse. No, I got you here because I hope you might write something good about our Rosie the Riveter campaign.'

'Oh?' Groaning within, Rochester wondered how much this lunch was going to cost, in return for a dull piece of puffery which inevitably Sid would mock him for. Foxy Sefton was a useful source of innocuous gossip when she wasn't promoting her charitable causes, and this lunch was a trade-off. But it promised to be boring.

'Let's save the jollifications until we have some lunch in front of us,' he said. 'While we have this moment, let's talk about Guy.'

Her eyebrows shot up. 'What's he been up to now?'

Those days in Montmartre were not so long ago, when Guy wore no shoes, she had a wardrobe full of Lanvin dresses, and they lay in bed till three. In the end – what was it? – was his art more important than her heart? Or was her ambition such that she always dreamt of a stately home, a title, financial security? Whatever it was, they'd drifted apart – Guy clinging to the memories, Foxy putting the past behind her.

'Nothing, nothing,' said Rochester. 'It's just that I saw him the other day – he was telling me about Archy Blackwater. He didn't look happy. I wondered if this job of his has got on top of him.'

'D'you think so? I thought he was doing rather well.'

'The Blackwater business,' replied Rochester, fishing. 'He seemed troubled by it.' *Go on, say something, Foxy, you always know what's going on. What's the Blackwater story? Come on – earn your ruddy lunch, girl!*

'They ask an awful lot of him, Ted.'

'Obviously there's a problem, though. Archy was found in his car – could it be suicide? Seems such a strange place to be found – I would have thought Windsor was out of bounds to the likes of Archy. What does Hugh say?'

'My husband never gossips, you know that.'

I remember you when you were just a fashion model, Fox – don't go all grand on me, thought Rochester, but he said, 'Well, have you heard anything?'

'There were a few unpaid bills, yes.'

'Many?'

'Possibly. He had debts of another kind, too – I'm sure you know that.'

'Blackmail?'

'Such an ugly word. Are we going to have another, or shall we go down?'

Rochester thought of his empty pockets and the cashier shaking his head with a tired grin. He raised his hand and clicked his fingers.

'Another. You were saying.'

'Are you pumping me, Ted? Not wanting to talk about Guy but actually digging for something on Archy Blackwater? Why not go and see Lally? She'll have plenty to say, though it might cost you more than a couple of sidecars.'

Rochester was immune to such snubs. 'Actually, I was thinking of writing a piece saying Buckingham Palace is struggling to cope with the death of their former courtier. That it revives memories of the abdication and the brutal way those who had been loyal to King

Edward were cut off – the door slammed in their faces. You know who I mean. Perry Brownlow, the Duff Coopers, all the others. And Archy, of course. Did he kill himself because of the shame of being ousted from the royal circle?'

'I don't think that'd be helpful to Guy. He's doing his best to sort things out – he told me so on the phone this morning.'

'Ah!' said Rochester. 'So there is something!'

'You'll have to ask Guy. Now, can we talk about Rosie the Riveter? It's a campaign that has been a huge success Stateside and I want to bring it over here – get more women into men's jobs in the factories and . . .'

Rochester was humming a little hum in his head. The Riveter story could write itself – he'd stumbled across something far juicier . . .

'Whatever you do, steer clear of those Russian boys. They're dangerous – not to be trusted,' said Simon in a half whisper.

He was perched with Elena in an unheated dressing room in Burnley's vast old theatre, shivering despite their recent warm-up exercises onstage. Outside, the Lancastrian rain fell with a vengeance; it was hard to believe this could be June.

'Step carefully around Constant,' Simon continued, 'and steer clear of Margot.'

Elena looked down at her shabby suitcase and down-at-heel shoes, sighing. 'They won't be speaking to the likes of me.'

The dream had been realised – Elena had been taken on as a relief ballerina by the Vic-Wells company, posted to their temporary base in the sooty northern town, but though only newly arrived she was already learning that onstage performance took second place to backstage politics.

'It's all over between them. Well, almost all over – Margot thought it would be for ever, but he's gone to live with his mother,' said Simon. 'He might even go back to his wife.'

'I thought they were devoted to each other. Everyone at Volkova's says so.'

'First he was in love with her, but she wasn't. Then as he lost interest, she came around. Artistically they're inseparable but in matters of the heart . . . I think she got fed up walking the streets trying to find him, having to pick him up from the gutter, hose him down.'

'He was pretty drunk the other night.'

'He's *always* pretty drunk, but still a genius. Oh, and by the way – wandering hands, darling.'

'I'll watch out. What was that about the Russians?'

'There's a small gang of them – you must have seen them at Volkova's – they're little toughs. Good dancers but bad people.'

Elena smiled at him. 'I expect you to protect me, Simon.'

'Me?' he laughed. 'Oh . . . no, Elena. I'm not . . . and in any case I'm off back to London. We're doing a fresh production at the New Theatre with a couple of try-outs called Norma Shearer and Beryl Grey.'

The names meant nothing to the Austrian – that she'd got her cameo part in *Swan Lake* was all that mattered; she hugged it to her like a small kitten, fearful it should escape.

He glanced up at the dirty skylight. 'Stopped raining,' he said. 'Shall I walk you home?'

The Vic-Wells Ballet, half in and half out of London, endured the war either with stoicism or resignation. Few found Burnley's dirty streets and tired buildings a match for the excitement of the West End, but the townsfolk had taken in this bunch of artistic cuckoos and made them welcome, with full houses every night at the theatre, and open doors in their homes. And the Nazi bombers had found the town, important enough a target with its cotton mills and coal mines, just beyond their reach. The broad streets of Burnley were safe, if mostly rain-sodden.

They splashed their way through the puddles, avoiding the squadrons of cloth-capped men making their way home for tea. Their steps took them past long terraces of soot-blackened homes and empty shops until they reached the cobbles of Sandygate, where they made a swift turn down an alleyway and into the back-yard of a tiny house.

'That's a ginnel,' she said, throwing a thumb over her shoulder. 'See, I'm learning the local lingo!'

They eased their way past the outside brick privy and into a downstairs room at the back of the house. With the kettle on the gas ring, they settled down to the perennial gossip which takes the place of food in the world of ballet. The stage back at the Vic was given over to a production of *Troilus and Cressida* tonight; they would not be on again until tomorrow's matinee.

As they sat, Simon gazed critically at this newest recruit to the company. Giving her a job had altered her physically, and for the better – her pinched features had filled out, the permanent frown that dusted her brow had disappeared, and her body seemed to have altered proportion. *You are beautiful*, he thought dispassionately. *There could be a chance for you now you're in.*

'I'm off the day after tomorrow,' he said. 'Just remember to keep smiling and never, ever be late.'

She made the tea and handed him a cup. 'Thank you,' she said quietly. 'This . . . this astonishes me. When I left Vienna I thought I was finished. I know you put in a good word for me. Is there anything I can do in exchange?'

He leant back and looked at her. 'Just stay safe.'

'We're safe enough up here. No bombs.'

'That's not what I mean. Those Russians, they wouldn't have got into the corps de ballet normally, but with so many of our lot in the army, there was no choice. But they aren't like the rest of us, Elena.'

'I've seen them in class. They're accomplished, what more can you ask?'

'I can't really tell you. But when I'm gone, stay as far away from them as you possibly can. When you get on the tour bus, sit with the girls.'

'Jealous?' She smiled. Maybe, now she had a job, there was room in her heart for romance once again.

Simon stiffened. 'Not in the slightest,' he snapped. 'There's something odd about them, something wrong. Stay away, Elena, stay away!'

She didn't tell him then what they'd done, that could wait till tomorrow – this moment was more important. She put her head on his shoulder, shut her eyes, and pictured the curtain rising on her glittering new career.

CHAPTER SEVEN

The name meant nothing. It was ordinary, without any embellishment, a name that had none of the distinguishing characteristics you might find printed in the pages of Burke's Peerage. Lady Blackwater had repeated it several times but claimed to know nothing more about the man to whom it belonged.

They were close, her husband and the man, she knew that. Were they lovers? She did not know.

What an extraordinary woman you are, Guy thought – tough as nails and completely unbending. My friend Foxy is a countess also, with a stately home and estate quite the equal of Blackwater Abbey, but charming with it. What makes you so haughty, so distant, so chillingly tribal?

As he closed the taxi door behind him and ordered the driver on, he reasoned that Lally Blackwater was determined at all costs to protect the family name, a name that stretched back to before the Norman Conquest. And as the old car ground into gear and trundled out through the ceremonial gates towards Waterbeach Station, the thought suddenly struck him that someone quite so feral could easily be the killer herself.

The idea grew as they bounced slowly through the Cambridgeshire lanes. Did she hope that, with the chances of her son surviving the brutal Stalag Luft regime being slim, he may never come home? And with her husband out of the way, she'd finally have full control of Blackwater Abbey, to do with as she wished? To live handsomely off the family riches, accumulated over centuries, to aggrandise herself now and get back in with her chum the Princess Royal?

The obliging Gwendolyn had revealed that, as Archy Blackwater's secret life gradually became known, so Princess Mary's visits to the Abbey petered out. With the offending peer now permanently out of the way, would Mary come back to make the Abbey famous as a favoured royal watering-hole? The irony was that though the royal train repeatedly crossed Blackwater lands on its journey to Sandringham, King George had never once stopped in to say hello, not even for a cup of tea.

The train would be an hour late, he was informed at the ticket office, so he sat on a green bench and watched a huffing, clanking goods train wend its way slowly and deliberately through the station. He took out his sketch pad and started to make notes.

Lally BW – murdered Ld B?

Couldn't have – surely not strong enough?

He paused and thought about this. She was fifty, but fit. The horses in the stable yard told him that she hunted – not a pastime he particularly admired but certainly one that required courage, daring and a level of fitness and muscularity to be able to control the massive stallions the local Master of Foxhounds expected to see in his hunting field. So yes, it was possible she could have delivered the fatal punch – and the fact that there was no sign of a struggle around the body did suggest that the peer knew his killer, allowing him or her to come close enough to throw their fist at his throat.

Why were they at Fort Belvedere?

Might Gwendolyn tell me if her mistress had gone missing at the time of her husband's death – a sudden trip to London, perhaps – or would she feel loyalty to the woman who'd employed her all these years?

He wondered if he had time to take the taxi back to the Abbey, but when he went out into the station yard it had disappeared, and he knew from bitter experience his shoes were no match for the journey. He'd have to hope that a telephone call to the secretary would suffice – though it was never the same asking direct questions when the person you're speaking to is separated by miles and miles of telephone wire. There was always an excuse for them to hang up or change the subject – much less easy to achieve when interviewer and interviewee were eyeball to eyeball.

The old locomotive hove into view and wrestled itself to a noisy, grumpy halt. Guy climbed aboard but as he was making for the rear of the train, he spotted the unmistakeable form of Scabbard, sitting precisely as he'd last seen him four or five hours ago.

He walked past the compartment, then paused. He turned back.

'Mr Scabbard!'

'Ah. Um.' Guy could tell that the man wanted desperately to be left alone.

'Successful trip, I hope?'

'I never talk about work, Mr, er . . .'

'Harford, Guy Harford. Would you like to see my Palace pass again?'

The man pursed his lips and exhaled a quantity of air through them. Public mention of the P-word was something he heartily disapproved of, and he was not partial to sarcasm either.

'All the way back to King's Cross, Mr Scabbard?'

'Mm.'

'How lovely. I gather there's a chance of a cup of tea after Cambridge.'

'Nn,' said Scabbard with the merest nod of his head and a pat of the Thermos by his side – he'd come prepared, as all King's Messengers do. One more jibe from Guy and he'd probably get up and move to another compartment.

Guy gave up trying to get a rise out of the mumchance emissary, sank into a corner seat and got out the sketch pad again.

Why am I doing this? Now it's only Lally BW who wants to know who killed her husband – nobody else cares. And if it was she who did the dirty deed, why am I bothering?

Esme F-F/Caroline S – biggest gossips out, they must know something.

He put down the pad, then picked it up again.

RODIE – where the devil has she got to?!?

Then, settling back in his seat, he proceeded to draw a caricature of the man opposite, with a large bulbous nose and weighed down by a hundred medals and royal decorations. He placed a crown jauntily on the man's head then shut his eyes and went to sleep.

◆ ◆ ◆

'Come down, blast you!
'Blast you, come down!
Charlotte the parrot was doing her nightly aerobatics up and down the tall-ceilinged studio, enjoying the novelty of the new phrases she'd learnt since she came to live in Chelsea.

'*Damn you, Charlotte! Damn you!*'

After a lifetime of being the bosom companion of King George V, sharing his breakfast table to the annoyance, not to say exclusion, of George's queen-empress Mary, she'd been shunted off the moment George uttered 'Bugger Bognor' and departed for that great throne room in the sky.

The parrot had been inherited by the Duke and Duchess of Gloucester – an experiment which neither bird nor royals enjoyed. Charlotte took exception to the duke's incessant whinnying giggle; Harry Gloucester to the presumption that she should sit on his shoulder while he was reading the newspaper. What had been good enough for Papa was not good enough for him.

And so Charlotte, the most regal of all plumed birds, had come to live with Guy and Rodie in their artist's studio just off Cheyne Walk. The arrangement worked better for the bird – more airspace to flap around in, a big echoing room which agreeably amplified her squawks – but not for Guy, fed up with never being able to capture her before plonking the finely embroidered, monogrammed cover over her cage for lights-out.

Rupert, who'd had a taste of Charlotte when he and Guy shared a flat in Pimlico, ducked instinctively as she made a low pass over his head. Finally Rodie coaxed her down with a piece of cheese and pushed her firmly into her cage.

'*Where's the captain?*' chattered the bird grumpily. '*Bless my buttons!*'

The heavy cover put paid to further complaints.

'So tell me in detail – your trip back to the Fort.'

Rodie sighed. 'Nuffin' to it,' she said. 'I told you – window open, step in, just like last time. No security at all, it's shocking really.'

'How'd you get there?'

'Bicycle. The Fort's far away from other buildings and because it's unoccupied, there are no patrols. Not regular ones anyway. I arrived just as dusk was falling – not too dark that I couldn't see to get around the house, but I took a couple of torches just in case.'

'And?'

''E got in through the butler's door, the poor fella, no doubt about it. It's the nearest entrance to the drive and 'e must have used it a few times when the prince – the duke, the king, oojamaflip – lived there. Door was on the latch, no signs of forced entry. All the other doors were tight. I worked the place over, gave it a good four hours – servants' quarters an' all. It's a big building but not that many rooms considering.'

'And?' he repeated.

'In my business it's always best if you start at the top of a house and work down – I dunno why, but that's what I was taught and I stick by the book. I went through the main part first, then the staff annexe. In the main house there were odd bits of furniture which had been left behind, pictures on the wall, a few books, but the house had been pretty well cleared out. There was more bits and pieces on the staff side, a sitting room and bedroom that had been lived in, I suppose by a caretaker, but not for months and months. You can tell from the smell of a house whether people have been living there recently, and they hadn't.'

'And no clue as to what Lord Blackwater might have been doing there?'

'I'm coming to that. Downstairs it's like a stately 'ome, very regal like, but upstairs the place is a bit of a hotchpotch – bedrooms with their own bathrooms, all very new, and then others that had been painted nice but not spiffed up, if you know what I mean. So I reckoned there was two classes of guest 'oo stayed there – the ones the Prince and Mrs Simpson wanted to impress, and the others who were probably just hangers-on.'

'That seems reasonable.'

'That lot had to share bathrooms. Anyway, I went through the whole floor. There was *her* bedroom – huge, looking out over Virginia Water. All the furniture gone, though. Then two interconnecting bathrooms and on the other side obviously what must have been the Prince of Wales's room.'

She got up and pirouetted across the room to the drinks tray. 'What is it about these people, Rupe?' she said over her shoulder. 'If you've got someone to love, don't you want to be with them day and night? Cuddle up nice and cosy? But them – separate bedrooms, I ask yer!

'After that there was four smart bedrooms and then all the others. I sniffed around and after a bit I found where Blackwater slept. Wasn't that clever of me, Rupe?'

'It's what I pay you for. How did you know?'

'My nose, darlin', my nose!'

'Get on, tell me what you found.'

'It's not what I found, it's what I didn't find, mate. You go into a room that's been stripped of its furniture, what you got to look at? Nuffin'. So you walk round the edge, you look out of the window, you open the cupboards. You look up the chimney, you kick the wainscot – that's it, you're done. On to the next room.

'But, Rupe, it always pays to turn the carpet back. And, hey presto, there was 'is lordship's little hidey-hole. Loose bit o' floorboard. Bingo!'

'Really? What was in there?'

She produced a foolscap envelope and brought it over to the table where Hardacre was sitting. Opening it up, she scattered half a dozen pieces of paper in front of him. 'There y'are!'

Hardacre looked at each one, reading and rereading. 'Love poems. Erotic. All in the same handwriting. Have you actually *read* these, Rodie?'

She laughed. 'Takes all sorts!'

'And this one,' he said, picking it up. 'On headed writing paper.' The coat of arms with two bears had been printed underneath it:

BLACKWATER ABBEY

WATERBEACH

CAMBS

TEL: WATERBEACH 301 CABLES: BLACKABBEY

'Not much to go on,' said Hardacre finally, 'but well done for finding them. We have samples of Blackwater's handwriting so we can check if this is written by him. But it doesn't take us further forward because there's still the question: what was he doing there? If he went back to the Fort to retrieve the poems, surely he knew where they were hidden and could have picked them up and got away. Why did he leave them there?'

'Look again,' said Rodie. 'Not the poems, the envelope.'

'Brown. Foolscap. No writing on it. Hasn't been sealed – the gum is fresh even if it's a bit dirty.'

'You're missin' it,' she said. ''Ave another go!'

Irritated at being made to look so ineffectual, Rupe looked again inside the envelope, then put it to his nose and sniffed.

'All right, Miss Smarty Pants,' he growled, 'what am I missing?'

'Look at the front of the envelope. See that oblong shape? That's caused by dust falling through the floorboards from the carpet above. Almost invisible, but not if you look closely.'

'And?'

'When I pulled up the loose bit of floorboard there it was, all by itself. I thought I'd found something really useful, but when I opened it up and read those poems, they were nothing but a bit of fancy writing. Him dreamin' about his boyfriend.

'Then I took the envelope over to the window and you could see the oblong. Inside the oblong, it's clean and fresh, outside the oblong there's a layer of dust – not that obvious but it's there.'

'So something had been resting on top.'

'And, Rupe, had been taken away. A book? Another envelope? A diary? A box?'

'So it's possible that Blackwater had come to the Fort specifically to retrieve whatever that article was. He was with someone, we don't know who. He went up to the bedroom, opened up the floorboard, took out whatever it was and then – was the carpet back in position when you came into the room?'

'Yes.'

'So he had time, he wasn't in a hurry to collect this thing and roll the carpet back. But he was happy to leave behind incriminating poems.'

'Looks like it.'

'But why take one thing and not the other? Why, since you've gone to all the trouble of driving from London, risking arrest for breaking and entering, all that – why not take the poems too? Or was there something so special about whatever this other thing was?'

'Maybe he'd gone there specially to give it to the person who killed 'im.'

'This is going round in circles! We might have a better idea of where we're going, who his murderer is, if we knew what it was that's missing.'

'Letters.'

'Most likely. Though you mentioned a diary – could be that. A man like that, with a reputation to preserve – illegal dalliances, that sort of thing. Maybe he liked to write about it, maybe it gave him a thrill.'

Rodie was pacing up and down, buoyed up by her discovery but trying to find answers to questions that refused to form in her mind.

'What happened when the Prince of Wales cleared out of the Fort? What happened the next day?' she asked.

'I asked about that. Apparently the new king ordered the place to be mothballed and the staff dispersed. Later, the ex-king's possessions were moved out, but apart from a caretaker left on the premises, the place was shut up tight as a drum as from the following morning.'

'So nobody allowed to go back there?'

'No. On the King's express instructions, Fort Belvedere ceased to exist. Probably if he could have taken a bulldozer to it, he would have – to him, it represented everything that was wrong with his brother. The people, the cocktails, the jollity and the gramophones.'

'Blackwater was in France with Mrs Simpson by then.'

'And when he came back he was cold-shouldered by the new royal court. If you're saying, did he go back to the Fort when he came back to England, the answer's no. I was told that whatever possessions people had left behind were packed up and sent back to them – there was no question of them coming down to the Fort to pick them up.'

'So Blackwater never had a chance to retrieve his poems and his . . . whatever it was.'

'Never.'

Rodie was rubbing her hands together as she paced, thinking. 'That was December 1936,' she said. 'And here we are six and a half years later. If he wanted to pick up this . . . thing – whatever it is or was – why wait all that time? There must have been many opportunities before that.'

'Maybe it wasn't him who wanted it, but the person who accompanied him.'

Rodie glanced at her watch. 'Look,' she said, 'Guy's going to be home any moment. We're goin' to the flicks. I haven't seen him for days – can we talk about it again tomorrow?'

'OK,' said Hardacre. 'But don't mention any of this to him.'

'Whyever not?'

'He's been taken off the case. The royals just want to forget about Blackwater – too strong a reminder of the abdication for them. As far as they're concerned he's dead and there's an end to it.'

'But—'

'I'm sure you and he have lots of things to talk about,' said Rupe. 'And if he starts badgering you with questions, ask him to marry you – that always shuts him up.'

'Ha ha.'

'Seriously, Rodie – he works for the Crown, we work for the government. He works for a group of people who never want to hear Blackwater's name again, while we urgently need to find out whether there was a Nazi plot to eliminate him because he might blab about Charles Bedaux. London's full of disaffected people – people who're angry the war has gone on too long, people who still believe that Germany can conquer communism while we lily-livered Brits would tolerate it and let it grow.

'There are small ethnic groups around the place who are for hire, who could do the Nazis' dirty work for them – I'm thinking particularly about the refugees who came flooding in when war was declared. So many of them we know nothing about – what they're doing, what they're thinking. Will they betray us? Are they the Trojan horse?'

'The Trojan what?'

'Leave it like this, Rodie. Tell Guy you went to the Fort, which is true. Tell him you found nothing, which is almost true. Tell him all that's over now and you've been put on another job altogether.'

'But I haven't!'

'You just have,' said Rupert, smiling grimly and gathering up the papers on the table in front of him. 'That sounds like his key in the latch now. What film are you going to see?'

CHAPTER EIGHT

In life, everything's a trade-off, thought Guy bitterly as he trudged his way up the winding alley to The Pig and Whistle. I get mixed up in a mysterious death then told to forget it. I'm forced to take a tiresome train ride – twice – to face a withering broadside from a battleaxe of a woman with not a shred of humanity in her. I'm told to go and make sweet noises to one of London's most notorious courtesans and now here I am, sucking up to a polecat journalist who lies with every breath he takes and nearly lost me my job more than once.

And for what? All so I can sit in that studio and paint my way through this war when I should be fighting it. If the doctors can't fix me up, or at least pretend that I'm fit, I'll have to get myself away back to Tangier and join the French Foreign Legion. Meantime, I do my best to support the royal family and stop the secrets from sluicing out.

Blackwater, King Zog – it's all about secrets. And keeping a lid on them.

When he pushed the door open Rochester was already there, a vengeful smile hovering on his lips. He'd been long enough in the game to know that if a Palace official telephoned and suggested a drink, it wasn't to give him a story, but pump him for information. Guy already owed him big time for the lowdown on Archy

Blackwater – then he'd had to sit through an unspeakably boring lunch with Lady Sefton and a friend who turned up unexpectedly and ordered champagne cocktails and talked about friends whose names he didn't know. All that, and having his ear bent with tales of Rosie the Riveter – this meeting was going to cost Guy Harford a great deal more than the price of a drink!

'Guy! Old friend! Lovely to see you again!'

'Don't overdo it, it's just a drink, Ted. What'll it be?'

'Another of these.'

'Coming up. Now what I wanted to ask you—'

'No, no, no,' replied Ted with an oily smirk as Guy returned from the bar. 'Fair's fair, old chum. I gave you a load of information about Archy Blackwater. My turn to ask a few questions.' He was still furious at his editor's contempt for the page-one scoop on the Blackwater case.

Guy sat back in amazement. 'Sorry,' he said, startled, 'that isn't how it works, Ted. We meet, we have a drink. If you're lucky I tell you something to help feed and clothe you.'

'And I write flattering articles about the family you serve. That feeds and clothes *you*, Guy.'

The man had a point but Guy ignored it. 'I gave you the scoop on Blackwater. Your paper ran it on page one. Every other newspaper followed it up the next day, showing what a valuable piece of information it was, Ted. It's *you* who owe *me*, not the other way round. I need some information.'

Rochester took a thirsty gulp of his drink and put down the empty glass, looking at Guy in anticipation. Who was going to blink first?

'You've had your drink. Now answer my questions.'

'Ask away, my friend. I really don't know any more about Archy Blackwater and his life of vice.'

'It's about somebody else.'

'Oh? Who?'

'Fanny Goldington.'

'*Fanny?*' Rochester hooted. 'Well now there, Guy, you really *are* talking about a life of vice!'

'Tell me what you know.'

'Not so fast! My editor needs more on Blackwater – what *was* he doing at Windsor? Seems such a weird thing to do, going back to revisit the scene of the crime. He'd been ruthlessly chopped off the Palace invitation list by the new management – he had absolutely no reason to be anywhere near the Castle.'

Guy thought for a moment. He could see in Rochester's eyes the hungry need for an extra morsel, and wondered what titbit he could hand out without giving the whole game away.

'In a minute. First tell me what you know about Fanny Goldington.'

Who's going to win this poker game? thought Rochester. 'All right,' he said after a pause, 'all right! But then you give me something on Blackwater.'

'I might.'

Rochester played with his empty glass. In truth, like all journalists, he adored being asked for private information so he could display his superior knowledge – but he tried hard not to let the floodgates open too swiftly or too wide for fear of it showing.

'On her third husband, as you're possibly aware. She's finally found love, and this time it's for real.'

Ah, then you don't know about King Zog, thought Guy. *Good.*

'Now she's got what she always wanted – a superior title, a house in Mayfair, a chauffeured Rolls Royce and a bottomless bank account. She once told me she never wore a pair of shoes more than twice.'

'Paid for by . . .'

'Herself, of course. They call her the *poule de luxe*, Guy, the luxury chicken – it's quite staggering how she managed to sleep her way to the top! I used to know her quite well before she became a marchioness but she doesn't talk to me these days, far too grand. The things I could tell you!'

'Go on, then.'

'We were on the Lido in Venice with a group – Lady Diana Cooper, Cecil Beaton, Marlene Dietrich, those types of people – and she was looking at them all as if they smelt. "You may think it fun to make love," she said to me, "but if you had to make love to dirty old men as I do, you'd think again."'

'Pays the bills, though.'

'She told me once she bought two hundred and fifty pairs of shoes in a week – she has a thing about them – so then she had to go to work to pay for them. Knows the detail of every rich man's ceiling from here to the Place Vendome and back again.'

'Ha ha.'

'Why d'you want to know all this, by the way? She's not suddenly on the Palace guest list, is she? I know for a fact the Queen despises her way of life – they knew each other in the '30s, and of course Her Majesty is pure as driven snow. Can't say the same about old Fanny now, can we?'

'War, Ted – the war. Changes everything.'

'You mean she . . .' Rochester laughed, shaking his head in disbelief and taking out a small notebook. 'Nothing now,' he said, hastily looking up at Guy, as he scribbled something in it, 'but in a week or two people will be fascinated to read that scarlet is the latest fashionable colour at the Palace – with the sex queen of Mayfair supping with Their Majesties. They say her mouth is as foul as her legs are shapely.'

What a rat you are, thought Guy, but if you want to think Fanny's going to be dining at the Palace who am I to stop you?

'What else do you know?'

'Fanny? Well, she came from the suburbs, somewhere in South London. She was pretty but nothing more, but then she shared a flat with Gertie Lawrence – the actress, you remember – and fell comfortably enough under a general she was introduced to. Old enough to be her grandfather. He introduced her to a financier called Edgar, who set her up in a flat near Harrods, then she met Vincent the Viscount. He had no money, but by this stage she knew how to get it all right. What she wanted was a title to go with it, and Vincent obliged in return for a set of golf clubs and the knowledge he didn't have to work any more – like a pimp he could just live off her earnings.

'That worked for a bit, then she decided she'd prefer to be married to an earl – that old poodlefaker Rex Portlemouth – and finally she ended up where she is now, as the Marchioness of Goldington. The Mayfair flat grew into a house, then along came the Rolls. And all the while she was keeping up the good work, dontcha know,' added Ted with a wink.

'How old is she?'

'Fifty, I'd say, but looks thirty. All that exercise! Now tell me the *real* reason you're asking.'

You may be a rat but you're not such a fool, thought Guy.

'Are you in need of a story, Ted?'

A pleading look came into the journalist's eye. 'T-tell me what you know,' he muttered hoarsely. He was thinking of Sid, the contemptuous editor.

'Why don't you ask the police if there are any suspicious circumstances surrounding Archy Blackwater's death?'

'What? *Are* there?'

'Ask them, see what they say. They may say no, they may tell you something else.' I'm teasing him now, thought Guy, but he deserves it for being so utterly horrible.

'S-suicide? In his car? Couldn't get over being cold-shouldered by the royal family?'

'Keep guessing,' said Guy with a grim smile, and he got up to leave.

◆ ◆ ◆

He wandered slowly back to the Palace, unsure of his next move. He didn't take Osbert Lothian's instruction to seduce the Mistress of Mayfair terribly seriously, but such was the bizarre nature of his job that you could never tell what was coming next.

Aggie was her usual prickly self when he arrived at his small office in the mews. 'Drinkin', is it, Mr Harford?'

'Only in the course of my duties. You know otherwise I don't touch a drop. Rather like yourself.' One day, looking for a pencil sharpener, he'd discovered a half bottle of Johnny Walker in her bottom drawer, hidden in her knitting. It helped explain those pink cheeks on winter afternoons when the heating was turned off as dusk fell. The King was strict when it came to extravagance among his staff, but not about their drinking.

'Ay, well,' she said, shuffling some papers. 'There's a few notes come down from Major Lothian. Go and see Mr Morgan, he says. He's been under the weather and feels nobody pays attention to him any more.'

'Remind me who he is,' said Guy, perhaps too crisply. But really, this latest item to add to the job tally – visiting the sick – was beyond a joke.

'Ach, ye should know the name, very important man. The old king's valet. Lives like a king himsel' in that huge apartment over in St James's Palace.'

'Valet, did you say?'

91

'Ay, verra important. He was the power behind the throne in the old king's day – King George placed great reliance on his wisdom and judgement. He was with His Majesty for years and years and the King treated him more like a friend.'

'His *valet*?'

'Don't be such a snob, if you don't mind me saying it, Mr Harford. The most important people round here aren't necessarily the ones with the grand titles and the big wage packets. It's who catches the King's eye. Or the Queen's.'

'Like poor old Ed Brampton.'

'Aye, he was sweet on her, and she loved him for it. In the same regiment as her brother who was killed in the last war. She sometimes used to hold his hand when he talked about what they went through together. He was only an assistant to the Assistant Private Secretary – like you, Mr Harford – and he probably wouldn't have got a job anywhere else, what with that wooden leg of his. But she adored him and he was far more important to her than someone like Tommy.'

She pretty soon skittered away when it emerged Ed had been murdered, thought Guy, but fair enough – a queen has her reputation to preserve.

'Anyway, I don't think old Morgan ever held the King's hand but you can never tell. He was given this huge apartment and certainly you never crossed him if you wanted to stay sweet with the King.'

'So what am I supposed to do?'

'Take him a bottle of champagne, drink it with him, let him chat to you for an hour or two. Tell him the present King asked after him. Just like poor old Major Brampton used to do. You never know, you might learn something from him – he's a mine of information, even if he is a . . .'

'Yes?'

'Pompous old bore, I was going to say. Servants who get above themselves, Mr Harford! Hoity ruddy toity if you ask me – they're the worst!'

Guy groaned inwardly. 'Anything else from Lothian?'

'There's a list here, quite long. Keep you busy for the rest of the week.' She said it triumphantly – nothing she liked better than to see her boss worked off his feet.

'Anyone telephone?'

'There's a list on your desk. Oh, and someone calling herself Lady Sutch rang, several times. Wants to invite you to lunch. Now I'm going over to see the Master of the Household, he always makes sure I get a nice cup of tea.' She took out a powder compact and pertly dusted her nose, only narrowly avoiding falling into the hoity-toity trap herself.

Guy waited till she'd squirted on some perfume and departed before picking up the phone.

'Caroline? Guy Harford here, sorry to have missed you earlier. How's everything?'

'Hew is having such trouble with his sheep, Guy. They keep him up day and night, dying in droves. Why is that? I don't like to bother him when he's so busy, what with the downpours they're having in North Wales just now. I'm camping at Esme's.'

'Sorry to hear it.'

'But here in London, Guy – all serene! The sun shines every day and I feel younger and younger.'

'Is there anything I can—'

'Darling, there most certainly is! You can take me out to lunch! Failing that, I can take *you* out! Hew's just sold a ghastly old painting for a huge amount of money and he's finally going to fix the roof! It's been dripping for years!'

'Well, that would be nice, but—'

'Of course there's a nasty patch on the wall where the painting was, and we can't afford to repaint the whole hall *and* do the roof. It's vast – acres, darling! But then I had this idea, Guy – *you* can paint my portrait like you promised me all those years ago, and it would cover the patch perfectly!'

'Caroline, it was lovely to see you the other day and we must have lunch some time. But I've got my hands full here at the Palace, not doing much painting at the moment.' The lie slipped out easily enough – did he *ever* really promise to paint her? Certainly she was decorative enough with her long, skinny legs, pink cheeks and mountain of russet curls, but she lacked personality – the one crucial element he sought to lay down on the canvas.

'I heard about your exhibition. A woman burglar. It caused a small sensation – you found time to paint her, didn't you?'

'Caroline, let me put it this way: I'm not accepting commissions at the moment. The war, other commitments – you know how it is.'

There was a snort at the other end of the line. 'Hew's promised me he'll pay whatever you ask. That roof can survive another winter. Go on, Guy – tell you what, I'll sock you lunch at The Ritz.'

He thought about this carefully for a moment. 'You remember us meeting the other day in Bury Street?'

'And you looking very trim and handsome, darling!' Her voice tinkled.

'We were talking about Fanny Goldington and . . . her friend. The one she was lunching with.'

'Oh *that* old fat fraud! And such an ugly name, darling – Zog! Sounds like a plant pot!'

'What more do you know about them?'

'Very little – why d'you ask?'

'Tell you what,' said Guy. 'Go and have a chat with your chum Esme and see what the pair of you can come up with on Fanny and her royal friend. I know at heart you're a couple of supersleuths.'

Or to put it another way, satchel-mouthed gossips.

'Why, darling?'

'Could be very useful to people I know. Very. Get going, see what the pair of you can find out and I'll buy you both luncheon. Maybe not The Ritz, but I know somewhere nice and cosy.'

There was a squeak of excitement down the other end of the line. 'Oooh!' gasped Caroline Sutch. 'How exciting! War work – I'm doing war work!'

'If that's what you want to call it,' replied Guy briskly, and put down the receiver.

CHAPTER NINE

An ancient tableau unfolded before Guy as he walked through the arched gateway, past two Gurkha soldiers and into the Tudor red-brick splendour of Ambassador's Court.

Once this had been a palace in fact as well as in name, with both Charles II and James II born and baptised here, and used as a bolthole by Henry VIII. Those ancient queens, Mary Tudor and Elizabeth, had enjoyed its comforts, and Charles I spent his last night on earth here before being taken down the road to Whitehall to have his head cut off. Here, so much more than at Buckingham Palace, lay the links that stretched back nearly half a millennium and made St James's the senior royal palace.

Guy unhurriedly made his way through Engine Court, Friary Court and Colour Court before arriving at the black-painted door-way with a hand-painted sign proclaiming it to be the residence of Ronald Morgan.

A young footman answered his knock. 'Hello,' said Guy, smil-ing. 'Champagne for the patient!'

'More like impatient, if you ask me,' sniffed the young man, not yet old enough for call-up but already with the world-weariness of an ancient mariner. ''E's upstairs, follow me.'

'Thank you.'

'You're Mr Harford?' came over his shoulder.

'Yes.'

'You're late. 'E don't like to be kep' waiting.'

Guy moved forward through the hall and looked about the spacious apartment in wonderment – a wide staircase, Tudor panelling, painted pillars and lead-light windows greeted his gaze, together with a selection of distinguished portraits in gilt frames. All this for one old man, he thought. Would he merit such a palazzo if he lasted the course?

If anything the upper hall seemed more palatial than below, and in a room at the far end sat an old fellow in a silk dressing gown and embroidered slippers.

'I won't get up,' he said, indicating that here was a man who need show deference only to his sovereign, and that sovereign was long dead.

'Hello, Mr Morgan,' said Guy, shielding his irritation. 'His Majesty asked me to bring you this.'

'Let me see.'

Guy handed him the bottle of Pol Roger '32, peeling back the linen napkin which had kept it cool on its short journey from Buckingham Palace.

'I'm more used to getting the '27,' grumbled the old man. 'His Majesty knows I hate young wine.'

Guy looked at the man's cloudy eyes and wondered if he was talking about the present king or his father.

'Tommy Lascelles asked to be remembered to you. He says do you remember the Durbah of 1911?'

'Better'n he does,' the old man snorted. 'He can only have been a subaltern back then. Has he got the top job yet?' Everyone was talking about Tommy getting rid of his boss, the much-hated Alec Hardinge.

'I wonder,' said Guy deflecting the question, 'shall I open it now? It's past eleven o'clock.'

'Seven minutes past,' said Morgan, enjoying this moment of superiority. 'You new lot don't know the meaning of punctual. That's why His Majesty always kept his clocks half an hour fast – then he was never late.'

What an ogre he must have been to work for, thought Guy. 'Glasses, Mr Morgan?'

'Call me Ronnie. Over there on the tray.' He shifted his slippered feet and Guy noticed he was wearing silk socks; how magnificent.

'What a remarkable place,' said Guy, genuinely enough. 'Is there a Mrs Morgan?'

'Long gone. Tomkins takes care o' me. Cheerio.'

With the first sip his countenance altered, a slight flush came to his cheeks, and he leant forward engagingly. 'That's better,' he said. 'Me heart-starter! At my age you need something to get it going. Come and sit down and give me all the news.'

'I don't know that I'm much good with—'

'Old Major Brampton used to bring me all the latest. He was very close to the Queen, you know. She's a real one for the gossip.'

'I'm afraid I don't see so much of HM, Ronnie; I spend most of my time chasing round after Tommy. Only recently I seem to be seeing rather a lot of Osbert Lothian – he's doing a stand-in job in the private secretary's office.'

'Man's an idiot,' wheezed Ronnie. 'I remember him back in the old king's day, used to walk about with a poker up his arse and a stink under his nose.'

Oh, thought Guy – I think I'm going to like you. 'Top-up?'

'Go on then. He was in the Black Watch till they found a way of getting rid of 'im. Bit of a mix-up with the mess funds. An' if you believe that, har har! But his sister took the present king's fancy long ago, so 'e's got a job for life.'

They drank and smiled, having quickly discovered each other's wavelength. Guy wished he'd brought a second bottle.

'I'm not a courtier really,' he said, smiling. 'I'm only at the Palace by accident.'

'You're not the first and you won't be the last,' said Ronnie. 'I could tell you're only passing through, like in the navy where they have those zigzags on their cuff – Wavy Navy. Temporary gentleman.'

'That's about it.'

'It's a good life if you don't buckle.'

'Tell me something about life with the old king. I have the feeling you saw him as a real person, not as an emperor.'

Ronnie stretched slightly, delighted this stray fawn had come to sip at the fountain of his knowledge. 'No man is a hero to his valet they say,' he began imposingly, 'but old King George was always a bit of a hero to me. And all those sons of his used to complain about what a rotten father he was, but he was only trying to knock them into shape.' He sighed contentedly after each sip of champagne. 'Have you met Queen Mary?'

'Almost.' Guy remembered the old girl giving him the runaround when he was dispatched by Lascelles to carpet her for buying black-market sausages and for sending money to her German relatives – jailable offences in wartime.

'They were such fun together. Both looked a bit pokerish,' he laughed, 'but in the privacy of their own home, well!'

'Really?'

'There was an old record they used to play, "The Departure of the Troop Ship", just a load of old noise really but it used to bring a tear to His Majesty's eye every time. At the end a military band plays "God Save the King" – and he and Queen Mary used to get up out of their chairs and stand stock-still while it played. I promise you, Mr Harford, made me weep with laughter every time!'

'He was a bit of a monster, though, from what I've heard?'

The old boy shook his head. 'One Easter, 'e said to me, "Ronnie," 'e said, "we're in dire need of rain. But I don't want my people gettin' wet over the Bank 'oliday." He cared for his people, see. More'n his sons do, that's for sure. Sometimes when we was out for a drive – I motored him too, 'e liked to chat to me – 'e'd tell me to stop the car so he could just look at the people. 'E loved them – and they loved 'im.'

He adjusted the silk scarf at his neck as if the late majesty was about to pop his head round the door. ''E 'ad some funny ways, though. It was my job to dress 'im ready for dinner, and what 'e loved was people coming in to watch 'im get ready. Putting the cufflinks in, brushing 'is 'air, straightening 'is tie. It was like something out of Versailles, if you know what I mean. A bit of a show-off. The present King's a bit funny that way as well.'

'Did you have much to do with His present Majesty when you were still in service? When he was Duke of York?'

'Oh yars,' said Morgan, shaking his head. 'Not a patch on 'is dad, though 'e does 'is best, poor chap. And anyway, it's she what wears the trousers. That's why she and Tommy don't get on. Tommy tells the King what to do – that's 'is job, and very good at it he is, I have the utmost respect unlike some of those other wallahs – but then *she* tells the King what to do. Guess which one His Majesty listens to.'

'I got the impression that—'

'Old Tommy thinks her judgement's poor and somehow she got to hear of it. That's why they're a bit cool towards each other, surely you've noticed?'

Guy looked at the old fellow, his lifelong service to the old king a suit of armour against present-day attack from the new regime. Here, in this sanctum, he reigned as if he wore the crown himself. How refreshing not to care about what people think – unlike almost everyone else in royal service. You're above it all, thought Guy. Why have I never met you before?

'Queen Mary, though, she's a long, cold drink of water. I remember 'er advising the present Queen when she married Bertie. She said, "Don't have any friends, Elizabeth. It could be embarrassin'."'

'What did she mean by that?' Without asking, Guy topped the old boy up; obviously chatting was a thirsty business.

'Restrict yourself to the royal circle. Keep everyone else at arm's length. Be friendly, but don't 'ave friends. It seems to work, but it's 'ardly natural, is it?' He picked up a small bell and rang it.

Tomkins slithered into the room as if he'd been listening at the door. 'Put another bottle, on ice, Tommy! Only see if you can find the '27 – this one ain't so good.'

'Oh no,' said Guy, 'I can't be drinking your wine, Ronnie. It's precious in wartime, you hang on to it.'

'Don't you worry, I have my own supply, but don't tell the King that. Thank him kindly for the bottle, won't you, though. I like to keep on 'is good side even if 'e's not really my cup of tea. I preferred the Prince of Wales, to be honest, even if 'e was a bad boy.'

A thought struck Guy. 'Did you ever go down to Fort Belvedere?'

'Two separate staffs,' he replied, shaking his head. 'Each guarding their master very jealous-like. King George, 'e hated the prince's friends, and the prince ended up despising 'is father. Rode 'im too hard. So they didn't mingle, and neither did their staffs.'

'Did you know Lord Blackwater?'

'Oh yes, funny fella, but always very nice to me. Very grand, like all those old families – but 'e 'ad an eye for the pantry boys, 'e did. Naughty.'

'Know him well?'

'Me?' the old boy laughed. 'I wasn't 'is kind.'

'You heard that he'd died? It was in the newspapers. I've been trying to find someone who knew him down at the Fort. Unfinished business, sort of thing – I get asked to do a lot of that.' He laughed apologetically.

''Oo you want then is Rufus, used to do for the prince. Footman. 'E works for Princess Marina since the abdication, but 'im and Lord Blackwater used to get on . . . handsome.'

'And where . . . ?'

'Out at Coppins, the country 'ome. Old Marina doesn't come into town very often. She's not that welcome at the Palace since Prince George died.'

'Oh?'

'The Queen – Elizabeth, not Mary – thinks of her as foreign. She don't like foreigners. Don't like abroad.'

'Well, she *is* foreign. Greek. Via Paris. I used to see her sometimes walking in the Tuileries when I lived there before the war. A very striking woman.'

'Queen Elizabeth ain't that keen, and it's not just 'er looks. Marina once let slip that she considered herself more royal than the royals in Buck House, and Her Maj took agin.'

'Is she? More royal?'

'The granddaughter of kings, twice over. Our Queen isn't – just the daughter of a Scotch Earl, and how many of those are there? Two a penny! But anyway, if you want to find out something about that scamp Blackwater, you hop over to Coppins. Twenty minutes from Windsor.'

'What a mine of information you are, Ronnie.'

'Come again. Only bring the ruddy '27 next time.'

The summer heat beat down on his old straw hat on the ten-minute walk back to the Palace, wilting the pitifully few flowers at Canada Gate, but back in the office the temperature was barely above freezing.

'Where *have* you been?' snapped Aggie. 'Tommy wants you. Now!'

'I thought he was up at Sandringham with HM.'

'Back this morning. Asked for you *several* times. Get up there now, Mr Harford, if you know what's good for you.'

Guy took the familiar journey at a trot. Tommy Lascelles was a fair boss but inclined to be a bit hair-shirt with unpunctual employees.

'Sorry, Tommy. Drinking champagne with Ronnie Morgan. He seems to have a peculiarly advanced palate. Can you honestly tell the difference between a '32 and a '27?'

'Rrr,' came the reply. Lascelles looked as though his stiff collar had shrunk a size and his eyes were bulging slightly.

'I'm here now. What can I do to be of help?'

Lascelles stared across his desk like a Victorian headmaster. 'We've had this conversation before. You know Lady Sefton, I think.'

'We're old friends, yes. In Paris . . .'

'One of her closest friends is the Duchess of Windsor, is it not?'

'I believe so, though she never talks to me about—'

Lascelles leant forward and thumped the desk. 'Well, she can start talking now!'

'I beg your pardon, Tommy. What's she done?'

'It's not *her*. It's the damned Simpson woman – she's put a hex on the Duke!'

'Sorry, I don't quite follow.'

'Look at this,' said Lascelles, tossing a cablegram across to Guy. He picked it up and read.

PRO BHOUSE

URGENT TLASC TOP SECRET

EX WASH DBL

TONIGHT NEWYORKPOST CLAIMING DUKE WINDSOR
ABOUT TO TENDER RESIGNATION GOVERNOR BAHA-
MAS. ALSO STATES HRH ATTEMPTING TO BECOME
UNITED STATES CITIZEN. AUTHOR OF THE ARTICLE
CORNELIUS VANDERBILT. ADVISE ACTION DBL.

'Is this such a surprise, Tommy? I heard things weren't going so well in Nassau.'

'I don't think you can have read it very closely,' came the grim reply. 'This message says two things – what are they?'

Guy read the short message again. 'That the Duke's resigning from his governorship of the Bahamas. And that he wants to become an American citizen. I don't see . . .'

'You don't see? You don't see *betrayal* written all over this cable? In fact not one, but two betrayals of the crown? The Duke, who's a public servant, *abandoning his post* when his strict instructions are to stay there and do a job of work? And then he's applying for American citizenship? What can the man be thinking of?'

'When you put it like that, Tommy, of course. But can he actually resign?'

'The trouble with that person is he does what he ruddy well pleases and nobody can control him – not Churchill, not the King. The only one who can is *her*. He's a loose cannon which will crash against the bows of the ship and let the water in, don't you see? Just as our relations with America are at the very best and we're all pulling in the same direction. The King's off to North Africa shortly where he'll be mixing with the American high command – how's that going to make him look when they discover a British king can be bought for a dollar?'

'I'm afraid I didn't quite take all that in immediately, Tommy. Is there anything I can do?'

'Go and see the Sefton woman. You have some influence there, I hear. I'll talk to her husband, but in the past he's always said, "She's her own woman, she's independent, I can't make her do or say anything." And I think out of respect for his closeness to the King, Lady Sefton doesn't share every secret she has with him.'

Lascelles fixed Guy with a steely gaze. 'I gather the same rules don't apply in your case. You were in Paris together before the war. She talks to you.'

'We weren't that close,' Guy lied.

'Rumour has it otherwise,' said his boss smoothly. 'There's another message hidden in that telegram. Have you spotted it yet?'

Guy picked up the paper once more and turned it over in case he'd missed something on the other side, but there was nothing. He turned it back and scanned the crude capitalised print.

'Ah,' he said. 'Vanderbilt.'

'The richest family in America and one of them has to stoop to being a . . . *journalist*!'

'I think he's a bit more than that. He owns several newspapers.'

'And he's a cousin of your friend Lady Sefton, I discover. Whose best friend is the Duchess of Windsor. D'you see what I'm getting at, Guy? The Duchess clearly wants this information out in the public domain. She wants America to know that her husband will soon take the Oath of Allegiance and in doing that, toss away a thousand years of his nation's heritage. What will that look like to our people fighting to the death in this war? That their former king's jumped ship, abandoned them to their fate? And to the people of America? "Oh, he'd rather be one of us – what the hell is wrong with his own country?"'

'Yes, Tommy. Dreadful.'

'It's betrayal, Guy, pure and simple. Go and see your friend Lady Sefton and ask her what the hell is going on. Do it *now*!'

CHAPTER TEN

For once she looked flustered. The trademark flame-red hair was disarrayed and the Parisian chic for which she was so famous seemed to be missing.

'Nothing to do with me, Guy, I assure you,' she muttered, but she looked away as she said it.

'This is serious, Foxy! Tell me what you know!'

They were sitting on a bench in St James's Square and a sudden summer breeze lifted her skirt. A gloved hand clamped down firmly on her thigh while the other reached to grab her hat. 'There's nothing I can tell you,' she said. 'Obviously I understand the seriousness of this, that the King and Queen must be beside themselves with worry that the Duke's about to let the side down. But I really don't know anything more than that.'

'The problem for us is that all communication between the brothers is at a standstill,' Guy explained. 'The Duke talks to Winston, but not to his family. Tommy says nobody has any idea what's going on in his mind. There's been a lot of press criticism of his governorship, and the local businessmen who really run the place take no notice of him. Then the pair of them keep making trips to the American mainland to go shopping – they've been given a rough ride over that. So I can see they're fed up, stuck in a backwater like that. But what on earth can he be thinking of, becoming an American?'

'Wallis never said anything to me about it.'

'Look,' said Guy, 'I know we agreed long ago that I wouldn't ask you about the Duchess – it would embarrass us both because whatever you told me I'd feel obliged to report back to the Palace. But this is different. Think back – what's going on in the Duchess's mind?'

She twisted uncomfortably on the seat, then got up. 'Come on,' she said, and under the stony gaze of King William III spurring his stallion on to who knew what military victory, they started a circular walk around the gardens.

'I'll be frank,' said Foxy. 'Wallis feels hounded. Hounded by the British, of course – we know the knives are out for her – but hounded by her own people too. She told me she'd learnt that the FBI have opened a file on her and David. When they made their first visit to Miami a couple of years ago, they were tailed by an agent.'

'Understandable, I suppose.'

'She doesn't see it that way! David was very upset when he heard about it – being followed around like a common criminal, he said.'

'I'm sure they do it with every visiting foreign dignitary,' said Guy.

'No, no, you don't understand – they're being *investigated*. Her letters are being censored – I know, because when she writes to me there are lines crossed out and the envelopes are re-sealed. The head of the FBI, Hoover, has assigned some big guns to make trouble for them – a special assistant to the Attorney General called Alexander Holtzoff, and a sidekick spy called Fletcher Warren.'

'Why?'

'I have no real idea. There was all that fuss about their visit to Germany and meeting Hitler before war broke out. Wallis's Paris lawyer has been arrested on suspicion of being a Nazi agent. There's David friendship with Bedaux, who's in jail now in America. And then their best friend in Nassau, a man called Wenner-Gren, has been blacklisted by the US authorities and has fled. All these people with Nazi affiliations – that could be it. But it could be something else.'

'What?'

'There's a man called Berle who's President Roosevelt's top spymaster. He seems to be in charge of it all, and determined to get them for something or other. Their old friend Vincent Astor sailed out to visit them, all very friendly, but he was actually spying for Berle. They feel naked and alone, Guy! David gets no support from London, and almost none from the British Embassy in Washington DC – as a couple they're being hung out to dry.'

Guy halted, looking up at the grand greystone building where the Prince Regent had received news of Wellington's victory over Napoleon. Wherever you went in London, it seemed, you were reminded of centuries of Britain's great royal heritage – but what it had come down to now was an exiled ex-king being hounded by a ruthless spy-hunter longing to splatter mud wherever he could.

'This is just awful,' he said, shaking his head.

'There's more,' said Foxy, chewing her gloves as they walked on. 'There's a move to get David and Wallis dismissed – shoved out of the Bahamas – being led by a man called David Bowes-Lyon.'

'The Queen's kid brother?'

'That's him. Apparently he's a big cheese now in the Washington embassy. So picture what it must be like for them out there, attacked on all sides like that.'

'Is this on the orders of Her Majesty? *His* Majesty?'

'I have no idea,' she replied, shaking her head. 'All I can say is, people haven't a clue what the Windsors are going through.'

Dwarfed by the enormous oaks overhead, they'd completed one circuit of the square and now they started out on a second. The way they whispered to each other, their heads so close together, people sitting on the grass munching their sandwiches assumed they were lovers.

'So if I've got this right,' said Guy, 'the Duke and Duchess are under siege from the US authorities. Yet the Duke still wants to become an American citizen. That all sounds a bit loopy.'

'Look, I don't know what's in their minds – Wallis's letters give you clues but don't tell you the whole story. We've had a couple of telephone calls but she can't say much – who knows who's listening?'

She stopped and turned to him. 'You were talking about betrayal earlier – what David has done since he stepped down from the throne. Well, that works both ways, Guy. I'm an American and I can see the problem from the other end of the telescope. The difficulty with you British is you're obsessed with your royal family and can't see the wood for the trees.'

'Nothing wrong in that,' said Guy.

'Well, consider this, Mr Courtier. David and Wallis are doing their damnedest to serve Britain the best they can in that fly-blown hellhole they call Nassau. Possibly one day it'll be a paradise, people will invest there and turn it into one of the most enviable places on earth – it certainly has the potential. But right now it's pretty darn ramshackle, run by a local mafia and with racial problems you could not begin to believe. As Governor, David has done his best to rein in the Bay Street Boys, as they're known, and ease conditions for the native population. From what I hear, he hasn't done a bad job.'

'That's not what I hear,' replied Guy. 'I hear he lacks judgement. He's driven by resentment of the way he's been treated by the Palace and by Whitehall, and is constantly spooked by the idea of losing all his money. He chooses the wrong friends and sticks his nose into things he should steer clear of.'

'Have you ever been to Nassau?'

'No.'

'You should,' she retorted sharply. 'You might think differently if you could see things from their perspective! This needs sorting out, Guy!'

I wonder if that dubious pleasure awaits me, he thought wearily.

'Anyway,' said Foxy, turning on her heel, 'you asked me why, if they're being pursued by the US authorities, he wants to become a US citizen. The answer is, he feels he can handle the Americans – we think straightforwardly. What he can't cope with are the Tudor court politics – the backstabbing, the poisoning of minds – back at home. What's all this business about David Bowes-Lyon, for heaven's sake? What's all that about?'

'Well, as it happens I know something about him,' replied Guy. 'When I first came to the Palace he used to bring in a few friends from Fleet Street – show them a good time, give them a drink, give them something to tell their wives and hopefully their readers. Then he started something called the Political Warfare Executive. Not sure what it does, but he's been based in Washington DC.

'He's very popular there, I hear, because he's the Queen's younger brother – but he's been trading off his social status and thinks he's more important than he is. He has the ear of the Queen, of course, and she tells him things about the war he wouldn't hear in the normal course of events. Bertie, the King, confides in her and I'm afraid she probably passes it on.'

'But why's he got it in for Wallis and David?'

'Because of the Queen – she despises them. And, I gather, Bowes-Lyon's an intriguer – he'd enjoy making the Windsors pack up their bags and get sent off to some even further-flung corner of empire. Think what the American press would make of their being kicked out of Nassau – I think Bowes-Lyon would probably get a lot of satisfaction out of that.'

'His sister too.'

'I couldn't possibly comment. I work for them, for heaven's sake!'

◆ ◆ ◆

Rodie was on her best worst behaviour. She'd said no to The Surprise, partly because she didn't want to bump into that old goat Augustus John, but also because she wanted to go dancing – Joe Loss was on at the Hammersmith Palais.

But Guy was adamant. 'Hell of a day. I just want a drink, some supper and an early night.'

'You're getting old. Look at your hair, I can see grey in there! But come on, mate, show a leg – I want some fun before I die!'

So far he was winning the argument, digging in his heels and sticking to the pub. 'You go,' he said wearily. 'Sure to be lots of handsome American soldiers you can do-si-do with.'

'Go on, you ain't much of a dancer but we 'ave fun, don't we, darlin', when we go out?'

'Not tonight.' He looked round the crowded bar. They'd got the quiet corner table, away from the noisy throng where someone was attempting to get the drinkers to sing 'The White Cliffs of Dover' in time with each other – and in tune. Progress was slowed by the amount of orders being shunted back and forth over the bar.

'Safe enough to talk here,' he said, bending his head towards her.

'Go on,' she whispered seductively, 'the Palais.' She said it *pally*.

He shook his head. 'Tell me about the Fort,' he said gruffly. 'I need to know what's going on.'

'Nuffin' to say. I went, I came back.'

'And?'

'Like I said, mate, nuffin'.'

Guy sensed there was something she desperately did want to say. 'Is it Rupe? Has he told you to keep your trap shut?'

'Nuffin',' she sang. 'Tra la!'

'Because, you know, he's just too officious when it comes to security. For heaven's sake, Rodie, how long have we known each other? You can tell me!'

'We've known each other since I broke into your office at the Palace and left a rose on yer desk. An' what progress have we made since then, mister?' She waggled her third finger, left hand at him.

'Look, darling, when the war's over . . .'

'You never called me darlin' before,' she said, rearing away suspiciously. 'Whaddya want?'

'Just tell me about the Fort. For goodness' sake, it's an extraordinary experience we shared, finding that body there in that place. Tell me what's going on, won't you?'

'Honest, this war,' she snapped. There was a lull in the racket over by the bar and she waited till they started up again.

'Ter-morrer, jus' you wait an' see . . .'

She took a swig of her gin then put the glass down with a bang. 'It's like sleeping with the enemy,' she said angrily. 'You come 'ome from work and don't tell me what's goin' on, and I go about my business and I'm not allowed to talk about it either. We can't talk to each other, we don't talk to each other – what's the point? Can't we trust each other?'

He leant forward and gave her cheek a kiss.

'Oi!' she snapped. 'What's that perfume? Who've you been messin' about with?'

'Just an old friend,' said Guy, brushing the question aside. He desperately wanted to find out about her break-in.

'That's what they all say,' she said fierily. 'Go on, own up!'

He sighed. 'If you must know, it was Foxy Sefton. Old friend from Paris days. You remember her.'

'You're not two-timin' me, are you? Cos I won't have that. What are you doin', kissing her?'

'We had a chat at lunchtime. Business. She gave me a kiss goodbye. *And,*' he added, suddenly irritated, 'a kiss hello, too, for good measure. She's the kissing kind. But as you can see I've come home all in one piece.'

'You and 'er! You talk a lot about 'er – what is it with you two? Is it because she's posh and I'm not?'

'Bloody hell, Rodie! Just tell me about the ruddy Fort!'

The swell in community singing drowned out the angry row that followed.

Eventually the hothead with the Eton crop and the big black eyes calmed herself with another slug of gin and a wave to the barman to bring more.

'But since we're talkin' about her,' she said, 'you may as well tell me everything. It's only ever been bits and pieces.'

'OK, but then let's not talk about her any more. She's part of my past.'

'As long as she is, mate.'

'It goes back ten years or more. She sailed over to Paris after Jean Patou spotted her in New York and wanted her as one of his mannequins. I was in art school then, and we were together for a time and I painted her. Then she married another American called Erskine Gwynne, very clever, whose sister Alice was the mistress of Prince George, the Duke of Kent. Alice – Kiki, they called her – was a drug addict and got the prince into a lot of trouble. Plus people thought she secretly had Prince George's baby.'

'Sounds just like a bleedin' gossip column. No wonder you got a job at the Palace if you were goin' round with that lot.'

'Foxy's married to Lord Sefton now and is very right and proper.'

'Oh, the toffs don't do it – is that it?' she laughed scornfully. 'No sex, please, we're British?'

'Stop that and tell me about Fort Belvedere.'

'Take me 'ome then, and I might.'

Though it was late there were still vermilion streaks in the sky as they slowly walked towards the river. She put her arm through his and as they turned into Tite Street, he bent down and kissed her.

'You're lovely,' she said.

'So are you.'

She put her mouth close to his ear. 'Don't look now,' she whispered, 'but a geezer in a bowler 'at is followin' us.'

'Nonsense.'

''E is, 'e just ducked into an alleyway but I recognised 'im. 'E was in the pub, sittin' by 'imself. Got a newspaper but kept looking at you.'

Guy looked round into the dusk. 'Nobody there. Come on, let's get home. I want to go to bed.'

They walked on but after a dozen steps Guy suddenly turned sharply, just in time to see a man hastily beating a retreat up the street towards the King's Road.

He was moving at speed, and the light was almost gone, but the bowler hat gave the game away.

The man in a hurry, unless he was much mistaken, was Scabbard, the King's Messenger.

CHAPTER ELEVEN

In the half-light, the streets of Oldham didn't look so bad – no worse, certainly, than any of the other soot-blackened towns they'd trundled through on their way from Burnley to Sheffield. Tomorrow, they would give their cut-down version of *Swan Lake* in the sure knowledge that a city that had never had sight of a professional ballet would rise in rapturous applause.

For someone whose whole life was dance, and who came from a country so steeped in culture, it seemed strange to Elena that this was a land of brass bands whose repertoire never stretched as far as Tchaikovsky. And yet, as the bus made its noisy, smelly, bumpy progress across the roads of northern England, she had to confess that the welcome the Vic-Wells Ballet received wherever they went was overwhelming. The nation was slowly starving, living daily in hope of victory but with no immediate signs of it, abandoned by their loved ones who'd gone to war and who may never return, and in fear of the bombs ahead. Yet the sight of Frederick Ashton's disciplined choreography, performed by an amiable and handsome group of young people, came as an unexpected treasure trove, a jewel found in the mud. And after each performance the applause outmatched that of the previous night.

Sheffield did not yet know what treats it had in store, but the Vic-Wells troupe took nothing for granted. The shrill voice of their leader Ninette de Valois came down to them at the barre, in the dressing room, onstage – even in the tour bus. Elena sat, her eyes screwed up against the fading light, repairing her ballet shoes, thinking of the steps ahead and the roar of the crowd.

This was her first chance to demonstrate the skills honed long ago, it seemed, at the Staatsoper in Vienna, and she did not disappoint. Her welcome into the company had been slow and grudging, but her power and grace soon overcame the inevitable prejudice against a newcomer; indeed the personnel of the Vic-Wells group was now turning over rapidly as the company split itself between its cultural mission in the north and maintaining a presence in London, its spiritual home. There was scarcely time for the petty feuds and factions that normally dominate a tight-knit company.

Simon, her sponsor and protector, had returned to London to dance in a new ballet, *The Quest*, and she felt his absence keenly. There had been a last meeting over tea and chips in a café by the station, and she'd handed over a heavy parcel. 'Some reading for you on the train, my dear.' They hugged, but the kiss he gave her was brief and, to Elena, ambiguous.

She became friends with Hilda, the chain-smoking company pianist, but soon, against Simon's advice, was spending more and more time in the company of the newcomers, Mikha and Pyotr – so muscular and so Russian with their crew cuts and blond hair, dancing with precision and polish.

Simon had warned she should keep her distance – was it simply jealousy? – but she found the pair full of fun – boisterous and determinedly anarchic. Early on they'd told her a secret, ordering her not to mention it to anyone, but it didn't seem much of a secret to Elena and she'd shared it with Simon. Now, with the thrilling prospect of dancing before audiences again, it had fled her mind as she relaxed more and more in their company.

To others in the Vic-Wells troupe, the stars were to be revered – Margot Fonteyn, Bobby Helpmann, the young Moira Shearer and, of course, their dance master Freddy Ashton – but to Mick and Pete, as they became known, these great names were simply targets for their jokes and ribaldry.

They'd introduced themselves on a previous trip when they all took an overnight train to Wolverhampton. The heating was off, they were shunted – as always – into a siding to allow vital goods trains through and, while the rest of the company sank into gloom and exhaustion, Mick and Pete kept up a jokey double act designed, it seemed to Elena, specifically to please her.

'Oh *krasivaya* Yelena,' they yodelled, 'we would swim the Black Sea for thee. Be free, come to me, we make you see how beautiful you be . . .'

There was no food, the Thermos flasks had been drained hours ago, and the cold was getting worse, but this improvised double act managed to keep up their antics until they finally arrived at six in the morning into Wolverhampton.

'How can you go on so long?'

'It is war, dearest Yelena. We stay up all night because we will be dead tomorrow.'

In the dressing room, in that interminable wait to go onstage, they told Elena their story. How they fled Moscow in their teens, then found jobs in Norway.

'We were in love,' they chorused. 'Not with each other, with Marina Lee. She was such star, too big for Moscow.'

'Really?' Elena blinked. 'The home of the Kirov Ballet? The Bolshoi? She was too big for them?'

'Oh *da, da*,' they laughed. 'Far too big. She had to go to Oslo.'

'Oslo? Is there even a theatre there? I've never heard of a Norwegian ballet,' said Elena, 'and I know most of the—'

'The Revolution, darlink,' they yodelled. 'She could not bear another bowl of potato soup, so she flees to Norway years ago. And we follow her. She is divine. Why have you never heard of her?'

Elena laughed. But then they told her how the Germans invaded Norway in 1940, and how they escaped by sea to Holland, leaving Marina behind, before making their way to London. 'Those Germans!' they chorused. 'Have you ever *seen* such table manners!'

She felt safe beside them – maybe they were a couple and, uniquely for a ballet company, uninterested romantically in anyone else. But they would come and sit with Elena and ask her about the days at the Staatsoper in Vienna and what it was like working with the great Austrian names. She had danced before great audiences; they had not, and they loved to hear her tales.

As she watched from the wings she could see Mick and Pete were perfectly matched, achieving what was required with ease, so muscular were they. Their smiles thrown lavishly out to the audience, and their bulging jockstraps, ensured the matrons of the industrial towns they visited went away with happy memories. Elena could see that though neither would become a principal dancer, they had made themselves invaluable in the line.

'Our dream is London,' they said. 'We tear every muscle at Vera Volkova's class for two years. We have nice little flat in Soho. Then we are sent up here! Maybe when we are no longer able to jump or to carry hulking great brutes like you around, Yelena, we will open a little café and you will come.'

'Ha ha!'

They discussed the love affairs and intrigues involving the others in the company, especially Margot, their greatest star. The affair with Constant Lambert was a push-me-pull-you, with one cooling while the other heated up, then the other way around, but a recent arrival had been another principal, called Sheila Fleming. A fly had landed in the ointment.

'Constant can't take his eyes off her, even when he's conducting,' they said. 'That's when he's not prowling round after Laureen.'

'Who's she?' Elena dug her needle into the toe of her shoe.

'Darlink, beautiful negress who works as cigarette girl in low dive called The Nest. He gets all experience about nightlife from her. Ha ha!'

The boys both laughed a lot, but at night in the bus or on the train they would sometimes sit together and talk in Russian, their voices growing darker and less jokey. The horrors of the regime they'd fled had clearly left a mark on both, but it was something they never discussed with Elena or other members of the company.

One night after dancing *Les Sylphides* in Barnsley, they all sat sipping sherry from the bottle in the scantily furnished back bedroom of a terrace house on the outskirts of town. The further north they went, the draughtier the accommodation became.

'Tell us about Simon,' said Pete.

'There's nothing I can tell you that you don't already know. You two are a mine of information. Where do you get it all?'

'We torture people till they tell us everything,' said Mick, grinning.

'Then we torture some more,' echoed Pete with a fiendish laugh. You could almost believe them, the look in their eyes as they said it.

'Is he your boyfriend?' asked Mick suddenly.

'It's not like that. He's a friend. He's been so kind.'

'Such an unusual type to be dancer. As if only half of him is involved, while other half is hidden behind curtain.'

'That's an odd thing to say,' replied Elena. They're jealous, she thought. He's back in London while they're out here on the road.

'He does not trust us,' said Pete, his mouth turning down. 'Very suspicious. Why is that?'

'You know these English,' said Elena. 'Insular.' For a moment she wondered if their collective vocabulary stretched to the word, but they seemed to catch on.

'He's not little Englander, he like foreigners. But we think he spying on us.'

Elena looked in surprise at both of them, sitting opposite her in the bus with a sign on the window saying, 'No Spitting'. It was true that Simon wasn't like the other men in the company, there was definitely something 'other' about him – but even if there was, why would he spy on his fellow dancers?

And what about them was worth spying on? They were dancers! And who would he spy for, anyway? It was too ridiculous – but then, she thought, no more absurd than some of the rumours that swirled around the company, especially away from London when everyone shelved their lives to live the suitcase existence of gypsies and travellers with plenty of time to dream up fantasies.

'I suppose I understand what you mean. In Vienna, after the Anschluss, it was as if someone was always looking at you over the top of their newspaper in the Petersplatz or the Schweitzergarten. Like you, I had to get away from the Germans, so I know it when I see prying eyes. But Simon's not like that. Not at all!'

'We think he is,' said Mick, the smile gone from his face. 'You must watch out, Yelena.'

She thought it ironic that Simon had said the same thing to her about them.

◆ ◆ ◆

'But do *gentlemen* come here?' asked Fanny Goldington, not disapprovingly.

'We are artists,' said Guy, as if that were explanation enough. 'It's wonderful, don't you think?'

The big room of the Chelsea Arts Club was crowded with old men past the age of wartime service, a few younger uniforms and a gaggle of brightly painted ladies whose consumption of wine was no less rapacious than the menfolk.

'Are *they* painters too?' asked Fanny, pointing her lorgnette affectedly. She had an expiring voice, very femme fatale and, with her angular-cut silver hair, didn't look out of place in this haven of artistry, stuck in a narrow street near the King's Road. She was strikingly beautiful.

'Or life models. I thought it would make a change for you.'

'You're right. The Ritz these days is one extended *longueur* – same old people telling the same old stories. The only thing that changes is the number of medal ribbons, spreading like a forest fire across chaps' chests.' She said it *acrorse*. 'Heroes, if you believe what they say.'

'You can have beer if you like,' encouraged Guy. 'Comes in lovely silver mugs.'

'Certainly not!' She put on an affronted face, but it was just an act: the trick about Fanny Goldington was that everything she did was calculated to make a man feel better about himself, to encourage him to rise to the challenge of mounting a boarding party on her ship of love. She may accept or reject his attack, but first she would fill him full of the courage to launch it.

'Do painters drink wine? If so, I shall have some, thank you, Mr Harford.' She gave a little gasp at the sight of two bearded men in smocks shouting jokes at each other and bellowing loudly. Was there *no* man she did not find attractive?

'To business,' said Guy. 'I have to get back to my duties at two o'clock.'

'What?' she expostulated. 'Never a siesta after lunch? *Pas de temps de s'allonger?*'

Guy laughed. 'Afraid not, Lady Goldington. Duty calls.'

'Fanny.'

'Fanny.'

'So why have you singled me out, Mr Painter Man? Sending me a mysterious note saying you wanted to do my portrait?'

Guy smiled. 'I caught sight of you one night at The Milroy. You were wearing a bottle-green gown and I saw your shoulders. It's not always the face, though yours is a remarkable one.' This was no compliment but a statement of fact, which Fanny Goldington took for granted, rather as if one had said she had ten fingers and ten toes. 'I have a new exhibition coming up and I'd dearly love to paint those shoulders.'

'I asked people about you,' she said languorously. 'You exhibited last year at the Gardner Gallery. Very successful. A portrait of a woman burglar, everyone said – what a peculiar thing to paint!'

Not if you felt about her the way I do, thought Guy. 'Well, it certainly grabbed peoples' attention.'

'Do you want me to wear a mask, then? Like her? When you're painting my *shoulders*? I'm told I look particularly . . . you know . . . when I wear a mask. The menfolk tumbled over themselves into the Grand Canal when I wore one in Venice in '39.' She laughed, a breathy sound which was more an intake of air than a joyous noise, then stretched her shoulders back and stared hard at Guy.

Oh please, he thought, just stop it! You were in bed with a king last night, then you went home to a marquis. You don't want an impecunious painter with no title and no landed estates. Do give it up for a minute!

'A mask might well do wonders,' he said. 'We can experiment.'

'I like the sound of that, *Guy*.' She put her hand lightly on his wrist.

He smiled and took a sip of beer from his tankard. 'I'm trying to find as many different subjects for my next show as I can. I went out into the East End and got some marvellous faces, but I want it to include people from all walks of life. So I'm glad you've agreed to sit to me.'

'I love "*to* me". Sounds so much more intimate than "for" me. Somehow brings the artist much closer.' She turned her head away so he could view her striking profile – perfectly formed, its perfection made all the more intriguing by an unexpected Roman nose. She made a swishing sound as she crossed her legs and turned slowly back to regard him.

'You're really quite handsome, Mr Painter Man. Has nobody ever painted *you*?'

He marvelled at Fanny's non-stop performance – did she practise in the mirror every morning? Certainly it would be no hardship to paint her, if it came to that, and her obliging turn of the head to demonstrate her profile had given him just the angle he wanted. But that wasn't why he was here.

'Too busy trying to find subjects for the next show.'

'Well,' said Fanny, sliding her eyes sideways, 'don't you think you should include a royal subject?'

'Oh no,' came the hasty reply, 'can't mix work with pleasure – well, not pleasure exactly. I am, first and foremost, an artist – just working at the Palace pro tem. I wouldn't want to ask the family, and they wouldn't want me to ask.'

'No, no . . .' she breathed. 'Light me a cigarette, will you, darling?'

Guy obliged, infuriated that his hand trembled slightly as he handed it over.

'No, I was thinking of someone else – a crowned head, naturally, not some piffy-paffy princeling.'

'Oh?'

'King Zog, darling. I'm sure you must have heard of him.'

Just a bit, thought Guy. 'I've seen him around. A most unusual face. But what makes you . . . ?'

'We are old friends,' lied Fanny. 'He looks to me for strength, for inspiration. I am his backstop, his mainstay in this ungrateful land.'

'What makes him think we're ungrateful? We've offered him a safe haven, made sure he and his royal court are safe and well. Found them a home in Buckinghamshire.' He stopped suddenly, realising he could be displaying too much foreknowledge. 'Or somewhere like that. I read it in the newspapers somewhere. Bedfordshire?'

'Right first time,' she said, her eyes narrowing slightly. 'What I mean is that His Majesty feels unrecognised – that though he is the sovereign of Albania, he's not treated on equal terms with other exiled monarchs in London by the Palace.'

'Ah.' That much was true – King George couldn't bear the sight of the strutting five-footer with his comedy moustache.

'But he remains a sovereign. And just as our King is awakened every morning to the sound of bagpipes, Zog too rises to the music of his homeland.'

'Really?' Guy wasn't terribly interested.

'He has a chorus of his men stand under his window – rain or shine – and they sing to him. They sing "*Lumit Zot*", and thus he is reminded of his great and glorious heritage.'

'How reassuring.'

'They are devoted to His Majesty – so devoted they have learnt the whole song by heart. Five hundred lines of it.'

'Good Lord, do they sing it all to him every morning? Must make breakfast last till lunchtime.'

She parted her lips and a low, melodious sound came forth.

> *Lumit Zot I kjofshim fal*
> *Mbretin t'onë kerkush se ka.*

'So I learnt it too. Out of devotion to His Majesty.' It said every-thing for the Arts Club membership that not a single person raised an eyebrow at the sight of a silver-haired aristocrat bursting forth into Albanian tunelessness at lunch.

'An interesting melody.'

'Do you think so? The lines are arranged in decasyllables – such a tricky language, don't you know – and some of these songs are two thousand lines long. The song invokes the name of God and then reminds us all that there is no other king than that of the Albanians.

'*Ahmet Begun e kishin tradhëtue*
Kishin sjellë vodat me votue . . .'

She really does seem to know the whole of it but what a boring tune, thought Guy – does she really love him that much?

'Sorry,' he said, collecting his thoughts, daring to reveal too much knowledge of the man in question, 'but surely there's only been a monarchy in Albania for ten years? Then they kicked him out? And wasn't your anointed one just some jumped-up politician who woke one morning and decided to plonk a crown on his head and declare himself king?'

'You have a very twisted view of world history, Guy.'

'And when he got kicked out, didn't he take all the money with him? Bankrupted the nation, more or less?'

A vague flash of irritation passed over Fanny's brow. 'Clearly you're not keen on kings.'

'On the contrary, it's my job to like them.'

'Well then,' she said, looking serenely around the room then returning her gaze to Guy with a smile. 'Get wise to what you're being told. Paint Zoggie, then you can paint me. He'll pay you for both, and three times more than you'd get elsewhere.

'Do yourself a favour, Guy, and wake up!'

CHAPTER TWELVE

Ted Rochester was seated in his small apartment perched high over St James's Street, hands poised like a concert pianist over his type-writer. He was writing, not for his British readers but for the great American press. His disguise, under the name Charles Greville, gave him ample freedom to feed his hungry audience with a version of the truth as he saw it.

Here in London a pall of mystery billows around the recent death of the Duke of Windsor's old pal, Archy, the Earl of Blackwater.

Readers will recall my shock news that Archy died at the tragically young age of 51 not as a result of the current conflict, but from unknown causes. I revealed that the holder of the 353-year-old title had been found in his car in Windsor Great Park, not far from that stately pleasure dome, Fort Belvedere, where the Prince of Wales and Mrs Simpson turned their love affair up to white-hot before scampering over the horizon into obscurity.

The abdication, which brought the ancient House of Wind-sor to its knees, is six years ago now – but still those

royals in Buck House are feeling the draught. And the
latest news of Archy Blackwater won't make things any
easier for them.

For I can exclusively reveal that Archy's body was found
not in his car, but actually inside the abandoned fort.
Police sources confirm to me . . .

And that cost me a pretty penny in bungs, he thought as he pushed
a cigarette into his jade holder and lit it. Coppers are getting greed-
ier as the days roll by.

. . . that the earl's body was found in the very room
where the instrument of abdication, which relieved David
Windsor of his duties, was signed on 11 December 1936.
The earl had apparently died of a heart attack.

The question remains: what on earth was Blackwater
doing there? Revisiting his old hunting ground? Was he
on a secret errand for the Dook and Dookess? Or did he
just go there to die, like an old dog returning to his kennel?

Little has been heard of Lady Blackwater since the peer's
death – she remains sequestered on the 3,000-acre family estate in eastern England – but an adoring circle of
his London male friends have clubbed together to provide
a memorial service for the fun-loving lord at which Noel
Coward has promised to speak (and might even sing a
sad little ditty).

Archy Blackwater had many friends in New York, Long
Island and Palm Beach. Should any of them wish to get

in touch to provide more information to help clear up the mystery of his death – and help his family out of their unhappy frame of mind – it would provide welcome relief. Not knowing what the head of this ancient family was doing, dying in an abandoned building over which a long, dark shadow hangs, has caused them great distress.

You would be doing the King and country of Great Britain – and its police force – a huge service.

Let me thank you in advance.

As he rattled the paper out of the typewriter roller, he laughed sardonically.

'That'll teach that snooty bitch her manners,' he muttered. 'She doesn't know about the memorial service, and she won't be invited – the boys will see to that. She put the phone down on me when I called – not once, but three times – and nobody does that to Ted Rochester!'

He fed two more sheets, separated by carbon paper, into the Remington and rubbed his hands together. He was thinking about rewriting the paragraphs to make them even nastier when the telephone rang.

'Ah, Foxy!'

'Listen, Ted, that thing I told you about Archy on the phone last night – you're not to use it, understand?'

'Certainly not. We're not allowed to write that kind of thing.'

'I don't mean here, in Britain. You're not going to start spreading scurrilous rumours back home, are you? In that vile New York column of yours?'

'Why should I do that, Foxy?' He gently tapped his cigarette holder and looked dreamily out of the window across the Palace rooftops.

'You promised me you'd keep it to yourself. Just to remind you that the Duke and Duchess read your paper, and I don't want them upset. They're having a hard enough time as it is.'

'Trust me, Foxy. Are you going to the Bradburys' this evening? If so, I'll see you there.'

As the phone clicked the reporter turned to his typewriter again.

> STOP PRESS Friends believe that, despite police state-
> ments to the contrary, there is something deeply suspi-
> cious surrounding the circumstances of the death, and
> that Blackwater either committed suicide or was mur-
> dered. This raises huge difficulties for both the present
> king of the United Kingdom and its ex-king. Though other
> European countries decriminalised homosexuality many
> years ago, in Britain it is still a jailable offence.

'Their despair is our delight,' he cackled, hugging himself with the thought that with these few lines he'd put the boot into Foxy, Guy *and* Lady Blackwater all in one go. None of them, if they read it, could do anything more than rage at his infamy – he'd let the genie out of the bottle regarding Archy Blackwater's private life, and once it had been said, it could never be unsaid.

The telephone rang again. This time it was Sid, the editor.

'How's that Blackwater story coming, Rochester? There's a big hole on my front page needs filling.'

'Something you won't want to print, Sid.' He could hear his boss stiffen with excitement.

'I'll be the judge o' that, matey. Tell me what you've got.'

'You'd be surprised by the size of my lunch bill from The Savoy. They don't know when to stop adding noughts.'

'Never mind that, spit it out, man.'

'Suspicious death, Sid. Suicide – or possibly murder. And Blackwater's body was found in the building, not in his car.'

'What?'

'There wasn't a car. He somehow got into the Fort and was found dead there.'

'How are you going to write *that*?' asked the editor, deferential all of a sudden.

'Can't see how I can, Sid. There's a news blackout. Foxy Sefton gave me the story and my police contacts confirmed it, but only off the record – the condition being I don't print it but use it as background information. If I try to write it, they'll slap a D-notice on it which means the official censor gets involved – and anyway I have to keep them sweet or they'll go back to giving their biggest plums to the *Daily Mail*.'

He could almost hear the editor grinding his teeth, torn between running the item regardless and losing any future scoops to his arch-rival, the *Mail*, or spiking it. Your despair, thought Rochester, is my delight, Sid – don't ever tell me my stories are no good!

'Tell me what's on your mind,' said Rupe. It was Sunday afternoon and they'd gone for a walk on Primrose Hill after a trip to the zoo. 'Things aren't right, are they?'

Rodie looked up into the sky past the barrage balloons to the sight of a single Spitfire soaring majestically overhead.

'I can't do this any more, Rupe. I'm going to find something else to do.'

Hardacre stopped and lit a cigarette. Its smoke blew into her face and she tiredly pushed it away. 'What's the matter?' he said.

'This job is the matter!' she replied. 'It's ruinin' my life.'

He kicked at some fallen blossom. 'Get this straight,' he said in measured tones. 'You can't quit. Weird as it would sound to an outsider, you're doing important war work. You can't quit, not in wartime – you're under orders.'

'Try an' stop me!'

'Let me remind you how we got here. You and your chums were up in the dock at Bow Street on an aggravated burglary charge. You'd have gone to jail and you'd be there still, but between us, Guy and I got you off. On that day you became a civil servant, working for my department and doing what you do best – only this time on the right side of the law.

'Come on, Rodie, you've been brilliant – there's nobody to touch you in the criminal fraternity. And we need you.'

'Like that old poster, the geezer with the tache pointing at yer and saying, "Your Country Needs You"?'

'Yes, Rodie, we do,' he said encouragingly. 'You're a star, so get used to it.'

She laughed scornfully and stuck her hands in her trouser pockets. 'I know I'm good,' she said. 'I just don't want to do it any more.'

'Look at the way you went through the roof at the Duke of Kent's house! And you must still be the only burglar who ever broke into Buckingham Palace. You've got nerve, intelligence and a very special sixth sense.'

'It's cos I'm a woman.'

'That could well be it. So what's the problem?'

'I'm bored, Rupe. Bored, bored, bored! You wouldn't understand, but what makes me *exceptional* is the danger. When the chances of getting your collar felt are high and still you go in, do the blag, get out and get away with it, it gives you a thrill. These days if I got pinched you'd probably get me out of it in the blink of an eye – so where's the fun?'

'I've told you before – you get caught, you're on your own. The government can't be seen to be offering a career ladder and a gilt-edged pension to burglars.'

'Oh, you'd fix it, Rupe, you know you would – underneath that civil servant exterior beats a heart of gold!'

'Don't bank on it. Anyway, you can't resign – I'm your boss and I say what goes.'

'An' what yer going to do – dock my wage packet when I don't turn up at the office? I tell you, Rupe, after I brought that envelope back from the Fort I realised I had to give this up. I watched your face as you undid it, full of hope, only there was nuffin' there. It was a waste of me time. You told me what a jolly good girl I was for getting into the Fort – but I'd done that once already, dontcha see? There was nuffin' to it, just doin' the same old repetitive stuff. At least in civvy street I'd find something worth liftin'. All that palaver – for nothing!'

He stopped and turned to her. 'That's not it, is it? Look at me!'

She didn't. Instead she shook her head violently.

'Come on, Rodie, out with it – what's the real problem?'

It came out in a tumble. 'It's Guy,' she said. 'I love 'im, Rupe.'

'If I've heard you say that once I've heard it a hundred—'

'I think I'm losing 'im. 'E's spending time with that old girl-friend of his, Foxy oojamaflip. 'E's always been in love with her, that's why 'e ain't proposed to me. Or maybe it's because of what I do for a livin', or where I come from, or the clothes I wear. Or the way I talk – I'm not like all them other women 'e knows. *Debutantes.*' She spat the word out.

'That's why he's devoted to you. You're different.'

'You don't get it, mate. It's the way 'is face goes all moony when 'e talks about 'er – which ain't very often, 'e keeps it all bottled up inside. If you mention Paris, 'e puts 'is 'ead on one side an' you know 'e's thinking about those days before the war when 'e and this Foxy danced La Cucaracha together. 'E don't dance with me if 'e can avoid it.'

'He's tall, you're short. It must be difficult.'

'The vertical expression of a horizontal desire, isn't that what they say? Well, 'e's all right when 'e's horizontal but NBG when 'e's upright, I can tell ya. I think 'e still yearns after 'er.'

'But what difference would it make to your relationship if you stopped working for me? He'll still be doing that job.'

'Not when the war's over. 'E's going back to Tangier and I'm going with 'im if I can hang on to 'im that long. You don't know, Rupe – I put the radio on every mornin' and listen to the news, prayin' they're going to announce the peace.'

'Ha ha.'

'I knew you wouldn't understand. Then 'e brought some other woman 'ome the other day. Fanny somebody, posh and rich. Just 'is type. "Oh, Rodie," he says, "I am going to paint Fanny's portrait. Would you pop over to Winsor and Newton's and get me some rose madder oil paint, I've run out."'

'Fanny who?'

'I'll think of it in a minute. Anyway 'e wants me out of the studio while 'e does some preliminary sketches. Ha ha, Rupe, ha ha!' she said bitterly. 'It'd take an hour an' a half to get there and back. Meantime, what are they up to? She's sitting there lookin' at me through her stupid specs on a stick like the cat that got the cream just waiting for me to scarper so she can get 'er 'ooks in 'im. I think she thought I was the cleanin' lady, the way she talked to me.'

'Specs on a stick? D'you mean a *lorgnette*?'

'Like this,' said Rodie, holding up her right hand, throwing her head back and peering down at Rupert in a supercilious fashion.

'Fanny *Goldington*?'

'Could be. I wasn't really listening, I took agin 'er the moment she walked in. So did Charlotte,' she added, as if this made a difference.

Rupert's features hardened. 'Try, if you can, to remember what was said,' he said slowly. 'Just think about it for a moment – take a deep breath, then tell me.'

They walked on. 'There wasn't much else. They came in the door together. "Oh Rodie," 'e says, "I didn't know you'd be 'ere. This is Fanny . . . whatever 'er name is . . . Fanny, this is Rodie." So she looks round as though there's a faint smell under 'er nose and then sits on the couch over in the corner. "Oh perfect," 'e says, all joyful, "the light likes you there." All that painter tosh.'

Rupert looked at her. 'D'you think he really intends to paint her? Or is it something else?'

'There! You see! Now *you're* at it,' whooped Rodie. 'Something's 'appened, Rupe. 'E's going off the rails. She may 'ave a title and money but I tell you, down the Elephant and Castle we 'ave a short and very nasty word for 'er type. She looked like she was goin' to eat him for breakfast, lunch and tea. And 'er old enough to be me grandmother!'

They reached the bus shelter at the end of the path. One or two people were waiting for the bus but standing outside, catching the sunshine. 'In here,' said Rupert urgently.

'Listen very carefully,' he whispered as they stepped inside. 'I don't think for a moment Guy has any intentions with that lady – or with Foxy Sefton either, come to that. They're both married and, believe it or not, Rodie, he's an honourable man.'

'*Honourable?* Wassat when it's at 'ome?'

'You're very lucky to have him. But listen. Just as I don't believe he has any intentions towards Fanny Goldington, I don't believe he wants to paint her picture either.'

'I thought that, too. There's nothin' to 'er – who'd want to waste good oil paint on a face like that?'

'Now, now! What I'm going to tell you is . . .' He paused. 'Are you still working for me?'

'I 'aven't 'anded in my notice yet. Why?'

'Lady Goldington's one of ours.'

'Ours?'

'She works for the department. In a strictly non-professional capacity.'

'Oh!' said Rodie. 'So next time she comes around smellin' of eau de cologne, I'll say to 'er, "'Ello, Fanny, you're workin' for the Post Office too? Doesn't it play 'ell on yer feet? Oh no, you works on yer back, dontcha!"'

'Don't be ridiculous. She's a vital cog in the machine and you keep your trap shut. No, I want you to find out from Guy what the hell he's doing mucking about with her.'

'Paintin' her portrait. Or a bit of the other.'

'You said you didn't believe that. Ask him!'

''E never talks about 'is work. And I never do, on your orders. We 'ad hot words on that very subject the other night – are we obeyin' the rules, him with his palace job, me with mine, keepin' our traps shut? Or is it that we don't trust each other not to tell someone else what's going' on?'

'Well, I think—'

'You see, Rupe, that's what's tearing at our relationship. We live under the same roof, sleep in the same bed, but we don't talk to each other. Not about our work, anyway. An' it's like there's a great big chasm between us and we 'ave to shout across it to make the other hear. I can't go on like that!'

'Just this once,' said Rupe unbendingly, 'I want you to get him in a corner and ask him about this Goldington woman.'

'It won't make no difference, 'e's very tight-lipped. Or, put it another way, 'e just don't want to talk about what 'e does.'

'Does he keep notes? A diary?'

Rodie's features froze. 'Are you askin' me – are you *truly* askin' me, Rupe, to spy on Guy? The love of my bleedin' life? My future husband? The man I'd throw myself under a train for?'

'Yes,' said Rupert, as the bus arrived. 'That's exactly what I'm asking you to do. Nobody can get it out of him like you can.'

CHAPTER THIRTEEN

With the King now in North Africa celebrating the Allied victory against Rommel's army, Tommy Lascelles looked even more like a monarch as he sat impassively in his cathedral-like office at the Palace. Rumours were mounting below stairs that he would soon oust Sir Alec Hardinge as the sovereign's principle Private Secretary – becoming effective managing director of the House of Windsor.

Hardinge, hated by almost everyone from the Queen down, had been too long in the driving seat and become sloppy and dictatorial, and the word was that Tommy was just awaiting his moment. Lascelles himself denied it but took comfort, as the number two, from the words of an important ally, Harold Macmillan, who described Hardinge as idle, supercilious and without a spark of imagination. It was only a matter of time.

Lascelles' mission, as he saw it, was to protect the King and his family from criticism, and guide them on the path to becoming the world's most successful sovereign couple. Ruthless when he needed to be, he was, above all, clever. And, as the well-padded Foreign Office official was ushered into his domain, Tommy made up his mind that changes had to happen – changes that would affect both the King and Queen, and the unfortunate Hardinge.

'Sir Rex Tankerton,' murmured the footman unctuously before withdrawing.

'Ah, Tankerton,' said Lascelles breezily. 'Enjoyin' that knighthood of yours?'

Tankerton softly coughed. 'Well, of course, Tommy – not for myself you understand! But Lady Tankerton is delighted – this morning she ordered Garter King of Arms to create a family crest and coat of arms.'

'Rr-rr,' said Lascelles, who knew that Lady Tankerton's embraces were reserved for the weekends, while the rest of the week the mandarin kept himself warm at night in the arms of his steely assistant, Lady Inverary.

'I trust all goes well at the Foreign Office?'

'Swimmingly. How can I be of help?'

Lascelles eyed him shrewdly. 'That knighthood, so graciously bestowed by His Majesty, comes as a result of your actions last year in swinging the Count of Paris, who hopes to crown himself King of the French after the war, round to the Allied side. A good job, well done.'

'I think it will find its way into the history books,' simpered Tankerton with feigned modesty.

Lascelles lifted an eyebrow. 'In large part the mission was made successful by one of my people here, Guy Harford.'

'Ah yes. Harford,' said Tankerton, unabashed.

'Who didn't get a medal.'

'No.'

'Even though, despite the fact he works for me, he's on the payroll of the FO. *Your* payroll. You didn't see fit to put him forward for an award, though.'

'I got the impression,' replied Tankerton blithely, 'he didn't care whether he was given a medal or not. Heaven knows there are so many deserving cases these days . . .'

'Even though his actions will find their way into the history books – according to you. I think you might have tried a little harder to get him something, but that's your department, not mine.'

'How can I help, Tommy?'

Lascelles got up from his desk and came round to sit on a sofa opposite the official. 'The Bahamas,' he said crisply.

'Ah.'

'The view here at the Palace is that the FO dispatches back from Nassau are considerably less than adequate.'

'I wonder why you say that, Tommy! We have some very efficient, some very dedicated, men out there.'

'I'm glad you think so. No doubt in time their efficiency and dedication will be rewarded with a medal or two. But from the Palace point of view, they're completely hopeless.'

Tankerton fingered his collar. 'I say, come off it, Tommy, they—'

'D'you know the phrase *red carpet fever*?'

'I . . .'

'People who get close to the Crown, so close they think they're royal themselves, become rabid if anyone criticises the family. Foam at the mouth.'

'Yes, well . . .'

'I'd say a nasty epidemic has broken out in Nassau – so much so that it appears to have engulfed not only the island, but all the other bloody Bahamas as well!'

'Er, sorry, Tommy, I'm not sure I get what it is you're saying.'

'Only it's not the King who's the cause of this fever, it's the *ex-king*.'

'The . . .'

'Your people over there,' went on Lascelles, 'have failed in their duty to report all that's going on concerning the Duke and Duchess of Windsor – conspicuously so. They've fallen for the Duke hook, line and sinker. Gone native.'

'Now that's something we don't allow in the foreign service,' protested Tankerton. 'I really must object! At all times our people are there to serve the Crown impartially, and serve it they do.'

'But which Crown?' barked Tommy. 'The present one, or the past?'

'What,' said Tankerton irritably, 'appears to be missing? From the *Palace* point of view?'

'The King feels he's not being told what his brother is doing. How he's behaving. What his intentions are for the future. Who his *friends* are out there.'

'I think,' said Tankerton smoothly, 'that for a moment you should take a look at it from the other end of the telescope. The Duke's constantly in touch with Winston Churchill, he sends his reports to our embassy in Washington, he keeps us abreast of his future plans. I'd say that was pretty comprehensive.'

'No it bloody well isn't!' barked Lascelles. 'We have reports that he's ready to quit. We have reports that he's about to take *American citizenship*.'

'What? I haven't heard anything about that!'

'Then try reading the newspapers!' snapped Lascelles, reaching over to his desk and tossing Vanderbilt's press cutting at him. 'This is colossally damaging to the King, and we've had no word from your people about what's going on out there, even though they must know what's in his mind. That's what they're paid for!'

'May I correct you there,' replied Tankerton, suddenly on firmer ground. 'The UK mission in the Bahamas is to provide a successful bridgehead between the British Empire and its nearest neighbour and our closest ally, the United States. We're there for strategic, economic, political and social reasons – not to spy on a disgruntled member of the royal family who's been parachuted in, with absolutely no experience of diplomacy, to head the mission.' The bitterness was heavy in his voice.

'So you're saying that your people just get on with the job they were doing before the Duke and Duchess arrived, and more or less ignore them?'

'They have enough to do in these trying times without having to nursemaid a thumb-struck idiot and his piece of stuff.'

'*I beg your pardon?*'

Tankerton sniffed. 'I'm sorry, Tommy. From the Palace point of view it seemed like a brilliant move to get rid of the Windsors to save embarrassment at home. But their arrival in Nassau put more than a few noses out of joint, and if the intelligence coming back isn't as juicy as you'd like, it's because the Windsors are given as wide a berth as possible by our professional diplomats. The Duke and Duchess have their own team, and communication between the secretariat and the Windsors is generally done through them.'

'Gray Phillips and Vyvyan Drury. And that other chap, Fairfax.'

'Yes.'

Lascelles got up, a tall and imposing figure somehow made the more immense by the five hundred years of family history he carried on his shoulders. 'I've made a decision,' he said. 'His Majesty has been made to feel distinctly uncomfortable by the stories coming out of Nassau. It's all bad news – the native riots, the Duke's questionable friends – it's building up, week by week and month by month, and your people seem to be doing nothing about it.'

'It's not their remit. Plus, as I'm sure you're well aware from your own experience over the years, the Duke takes nobody's advice but his own.'

'And the Duchess's.'

'You'd know that better than I. What do you propose?'

A gleam came into Lascelles' eye. 'You seem to have made a striking success with young Guy Harford in Tangier last year. I'm going to ask you to send him to Nassau to sort this out.'

'Oh no, Tommy. No!'

'Why ever not? He earnt you that precious knighthood of yours – who knows what you might get this time around if his mission's successful? A dukedom? Who can tell?'

'Ha ha. Why don't you just send him yourself? No need to involve the Foreign Office.'

Lascelles sighed. 'Because though he works here, he's on your payroll – he's an FO man. Who knows, if you hadn't made life so difficult for him when he came back from Tangier the first time you could have a decent middle-ranking diplomat in your office today. As it is, he's done some sterling work here and we have high hopes for him after the war. Unusual chap,' he added, 'but on the whole quite satisfactory.'

Tankerton shook his head. 'The Tangier job was a one-off. He just got lucky. He has absolutely no experience.'

'Experience enough for Lady Tankerton to be talking to Garter King of Arms about your family crest. Come on, man, stop thinking like a civil servant and think like someone going into battle. This is one we have to win, and in my view Harford is the man to do it.'

'Do what, precisely?'

'Gather information, first of all. Find out what the hell's going on with the Windsors, see if they're truly rats about to desert the sinking ship. And then, advise. He's good at that.' Lascelles thought back to the day he sent Guy to tell Queen Mary off for buying black-market sausages and writing letters to her German relations, against wartime regulations. It had been a Pyrrhic victory in that the Queen skittered away to London to avoid seeing him, but the message he'd carried had the required effect – Guy's reputation as a negotiator was not enhanced, but the job got done.

'There's something else,' said Lascelles. 'It's highly convenient that Harford is a Foreign Office employee. It means from the Palace point of view he's deniable. If things go wrong, he's your baby, not ours.'

'Thanks very much.'

'We can't, at the Palace, be seen to be making contact with the Duke of Windsor. All communication to Nassau officially goes through the Washington embassy, and comes back through those bally telegrams he keeps sending the Prime Minister. We have no contact, which leaves the King untouched when the Duke finally kicks over the apple cart. Which, knowing him as I do, will happen sooner or later – the man's a loose cannon. A deplorable fellow.'

'So what's the plan?'

'We put Harford on an airplane. He'll stay initially in one of the outer islands where he can draw breath and sniff the air without drawing attention to himself. Then he can sail into Nassau and discover what's going on *unofficially*. I hope your people will be good enough to furnish him with all the information he needs, even if they don't write it down on paper.'

'It's all highly irregular.'

'Sorry, I started out asking for your help. This has now turned into an order – you will get Harford out to Nassau, you'll look after him while he's there, you will afford him all the help he requires, and make sure he gets home safely. Is that understood?'

'Well, I—'

'An order, Tankerton, *in the name of the King*. Is that understood?'

144

In Burnley all the talk backstage was about the company's new name. The Vic-Wells Ballet – or Sadler's Wells Ballet, it had never quite made up its mind – was about to take an historic step up.

The King, and more especially the Queen, had followed the company's fortunes with growing interest and the long-held dream of their boss Ninette de Valois – to emerge as the Royal Ballet ahead of the competition from other fledgling companies – looked as though it might finally come to pass.

There'd been a piece in the *News Chronicle* under Ted Rochester's name that had blown the secret, and though the management hastened to deny it publicly they confirmed to the gathered members of the company that it was true – they had won the royal seal of approval.

'It may take a year or two,' the dancers were told, 'certainly until the war is over. But as from this week, we are effectively By Royal Appointment.'

The stresses and strains of life on the road, the injuries and the thieving landladies, the laddered tights, broken slippers and constant hunger, all melted away with this one brief statement – for dancers live for only two things: perfection and acclaim.

Oh, and love.

'I've got a bottle of sherry,' said Elena. 'Come back to my digs and we'll celebrate!'

Mick and Pete beamed their handsome smiles, put on their day clothes, and walked her home.

It had been an extra special evening because one of the principals had fallen badly at rehearsal and Elena had taken over the part of Myrtha in the second act of *Giselle*, dancing it to perfection. She was slowly moving towards the heart of the company, and this realisation had given her looks a new bloom.

'I wish Simon had been here to see me,' she said. They drank the sherry out of eggcups, there was nothing else.

'Simon this, Simon that,' said the Russians, pricked by jealousy. 'Do we mean nothing to you?'

'Oh, I love you both!' laughed Elena. 'But Simon is my guiding light, my lodestar. He took care of me when nobody else was interested. He got me into the company – the competition, boys, you wouldn't begin to understand!'

'We had to struggle too,' they said.

'Not so much. What with everyone going off to war there aren't so many male dancers around.'

'You're wrong,' said Mick. 'When we arrived here—'

'Broke and penniless and without a farthing,' interrupted Pete.

'—London was full of Russian boys looking for a dance. We worked for the Anglo–Polish ballet for a bit, but they hate Russians, then for the Lydia Kyasht Ballet. But she was just too terribly grand, darling, world-famous – she knew the last Tsar and Tsarina, she was the toast of pre-Revolution Moscow. We soon cleared out of that – we're working-class boys from Petrograd!'

'We had a go at the Arts Theatre Ballet but they had no money and we didn't get paid,' said Pete. 'Was only when we started attending Madame Volkova's class that we stood a chance with Vic-Wells.'

'But now we're here, this is where we stay!'

'Well,' said Elena, beaming, 'where else would you go, now that we're The Royal Ballet? The King and Queen coming to each new production, and I hear Princess Elizabeth has fallen in love with ballet too.'

The boys laughed. 'You know what happened to royal family in our country,' they said, shaking their heads. 'Taken, shot, *disparu*. Don't you ever think it might happen here too?'

A look of horror crossed Elena's face – she loved the idea of royalty, and even more now that they, in turn, loved the idea of a Royal Ballet. 'What a terrible thing to say! Look at the audience at the end of every performance, standing up and singing "God Save The King". All the cheering!'

'They're cheering *you*, Yelena, not King. Royals came to Sheffield when bombed a couple of years ago – have they been back to see how everyone's getting on?'

'Don't be ridiculous! They can't be everywhere, it's not possible!'

'The world a better place without people wearing crowns, Yelena. The new world we live in, kings and queens are pointless, unnecessary. But they are so strong there's no way of getting rid of them except' – and here Pete drew his hand elegantly across his throat – 'this.'

'The only way,' said Mick, nodding.

'Well, I appreciate you come from a country that got rid of their sovereign, but so do I – in Austria we had an emperor until 1918. But he went peaceably. The blessed Karl,' she sighed. 'I wonder where he is now.'

'Sitting on Swiss mountaintop counting his gold, like they all do,' said Pete with a snort. 'The same will happen to the British royals.'

'When they lose war,' added Mick.

Elena took the sherry bottle and clasped it tight. 'I thought you were lovely boys,' she said, unhappily. 'Now I'm not so sure. Why talk about killing people when there's enough of that going on everywhere else in the world?'

'We are Russian,' they said simultaneously. 'Is our way. Don't worry, Yelena, we don't kill anybody.' With that they snatched the sherry bottle and, laughing, poured the remains of its contents down their throats.

Later, much later, as she lay half asleep on the bed, she could hear their voices through the open window. They were sitting in the backyard, watching the sun's first flickers rise from the purple dark, sharing a cigarette whose sharp aroma, fluttering through into the bedroom, had woken her. As was mostly the case on the bus or the train, when they were alone they spoke in Russian. It was rather soothing to hear it so beautifully spoken.

'*Chto my budem s etim delat?*' said one, and there was a mumbled reply. She couldn't understand any of it, but as she lay there half awake, half asleep, two words were often repeated.

One was 'Simon'.

The other was '*bleckvttr*'.

CHAPTER FOURTEEN

Dawn was rising over the Thames and in the great wide room the reflections of the early sun's rays shimmered on the ceiling.

'So that's it,' she said, bleakly. 'You're leaving me.'

'Mm.'

'You bastard.' The words, indistinct and unemotional, were spoken into the pillow. Guy turned over and put his arm round her.

'I told you, it's the same as last time. I'll be back.'

'I din' love you as much then as I do now,' said Rodie. 'It'll hurt more.'

'Just a few weeks. Let me get some coffee.'

He got up and walked out on to the gallery overlooking the studio floor. The night before he'd begun a new portrait of Rodie, painting over the sketch he'd done of Fanny Goldington. He'd suggested priming a new canvas, but Rodie liked the idea of her features being superimposed on those of the oversexed marchioness; a silent victory of love over lust.

'Did she . . . Did you . . . ?' she'd asked as he sketched, but he laughed.

'Head and shoulders, perfectly decent,' he replied, 'though her conversation most definitely wasn't.'

'Why did you pick 'er of all people?'

'Why not? She's a handsome woman, most unusual-looking, in fact, and, as an artist I have to think about what follows after the next exhibition.'

'Meaning?'

'I put her in the show, she brings her rich friends, they all want their portraits done. I get to pick and choose, rather than having to stop people in the street and ask.'

'Or bump into them in the pub, like you did me.'

'The Grenadier. I saw you across the room. You were stunning, I couldn't take my eyes off you.'

'Then why were you so nasty to me at the start?'

'Because you burgled my office at the Palace, you ass. What a ridiculous thing to do!'

'Showed I loved yer, though, didn' it?'

Guy toasted bread, put it on a tray with marmalade and coffee and brought it back up to the bedroom.

'No butter, no margarine,' he warned with a shake of his head.

'I don't care.' She was wearing his pyjama top and had stolen his pillows and was half-hidden in them. 'We never finished our conversation last night about that woman.'

'Which one?'

'Goldilocks.'

'Nothing left to say. She wants me to paint King Zog for some reason, only I can't now I'm off.'

'What's happenin' in Tangier, then? Thought you'd sorted all that out on your last trip.'

Guy poured coffee and dropped in a spoonful of sugar. 'It's not Tangier. And – before you do – don't ask me where. Further away this time.'

'That's a shame,' she said, pretending not to be interested. 'I wanted you to bring me back some of those herbs from your garden. Smelled lovely, they did.'

'Za'atar. I wish I could. In fact, I wish we both could be there now – I miss my house, I miss Dean's Bar.'

'*My* 'ouse,' she insisted. Guy had promised that it was hers should anything happen to him. '*Our* 'ouse! But will you want to go back, when this ruddy war is over? Life's changed, Guy – you've changed. You're a famous artist now – well, you will be soon! – and you like your job at the Palace, though you're always moanin' on about it.'

'It's not something I ever thought I'd do,' he agreed, 'but everything will change once the war's over. Life will be a lot less frightening, and a lot less exciting. And what will *you* do if I stay in London? Go back to your bad old ways? With me having to haul you out of a police cell every five minutes?'

'I dunno,' she said, staring into her cup.

'The last time I was in Tangier – when I drove down to Larache – I came back through the mountains and the wind was howling. I stopped in a village and there was a bunch of musicians sitting on the pavement – the sand blown by the wind had made big orange-coloured seams in the folds of their robes. That's what I want to paint, not rich courtesans.'

'Or me? Just using me for practice?'

He laughed. 'Go downstairs and take a look at what I did last night and ask yourself that question again. That face is a paradox – full of beauty, at the same time full of mischief. When you're sleeping you're one thing, when you're awake something quite else. I think I could be happy painting you for the rest of my life, whether we stay here or go back to Tangier.'

'So tell me where you're off to,' she said, sensing a vulnerable moment.

He saw that one coming and laughed it off. 'It's a long journey, and the job may take weeks. I'll try to keep in touch, of course I will, but you're now officially in charge here. All I ask is you stay away from that old goat Augustus John, and if you go down The Surprise, steer clear.'

'Because 'e might paint me again? An' make a better job of it than you do?'

He threw a crust at her. 'Farmyard morals, Tommy Lascelles said. You stay close to Rupe, he'll keep you safe. He's a good friend.'

Not as good as you think, mate, she thought – but at least if you push off I'm going to be spared having to spy on you.

But not yet. 'So what's the *real* reason you latched on to that Fanny woman? You fancy 'er, don't you?'

He lit a cigarette and went to stand by the window in his dressing gown. Down below the traffic was starting to flow along the Embankment, and men in uniform were marching briskly in ones and twos towards the Chelsea Barracks.

'Doesn't do any harm to tell you now, because I've been taken off the case. Where I'm going, what I'm doing, is far more important than trying to stem a flow of scurrilous gossip – something that is impossible to do. Like King Canute.'

She smiled at him vaguely. Canute's name went largely unmentioned down the Elephant and Castle.

'That woman – Goldilocks, you call her – is sleeping with King Zog. Among her earlier conquests – quite apart from the three lords she married – was Prince Harry, the Duke of Gloucester. The King has a very low opinion of Zog and was worried that she'd start pouring state secrets into Zog's ears. My job was to cosy up to her—'

'You did *that* all right!'

'—find out what she'd leaked – *if* she'd leaked – and get her to shut her trap.'

''Ow?'

'Oh,' said Guy, smiling, 'there are ways. She's not exactly free of gossip herself. Some things even she wouldn't like to appear in the papers. Even though she's bold as brass.'

'Well, from now on you leave 'er alone!' said Rodie firmly, levering herself up on her pillows so as to appear more authoritative.

'Whaaat?' laughed Guy, almost choking on his coffee. 'What *is* this? All sisters together all of a sudden? The woman you hated, the one who treated you like a servant? The woman whose face you had painted over!'

'She's one of ours. One of Rupe's, more like.'

He put down his cup with a clatter. 'Fanny? Fanny *Goldington*? A spy? Come on, she's just a good-time girl – pull the other one!'

'Instead of worryin' about your precious king's reputation, take yer blinkers off, Guy, and look about you at the real world. The war. Rupe explained it all to me.

'The Italians kicked your King Zog out of his country in '39. Now it looks like the Italians might be ready to surrender, and your Zoggie-Dog will be headin' back home. But things have altered since he left and everyone back home knows he stole all the gold. We need to know what's in his mind – is he goin' back? If so, will he be safe or will he be assassinated, or will some other regime take over? An' where better to find these things out than on the pillow?' She said it *piller.*

'Well!' said Guy, amazed. 'She has her uses after all!'

'If half of what you tell me's true, she's had many uses. I doubt she's sharing details of her nights of passion with Zog, she's too busy drillin' 'im for info for our department. So forget about 'er, Guy – and when she comes knockin' on the door for her next sit- tin', I'll send 'er away with a flea in 'er ear and a boot up 'er arse. Department or no department!'

He laughed aloud as he gathered up the coffee cups. 'Off to work,' he said. 'Then only a couple more days here before I go. Shall we go somewhere smart tonight? The Ritz? The Berkeley?'

'Those ain't my kind of places, you know that.'

'I distinctly remember Rupe telling me he found you one night in the downstairs bar at The Ritz, with Lem.'

'Lem wanted to go an' pick some rich toffs' pockets. I just went along for the ride. If you want to take me out, take me to the Hammersmith Pally, then we'll go and 'ave fish an' chips.'

Guy groaned. 'As stylish parting celebrations go,' he said 'that leaves a lot to be desired. I was thinking of buying you champagne. I don't think they serve that in Lisson Grove.'

'Give me a glass of milk an' that'll do. As long as I'm with you that's all that matters, mate.'

◆ ◆ ◆

Across town in the City of London, behind the great stone facade that housed the General Post Office, men and women battled to prove that Britain still maintained the most efficient postal service in the world. In the depths of war letters from loved ones were the nation's lifeblood, and a heavy burden of responsibility was placed on this largely invisible public service.

Further back in the building, though, down a long corridor and behind steel shutters, another vital national service – one that went without a name – also went about its duties. Here, the men wore no uniform and carried no visible rank but they were just as vital to the war effort. In big open rooms, desks were spaced far apart and conversations rarely rose above a murmur.

In a corner office, Rupert Hardacre sat opposite a grey-faced man who went by the faintly comical code-name 'Z', waiting for him to finish a calculation on a slide rule. Finally the man put down his pencil and leant back.

'Yes,' he said drily.

'One last thing on the agenda. The Blackwater business.'

'I hope you've got something. This thing's been going round in circles and ending up nowhere for I don't know how long.'

'Here's what we have,' said Rupert. 'It's not much. As you know, I'm in close contact with a Buckingham Palace official. For entirely different reasons he was investigating Blackwater's death. His motive is simply to ensure the King is protected from anything that may emerge – either political, or more likely of a more personal nature.'

'Not the Bedaux angle? The Nazis?'

'No. I think it's more along the lines of "how dare Blackwater die on royal property, and what the hell was he doing there anyway?"'

'I'd like to know the answer to the second part of that question myself. What's he got?'

'Nothing, and the investigation's been called off. He's been assigned to another project.' *Thank you for that information, Rodie, he thought. Let's hope Guy never finds out you're still telling tales.*

'So what's left?'

Rupert opened up the file. 'Our Palace man tried but failed to find out who the last person was to see Lord Blackwater alive. But we think we've found him.'

'Yes?'

'A chap called Green – ballet dancer awaiting call-up. In the weeks before Blackwater's death they were seen together on a number of occasions.'

'By?'

'We have a wide network out there,' said Rupert evasively. 'You know that. Sometimes it just takes a little longer for the facts to emerge.'

The man grunted. 'I take it they were man and wife.' The terminology showed his disapproval.

'Difficult to know, but probably. The information came to light because they had a very public row one night in a nightclub called The Nut House. The person who reported in with this had . . . ah . . . been detained after a police raid on a similar establishment in Soho.'

'Illegal activities,' said the man with a slight sneer.

'Call it that if you want,' said Rupert sharply, 'I don't!' The man looked up, then down again; it was not the moment to get into that sort of argument.

'Go on.'

'This chap is not what he seems. He's a dancer with the Vic-Wells Ballet and goes by the professional name of Simon Green, but what's of special interest to us is that in fact he's Simon Greenleigh, the son of General Greenleigh.'

'Auchinleck's sidekick?'

'That's the man. Very distinguished soldier, but very old-fashioned – unlikely to find much consolation in his only child making a career in the world of ballet. His own father was a soldier and, I think, the father before that too. So you see.'

'Have you approached him?'

'Green? Since Blackwater's death he's been up north, dancing with the touring ballet. He was due to come back to London a few days ago.'

'He killed Blackwater – you obviously think that. But why?'

'We can't have the answer to that till we know what the hell the pair of them were doing in Fort Belvedere. The place is abandoned, mothballed. True, Lord Blackwater was a permanent guest there during the run-up to the abdication – but that was years ago. These men were there for a reason – and remember, this investigation is more than just about the random death of someone who was once famous, it's about Nazi infiltration.'

'I have something to tell you that may be of help,' said the man. 'The very good men in E Section have been following various leads – nothing to do with your inquiry – looking into communication with the enemy. One line they've come up with is a series of communications that have been coming out of Norway – a number of coded messages dropped in dead-letter boxes in Cricklewood and Hendon, the London suburbs. Maybe some more elsewhere, they're still working on that. They came across them only by chance.'

'What do the messages say? How are they connected to this case?'

'Until you mentioned ballet I didn't think anything about it, but suddenly the pieces could be falling into place. We think the messages emanate from a woman called Marina Lee. She's a dangerous, dangerous woman – an extraordinarily gifted spy who stole the British battle plans that led to the fall of Norway to the Germans in 1940.'

'Is that known? Publicly, I mean?'

'Top secret. This Lee woman used a nurse's uniform to get into the British Expeditionary Force's headquarters and somehow she got her hands on the plans – astonishing how she managed it, but she did. She passed the information on to Nazi high command who'd given up hope of securing Norway, but now they knew what our battle plan was, it was like shooting fish in a barrel. She is an evil genius with a corrupt mind and a determination to wreak as much damage as she can on this country, for reasons we simply can't fathom. She's not a German.'

'I see the connection.' Hardacre nodded. 'The general in charge of defending Norway was Auchinleck, am I correct?'

'Yes.'

'Whose right-hand man was General Greenleigh. Simon Greenleigh's father. Is it stretching things too far to think that these signals coming in from Norway are for *him*?'

Rupert's boss rose silently from his desk.

'That's for you to find out,' he said bleakly. 'Why don't you go and have a nice little chat with our dancer-boy Greenleigh? I'm sure you have lots in common.'

CHAPTER FIFTEEN

The Royal Standard flapped lazily in the breeze over the Round Tower at Windsor. This ancient signal that the sovereign was in residence was a hoax: the King had been playing ducks and drakes with tradition ever since the outbreak of hostilities, often telling his subjects via this ancient device he was at home when he wasn't. Currently he was in North Africa.

Tommy Lascelles and Guy were enjoying the evening sun in the Great Court, watching at a distance the occasional arrival and departure into the Norman Gate. The table between them had a small whisky decanter, a silver water jug and some dry biscuits on a tray. The silence was all-enveloping.

'I wish you luck,' said Tommy finally. 'On the one hand, I hate to send you; on the other, I know you've been itching for action.'

'Glad to be doing something worthwhile, Tommy.' Anything rather than chase round after an ageing seductress.

'I'm afraid you're under the wing of that fool Tankerton again, because you'll be travelling as an FO official – this mission has to be deniable by the Palace. If anything happens to you, you were working out of Tankerton's office.'

'He's OK with that, Tommy?'

'After that knighthood, he does pretty well what he's told. Anyway, you have your written instructions from me, but don't take them with you – read them up and then destroy them.'

Lascelles took a sip of his whisky. 'The job, Guy, is this. You go to the Bahamas and find out what's in the Duke's mind – is he going to resign? Is he going to take US citizenship? Find out what the Duchess is thinking, and bear in mind she may say or do things that don't quite chime with the Duke's wishes. But she wears the trousers in that relationship, and much of his opinions are, these days, predigested by her.

'In my memo, I've laid out the difficulties he's got himself into – his association with men of Nazi sympathies. The hints that he's been money-laundering. And while you're about it, size up how his governorship is going – is he any good at it, or is he doing damage to the Crown?'

'D'you want me to try to speak to them?'

'Yes. But only once you've got the big picture. Take the Duchess a message from Lady Sefton – only don't take a real message, Foxy's a very leaky vessel and I don't want her knowing what you're doing – I'm sure you can manufacture something along those lines.'

'I expect so.'

'Tankerton's people will take care of your transportation. We haven't lost many airplanes over the Atlantic, but there is of course a risk. Make sure you've written your will and it's up to date, and that instructions have been left. Should the worst occur.'

Guy smiled. 'You said that to me before the Tangier mission. Funnily enough it helped me make up my mind about certain things. The thought of death.'

'Have a drop more. I'm dining with the Queen so I mustn't linger, but just to let you know that when you get there you won't fly into Nassau direct – I don't want the Duke and Duchess to know you're there until the time is right, and I gather they always go through the list of UK arrivals.'

'Right-o. Where am I landing?'

'There's an island near Nassau called Whale Cay. We have a significant ally there – in fact, she owns the island outright, several others besides, and you're to stay with her – she'll make you comfortable and plug you into all the right connections.'

Lascelles turned to face Guy with a lopsided smile on his face. 'Because you're an artist, a painter, I think you'll enjoy this. Your hostess is an oddity. She has tattoos, she dresses as a man, and answers to the name Joe. I think I can truthfully say there's never been a man in her life, but there've been quite a lot of women. Some famous names too, including Greta Garbo and Tallulah Bankhead. She never goes anywhere without a weird doll she calls Lord Tod Wadley, whose clothes, by the way, are made in Savile Row.'

'Good Lord.'

'That may sound eccentric, but she's a remarkable woman. Drove ambulances in the First War, races powerboats, once owned the smartest chauffeur-drive business in London. Then she inherited an eye-popping dollop of oil money and bought herself a slice of the Caribbean. You won't be disappointed with your stay there.'

'Sounds promising, Tommy. Any ground rules about approaching the Duke and Duchess?'

'Whatever you do, don't call her Your Royal Highness. If it gets out a Palace official has fallen into that elephant trap, we'll never hear the last of it.'

'I take it the brothers are still at battle stations.'

'Regrettably so,' said Tommy. 'So be discreet. But if you talk to the Duke, let it be known that you are indeed an official emissary from the King. The simple message to him – stay in post.

161

And whatever you do, just *think* of the consequences of American citizenship.'

'I honestly don't think he's going to take orders from a junior courtier like me.'

'Just remind him of this, and then he'll listen – when he left this country, he took with him far more money than was ever stated. If he'd stayed here he'd have been the richest man in England. By no stretch of the imagination could he, if he becomes an American citizen, escape the long arm of the Internal Revenue Service – like the Mounties, they always get their man. While he remains linked to the country he once ruled,' Lascelles said this with a tinge of bitterness in his voice, 'he is treated graciously in matters of personal taxation. It won't be the same if he switches teams.

'And,' he added, 'I can tell you this from personal experience. From the years I served him when he was Prince of Wales, the Duke lives in perpetual fear of having no money. For a man who was once emperor of half the world that may seem ridiculous – indeed it is – but that's his Achilles heel. You cannot bring the taxation point home to him hard enough or often enough.'

'Got that.'

'You know,' went on Tommy, 'I had Fruity Metcalfe on the telephone this morning. A man who gave his whole life to the Prince of Wales – he was equerry, best man, procurer, valet and who knows what else. Devoted to that selfish man, devoted, and it was terribly sad to hear him. "Without that missus around," he said, "he's excellent. But with her, or near her, and he's not worth tuppence ha'penny. And you can't trust him a yard."

'So,' he concluded, 'let that stiffen your resolve when you meet the Duke, Guy. Some still love him but to most of us, as Metcalfe says, he's not worth tuppence ha'penny.'

As he poured another whisky and watched the sun slowly fall behind the Round Tower, Guy thought again about his mission last year to curtail Queen Mary's illegal proclivities. It was pointless thinking they, the royals, could be told anything by mere mortals – but, as Tommy had said, it was his duty to try.

'Take care, and stay as safe as you can. You're an ingenious fellow and I sense you don't lack courage. Things will be changing around here soon, and I rather hope you'll think about staying on once the war's over.'

'That's very kind, Tommy, but I'm an artist first and foremost. Everything else – this included,' he said, sweeping his hand around the shaved lawns, 'comes second to that.'

'You seem to manage all right at present,' replied Tommy, getting up, 'and that's with a war on. I'm sure you could find the time to do both once the peace comes.'

'My home's in Tangier,' said Guy. 'That's where my heart is.'

'Ah yes, the Tanja Man! Well, there's plenty of time to think it over – who knows how long this wretched war will last – or even if we'll win it. I must go to the Queen now, but when you finally get to Nassau, see if you can single out Carey Fairfax, who's working as an equerry for the Duke. Give him my regards.'

'I will.'

'A fine chap. If,' added Tommy tersely, 'he hasn't gone native. Like the whole of that man Tankerton's crew.'

It was dirty, dusty and the windows hadn't been cleaned since the outbreak of war. Outside the sun shone but only streaks of it made their way past the layer of dirt and into the room. Within the confines of the Kilburn church hall, the only heat came off the bodies. Rodie cursed inwardly at the sight of them.

'Point your toe in front of you, little toe on the ground!'

Why? Why am I doing this?

'Heel to the middle of the instep, point to the front.'

When Rupe said 'e'd got something new for me to do, I jumped at it. Why the 'ell did I do that?

'Point to the side. Point to the back. Back straight! Straighter! Are you breathing properly?'

I could kill 'im. 'E knew what this would entail – did 'e make me do it just because I said I was quitting?

'Now rest and pay attention. *Retiré* is a step where one pointed foot is drawn up the supporting leg to lodge at the side of the knee so that the two turned-out legs – one straight, one bent – make the shape of a figure four.'

I'll give 'im what for when I get out of 'ere, this is murder.

'*Retiré!*'

Bastard.

'*Retiré derrière! Retiré á côté!*'

It went on for another half an hour. The other girls seemed to withstand the attacks on their muscles, managed to keep their ankles loose, smiled gracefully – unlike Rodie, whose grimaces drew the teacher's disapproving gaze more than once.

'Just before we finish, let's welcome our newcomer, Miss Carr. A very good effort for a first-timer, Miss Carr.'

Well, I read the book before I came, did'n I?

'So just to show everyone else how far they've progressed, give us all the five basic positions.'

Rodie did her best and finally the hour of torture was over.

'Just a moment, Miss Carr,' said the class mistress sternly, as the other girls struggled into their day clothes, glancing instinctively into the makeshift barre mirror hung up to allow them to glimpse their movements.

'Yes, Miss Railton?'

'I am always glad to see new pupils,' said the mistress, eyeing her through heavy spectacles, 'but I wonder whether you'll be able to manage this. I can see you've never had a lesson in your life – why have you chosen to start now?'

'I'm a civil servant, miss. We sit around at our desks all day drinkin' tea and getting' fat. I need the exercise.'

'Well, you certainly have the shape and form to be a dancer, and you're strong – but you're using all the wrong muscles.'

'I expect I'll get used to it.' Not if I can help it. Two lessons here, tops. I hate it.

'You're rather late to get started – to make a success of it, I mean. It's harder when you're older – your joints aren't so supple.'

'I'm twenty-four!' protested Rodie. 'A ruddy spring chicken!'

'My dear, most of my girls have been dancing since they were five. You've got too much catching up to do. But it's good to have you here – just keep doing the exercises, and I'll see you on Saturday.'

Like hell you will, she thought furiously as she struggled into her clothes and shot out of the door.

In the café on the opposite side of the road, a grinning Rupert Hardacre greeted her enthusiastically.

'How'd it go?'

'It was 'ell, mate, an' I ain't goin' back. The last classroom I was in was when I was fourteen. I don't like bein' told what to do, especially when it involves physical torture.'

He laughed. 'You must be the only person in Britain being paid to get fit!'

'I'm *fit* all right. I can climb up a three-storey building no problem, get in through the roof, do the business, get out again in no time. *You* couldn't, in that smarmy suit of yours!'

'Calm down and have a cup of tea.'

'Look,' she said, 'do I really have to do all of this? I've got the picture now. I don't see that any more lessons are going to make a difference.'

'I'm sending you to another class tomorrow. Down the road in Maida Vale. You need to absorb as much of the lingo as you can in as short a space of time as possible.'

The tea arrived and her hands shook as she lifted the heavy china cup. 'Can't I just get somebody to talk me through it?'

Rupert shook his head. 'No, my darling, you can't. When you walk through the door of the Vic-Wells Ballet you've got to know what you're talking about.'

'But I'm only going to work in the wardrobe department!'

'That's where the girls go to relax. If they start to chat to you, you've got to know what they're talking about. You've got to have suffered what they go through if you're to be convincing. Your cover is that you went to dance class when you were a child, but then had an accident that stopped short your career. But like all failed ballerinas, you can't leave the dance alone and you're thrilled to be employed, in even the lowliest capacity.

'The thing is, Rodie, you *look* like a ballerina, you *walk* like a ballerina. The way you skip around that studio, you could have danced all your life. That's where I got the idea – the other night when we were waiting for Guy to come home. But it's the girls you've got to convince if you're to get their confidence.'

Rodie put extra sugar in the tea. 'And just what are we going to get out of it?'

'I've no idea – but this is important. These messages that have been coming in from Oslo – they could be intended for one of the male dancers, Simon Green. He wouldn't be picking them up himself – too risky – he'd be using an intermediary. He's considered to be the pin-up boy of the company and all the girls have their eye on him. Listen to the girls and eventually when you've sized him up you can get a bit closer to him – if you can find him, that is, we're not sure where he is at the moment. But if you do track him down, be nice – he might take you out for a drink. And by sticking close you'll find out where he lives, where he keeps his stuff, and then maybe we'll get somewhere with this inquiry.

'If the Germans are sending messages into London, we need to know where they're ending up – who else is involved. If there's a spy ring we haven't yet detected, it could be that the people he's associating with are precisely who we've been looking for. So the more you can get to know him the better.'

'Seems a bit – what's that word you use – *elaborate* to me, Rupe. Surely there's a simpler way . . .'

'If you can think of a simpler way, let me know,' snapped Rupert. 'Our job is to stop any kind of enemy infiltration, nip it in the bud. The war isn't over – far from it! And anyway, Rodie, you're a bit of a perfectionist. Go out and do a good job. You'll enjoy it, smarming up to the handsomest man in the troupe.'

'I thought 'e liked blokes.'

'Girls too.'

'So where are you sending me tomorrow?'

'Madame Popowska's in Castellain Road. I gather she's a whole lot tougher than Miss Railton over there, a bit of a martinet, in fact – you're going to have your work cut out.'

'Honest, Rupe, I don't think I can. I ache, me legs are shakin' and you'll have to give me a lift 'ome, I can't walk.'

Rupert got up from the table. 'Come on, then. Have a hot bath – throw some salt in, that should sort you out. When's Guy off on his travels?'

'Very soon.' She wasn't telling any more, she'd said too much already.

'Well, this lot'll keep you busy for a bit. We don't want you sitting round in that studio moping after your lost love, now do we?'

167

Rodie stood up, shakily. 'You know you're more than a bit of a rat, Rupert Hardacre,' she said. 'I can still go and work in a factory.'

'And miss the excitement? You're made of sterner stuff than that.'

'Am I?' she said bitterly as she hobbled towards the café door.

CHAPTER SIXTEEN

'I tried to get you a decent bottle, but Fred Corbitt got quite shirty. Said you've had your ration for the month.'

'Don't you worry,' chuckled Ronnie Morgan. Today he was wearing a gilt-wired fez on his head and Moorish slippers with turn-up toes. 'I've got plenty in reserve, and if I ever run short my man Settrington usually obliges. We have a key to the cellar.'

'I brought you some malt whisky instead.'

'Well, that's very nice. What a gentleman you are.' The ex-valet beamed. 'Nobody else bothers much these days.'

'You said it was urgent,' said Guy. 'So I got over here as quick as I could, but I'll be honest, Ronnie, I'm just a bit busy at the moment. So if—'

'Sit down,' said Ronnie in lordly fashion, as if this ancient place were his own. 'Tomkins will bring coffee.'

Guy obeyed. It seemed odd, being bossed around by a septuagenarian flunkey – but then the Palace pecking order was never quite what it appeared, he'd long ago realised that.

'I did enjoy our little chat the other day,' said Ronnie. 'You're not like those stuffed shirts over there in Buck House. I don't know why a man like you puts up with all the nonsense, the bowing and scraping. For me it was a way of life, o' course. And, let's be frank, it was always going to be a cushy number once I became His Majesty's man. You could always get someone to do things for you, you din' do them yourself.'

And here's another mug, thought Guy. Here I am, getting ready to take my life in my hands and fly the Atlantic, with the very real risk of being blown out of the skies by the Luftwaffe, still with my packing to do, last-minute details to sort out with Tankerton, the transport to Northolt to be organised – but oh no, I'm here paying a courtesy call on the majestic Ronnie Morgan bringing him a drink he doesn't need.

'A word in your ear,' said the great panjandrum, as he lifted one elegantly clad ankle over the other – the way he did it, he might almost be sitting on a throne himself. 'About changes at the top.

'I liked the look of you when you came the other day and thought you needed to have your card marked. You know all about His Majesty's Private Secretary?'

'Hardinge? Yes.'

'He's about to walk the plank and not a moment too soon, the bad-tempered bugger. And your boss is finally able to take control of the House of Windsor.'

'I had heard something of the kind.'

'Hardinge's been driving His Nibs – His Majesty to you – crazy for years. Hopelessly out of touch, doesn't let anyone near 'im, and I tell you, Mr Harford, the Queen's gone right off 'im, did a long time ago. Tommy'll do a much better job – and that's good for you, see?'

'Well, thank you, Ronnie. I hope so. But if that's all, I'd better be—'

'Sit down, drink yer coffee and listen,' ordered Ronnie tersely. 'The fly in the ointment is the Queen's brother – goes by the name of David Bowes-Lyon. He's been trying to get rid of Hardinge ever since the war began – 'e's a nasty little man, but 'e's got the Queen's ear – both of 'em, in fact, ha ha! 'E tells' er things, and she passes 'em on to the Nibs and that's 'ow things get done. Mr B-L doesn't want Hardinge, doesn't like 'im, and – poof! – he's gone. Get my meaning?'

'I think so. But what's this got to do with me?'

Ronnie pressed a forefinger to the side of his nose. 'A little birdie tells me you're off on your travels,' he said. 'And you might bump into him. Bowes-Lyon.'

'You must be mistaken, Ronnie. I know for a fact he's in Washington.'

'An' makin' a right nuisance of 'imself, I hear,' replied Ronnie with a wink. 'Send the Duke my regards when you get there; don't bother with 'er, the sour-faced bitch.'

'I think you've got hold of the wrong end of the stick,' said Guy, alarmed. 'It's true I'm being sent off somewhere shortly, but it's not where you think.'

'I don't think, Mr Harford, I *know*. But I'm not talkin' about the gone-with-the-Windsors, I'm warnin' you about Mr B-L. I daresay you'll find yourself face to face with 'im sooner or later and all I'm saying is – watch out!'

Guy shook his head in wonderment. The more he worked at the palace, the deeper the intrigue. The whispers! The gossip! How could this old flunkey already know about the job he'd only just been handed by Tommy Lascelles?

'You know, Ronnie, you're a bit of a miracle,' he said, doing his best to hide his sense of shock. 'I daresay if I worked full-time at the Palace I should be petrified coming to talk to you – you seem to know everyone and everything!'

'Cham-*paaaaaagne*, Tomkins!' came the old boy's delighted response at this ambiguous compliment. 'Life in the old dog yet!'

He turned back to Guy. 'You just come an' see old Ronnie Morgan whenever you need a steer on anything. If I don't know the answer, I'll know someone who does.'

With the sound of a cork popping in the distance, Guy realised he wouldn't be escaping any time soon, so he sat back and watched the adenoidal footman enter, bearing a silver salver. 'Actually, there *is* something you might be able to help me with,' he said as the wine was poured.

This pleased Morgan no end.

'A couple of times recently I've bumped into a fellow called Scabbard. I wonder if you know him? King's Messenger, old soldier type. Probably about your age.'

'Arthur Scabbard? That old fool? We used to call 'im 'alf a Scabbard, cos he's not all there, Mr Harford. A bit away with the fairies.'

'I met him on a train. He was going up to Sandringham.'

'They're always sending 'im up there to get 'im out of the way. *And* Balmoral. 'E spends 'is life on trains and buses.'

'Is it important work he does?'

Morgan emitted a noisy laugh. 'Bless you,' he said, "e's just a hangover from the old days. Nobody has the heart to sack him. Did you notice his walking stick?'

'I don't think so.'

'It's a sword-stick. 'E says he'll run through any blackguard 'oo tries to take the King's pouch off him. Ready to lay down 'is life, 'e is.'

Aren't we all, thought Guy with trepidation, envisaging his transatlantic flight. 'I found our conversations a little unsettling. Spooky. It's almost as if he's sitting on a time bomb.'

"E was in the Boer War, you know. Got a bit rattled – 'ow do you say these days? – shell-shock? But 'e came to the notice of King Edward VII somehow and that's it, Mr Harford – once you're in, you're in. Honestly, all they do these days is give 'im the King's sandwiches to take in that pouch, only 'e don't know that because he'd never open it. No, not in a month of Sundays!'

'But, you know, he struck me as a bit unbalanced.'

'Why's that a worry, Mr Harford?'

'Well, this may sound very strange, Ronnie, or you'll think me a fool, but he tracked me down to the pub where I usually go for a drink after work, and the other night he was actually in there, watching. I didn't spot him but my companion did.'

'Maybe 'e lives local. Where are you, if you don't mind my asking?'

'Chelsea, down by Cheyne Walk.'

'Well, it could be. There are some Guinness flats down that way. And Peabody.'

'It's not that, Ronnie, he can drink wherever he likes as far as I'm concerned. It's just that . . . it sounds odd, but he followed me home.'

'Aaaaaah,' said Ronnie, clicking his fingers. 'Now I got you, Mr Harford!'

'What is it?'

'That 'alf a Scabbard, 'e's in old Hardinge's camp. They go back a long way together – grenadiers, you know. But Scabbard, 'e's like a knight in shining armour, 'e is. You're one of Tommy Lascelles' boys and Tommy's whipping away Hardinge's job from him. So, Mr Harford, you're the enemy.'

'What d'you mean, enemy?'

''E's what you might call simple in his likes and dislikes. He can be quite sweet if he feels you're batting for the same side but if not – watch out! He can be quite a nuisance when 'e wants.'

'What sort of nuisance? You're right that I'm off on a trip somewhere, but I have to leave behind my . . .' Did he want to say girlfriend? Companion? Fiancée? None of them somehow summed up his relationship with Rodie, but Ronnie was ahead of him.

'Lady friend,' he said.

'Yes. I don't want her being followed round by some old fool who's off his trolleybus. What should I do?'

'Don't you worry,' said Ronnie. 'I'll 'ave a word in the right quarter. You won't have any more bother. Now – more shampoo?'

'I really ought to be getting along.'

Ronnie filled their glasses. 'I sometimes get above myself,' he said, after a moment's thought. 'Happens to us all in royal service. We start to think we float on air. It'll happen to you, if you 'ang around here after the war's over.'

'I don't—'

'When I said I could take care of Scabbard, maybe I was a bit hasty. 'E's a bit of a loose cannon. 'E was devoted to the present king's grandfather, and to his father, and now to the King 'imself. But 'e couldn't abide the Prince of Wales – Edward VIII to you, we still call him by his old moniker – and when the old king died and the prince came in, Scabbard was warned to keep 'is trap shut. 'E used to say all sorts of nasty things about what 'e called the Belvedere Set, and he'd get 'imself into arguments with people who still spoke up for the ex-king.

'Now these people, Mr Harford, these royals, are our bread and butter. Sometimes they seem superhuman, other times they're just like the rest of us, and worse – but that's the game, see? We tell 'em every day how wonderful they are and everything's hunky-dory.'

'Cigarette, Ronnie?'

'Never touch 'em. Now if you'd said a nice fat Romeo y Julieta . . . Anyway, to the point. Old Scabbard's a stuffed-shirt kind of fellow – you'd never see 'im in 'is shirtsleeves or without that ruddy bowler 'at of his. An' when the Prince of Wales opened up Fort Belvedere ten or twelve years ago 'e went a bit peculiar.

'The old king used to send Scabbard over from the Castle with messages to 'is son – "Are you comin' over to dinner?" kind of thing – and, well, the Prince used to go there to let his hair down an' have parties with his friends. 'E was sick of all the bowin' and scrapin' but Scabbard couldn't get used to the idea. The way they couldn't be bothered to dress properly, hanging round the swimmin' pool in their jim-jams, gramophone records, all that. I remember 'im tellin' me once 'e was disgusted that most of the men wore *coloured socks.'*

Guy thought of the train journey from Blackwater Abbey and the look of scorn on the King's Messenger's face.

'Anyway,' said Ronnie, scratching away under his fez at his scalp, 'they 'ad to get rid of Scabbard PDQ when the Prince became King. 'E was a real liability. So they sent 'im up to Holyrood to get 'im out of the way.'

So that's where all the black sheep hang out, thought Guy, recalling Osbert Lothian's threat to have him banished.

''E came back after the abdication, of course, but that stint up in Edinburgh did something to 'im – it was as if 'is sense of honour, or duty, whatever you call it, had been splattered with mud. There were all sorts of stories about him – 'e'd get into fights with anyone who said something that didn't fit with his idea of what was right and proper. Fist-fights, Mr Harford, and nasty ones at that.'

'But, Ronnie, he must be nearly seventy!'

'E's a sturdy one, that Scabbard, like 'e's been pickled in vinegar. How's your glass?'

The morning was melting away. Whether the King approved or not, one of his better vintages was disappearing fast down their throats. 'This is delicious, Ronnie.'

'Roederer '37. A bit young yet. The point about Scabbard *being . . .'* he said, determined to make his point, ''e got a reputation for being violent. That knock on the 'ead during the Boer War, I suppose. There was one or two dust-ups that could have ended up in court, only the Palace police smoothed it all away, like they always do.'

'Why was he kept on then? As a King's Messenger?'

'Ah, now, there you see. The war comes and everyone in the Palace is put in uniform, on the King's orders. They must go and fight for their country. It leaves gaps that will probably never be filled again. So Scabbard got lucky and was kept on just at the moment when they were going to fire him.'

'Let me ask you something, Ronnie. He didn't like men in coloured socks, right?'

'Correct.'

'Didn't like anything unconventional. Exotic.'

'What, 'alf a Scabbard? 'E's a meat-an'-two-veg man. In all respects.'

Guy paused for a moment, wondering how wise it would be to put his next question. Given that Ronnie would be telling all his friends the moment he left the apartment what the question was, and who had asked it.

Oh hell, he thought, Ronnie probably knows the answer and I'll kick myself if I walk away from here without having asked.

He drained his champagne glass and stood up.

'I really must go now, it's been lovely,' he said. 'I'll come and look you up when I get back.'

'Watch out for that Bowes-Lyon. And send the Duke my regards.'

'One question, though.'

'Yes?'

'Do you think, given all the things you've told me, that Arthur Scabbard could have killed Lord Blackwater? Over at Fort Belvedere?'

The old servant raised his glass and peered over the rim at Guy. He paused for a moment.

'Was Blackwater, 'ow you might say, a lady's man?'

'Quite the opposite.'

'Then, yus,' said Ronnie, nodding sagely. 'That sounds like a Scabbard job all right.'

◆ ◆ ◆

The irritating thing about transatlantic telephone calls was they had to be booked well in advance and there was never a guarantee they would come through on time, or even at all. The other way around – New York to London – there never seemed to be a problem, and when Maury Paul, the famed society columnist for the New York Journal-American, put down his breakfast newspaper and picked up the telephone, Ted Rochester answered almost immediately.

'Cholly here.' He used the pen name of his column, Cholly Knickerbocker. It was a byline recognised across the whole of the United States.

'Hello, Maury, what a surprise. How's Fifth Avenue?'

'I rarely stray from Park,' came the lordly reply. 'Such a long way over, don't you know, and you can never be sure of the type of person you might meet there.'

'Ha ha. Wish I could be over there with you. A dry martini in the Stork Club is what I could do with right now. London is a helluva of a place.'

'You're at war, Ted – what d'you expect?'

'The last I heard, the US of A is at war too, but I bet you wouldn't notice it if you were stuck in the bar at 21.'

'Oh, we see a few uniforms around,' replied Maury Paul airily. He picked up his paper between finger and thumb. 'I've just been reading your Charles Greville column. One or two good tales there I'm going to dust down and add a little polish to.'

Ted bit his lip. Maury Paul was a useful contact and they often exchanged stories, but the New Yorker believed himself to be the best columnist ever to grace a newspaper's pages. And too eager to recount the size of the bribes he took from the rich and famous to keep their names *out* of his column.

Rochester seethed about this – on the one hand because, as a journalistic practice, it was spectacularly unethical, and on the other because nobody in London ever offered him so much as six-pence to keep his trap shut.

'What can I do to help?' he said through gritted teeth.

'This tale you have about Archy Blackwater's quite good,' Paul said condescendingly. 'I see here you're asking American readers for help in solving the mystery.'

'Early days yet, Maury. It'll take a week or so for any feedback to filter through to me here in London.'

'I'm an American reader,' teased Paul. 'And I'd like to help.'

'Oh. Ah! D'you have something for me?' Try not to sound desperate, Ted, even if Sid will slash your expenses even further if you can't come up with some sort of development.

'What can you give me in return?'

'Something on Princess Elizabeth,' came the instant response. 'The word's going round that she's fallen in love. Fallen so hard she's telling people she's found her future husband, only we can't get any kind of confirmation from the Palace so we can't run it.'

'*Really?*' squeaked Paul. 'But the girl's only sixteen!'

'Seventeen, just. That's why we can't run it.'

'So your future sovereign has got herself a man – I can do something big with that! Who's the lucky fellow?'

'Some obscure Greek royal, I've got his name somewhere. Never heard of him.'

'Well, that slightly puts my story for you in the shade.'

Oh, don't you worry, old fellow, thought Rochester. As soon as you're ready to print my Elizabeth story, I'll be able to tell it to my readers, quoting your newspaper. Because I know in advance what you're going to say, I'll be able to run it as a scoop before my competitors have even got out of bed.

'Not to worry, Maury. Happy to take anything off your hands, second-hand or not.'

The line crackled and faded, sending a shiver of fear through the London journalist. If he were cut off now, he'd have given away his prize scoop without getting anything in return. Who knew how long it would take to get a return call through to Maury Paul – it could be days!

'Still there, Maury?'

'Still here, Ted. Here's the dirt on Blackwater. Word has it, around the more excitable section of my society friends, that he kept a diary. Not an engagements book, but a full-scale daily memoir. Warts and all.'

'Good heavens! His inside story of the abdication would make a bestseller in its own right,' said Rochester, thinking greedily of the colossal royalties.

'There's more,' said Paul. 'Much more. You know that his was a white marriage, give or take.'

'Of course.'

'And that after the birth of his son, though apparently together, he and Lady Blackwater went their separate ways.'

'Yes.'

'According to the word going around here, Blackwater took delight in writing down every last indiscretion he, or anybody he knew, ever experienced. Men, I'm talking about, Ted – men. Given Blackwater's closeness to King Edward VIII, if any of it got out it'd create a wonderful scandal. Just what we need to lift your readers' spirits in wartime!'

'We could never publish that sort of thing over here.'

'But I can in the States. Now, my guess is that the diary itself must still be around – in London, at Blackwater Abbey, wherever. If it can be found it could be worth a fortune.'

Ted Rochester breathed in slowly. 'Yes, indeed,' he uttered finally.

'So here's the deal, Ted. You find the diary – it surely must be in England, he hasn't left the country since you went to war. You take all the abdication material, I get the pink gossip. We split the profits fifty–fifty.'

'Well, Maury, you know where Blackwater last was – you read it in my column. Fort Belvedere. But I can't see him hiking all the way out there from Mayfair with a ruddy great diary under his arm, so it has to be somewhere else.'

'Ask yourself, Ted – what the hell was he doing at Fort Belvedere?'

'That's precisely what I keep asking myself! But finding the answer isn't that simple. We don't bribe our police like you do,' he lied.

'There I can't help you. You're on your own. But just remember – fifty–fifty, Ted.'

Rochester put down the phone and poured himself a drink. The money he'd paid his police contacts had failed to unearth this treasure trove of information; he'd have to look elsewhere.

He sat looking down on St James's Street as a sudden summer squall sent lunchtime strollers skittering into shop doorways, while old gentlemen covered their heads with their early-edition evening newspapers and scurried into their clubs.

Newspapers, he thought, are everywhere in people's lives, yet what do they know? If I were a truly great journalist I'd find some way to track down this diary of Blackwater's and have a world scoop on the abdication. But I'm not. I've exhausted every avenue.

He sat and thought, and lifted his telephone receiver.

'Buckingham Palace? May I speak to Guy Harford, please?'

◆ ◆ ◆

They met again in The Pig and Whistle. The lunchtime crowd had disappeared and the private bar was empty. Rochester bought the drinks and in old-school 'attack when you want something' mode, wasted no time in going into battle.

'Princess Elizabeth and her boyfriend,' he broadsided. 'She's seventeen. A few weeks ago she was sixteen. What's all this about?'

'When you called you said it was important!' snapped Guy. 'I assumed it was something to do with the King in North Africa – but no, it's trivia!'

'Our future queen in love? And at such a tender age? That's not trivia where I'm sitting.'

'Look, Ted, I don't have any time to spare; I'm off to Balmoral.' The lie slipped easily from his lips since one need have no conscience in front of the most consummate liar in Fleet Street. 'I've still got to pack my bags and get my things together.'

'Don't you have a man to do that for you? I heard you're on the up and up at Buck House.'

'Don't be absurd. Now look, I don't have time for more than one drink. There's nothing in the Princess Elizabeth story.'

'I hear sweet words on the grapevine of a devastatingly handsome Greek.'

'You can unhear them.'

'Whose father bolted with the daughter of the most famous prostitute in Paris and whose dotty mother is holed up in Athens and has taken to wearing a nun's habit.'

'Forget it, I don't know what you're talking about, and there's nothing you can write, Ted, because it isn't true.'

'It's true, old chum, believe me. All right, I won't write about that if you help me with something else. Fair's fair.'

Guy screwed up his eyes. It wasn't the first time he'd had to deal with Ted Rochester's weasel ways.

'Archy Blackwater wrote a diary. At least a page a day about himself and all the famous people he knew. The King, the Prince of Wales, and a lot more besides. The book's missing – has it by any chance found its way into the royal archives? That Fort Knox perched on a hill in Windsor, where books and papers go in and never see the light of day? Which is paid for by the taxpayer *who isn't allowed to read a single word?*'

'No point in taking that tone with me, Ted. It's the first I've heard of it. I'll certainly ask around if you like . . .'

'Thanks, you're a pal.'

'. . . on condition you drop the Princess Elizabeth stuff. Write about her war work – that's what people really want to read about.'

'That's *not* what people want to read about,' came the instant riposte. 'They want to read about what makes her heart flutter. Love, love, love – it's what makes the world go round, Guy! Or maybe you effete courtiers don't know about that sort of thing.'

'Come off it. It's just gossip.'

'You're wrong! Elizabeth's the nation's pin-up – people are desperate to know about her romantic life.'

'Anyway,' said Guy, putting on his hat, 'must be off to Balmoral. If I come up with an answer on the diary I'll let you know – but I can't think why you're even asking me. Blackwater was a civilian, not part of the royal circle.'

Ted gave him an old-fashioned look. 'There's a tradition, y'know, goes back years,' he drawled. 'Anything in written form that could be damaging to the royal circle has a habit of ending up at the Royal Library – where they have a special incinerator set aside for just such articles. Just a nod or a wink if Lord Blackwater's diary is going to help heat His Majesty's bathwater, *if you please.*'

'No mention of Elizabeth?'

'No mention of Elizabeth.' Rochester smiled, thinking, I doubt they ever get to read Maury Paul's column up there in the wild wastes of Aberdeenshire. Too busy trying to stop their kilts lifting high in the breeze.

CHAPTER SEVENTEEN

The parrot was performing its usual evening aerobatics. It was difficult to concentrate while she did her best to emulate the Luftwaffe's finest, raining down liquid bombs on the populous below.

'*Say Fanny!*'

'Shut up, Charlotte.'

'*Say Fanny! Say Fanny!*'

'I suppose that tart of yours thought it was a joke, teaching Charlotte to say that,' Rodie snapped.

'I can only have left her alone for half an hour while I went and bought some tea,' he apologised. 'She drinks lapsang, so I had to go to the grocer in the King's Road. What a wicked woman.'

'So that ruddy parrot is going to be squawking her name from now till kingdom come. Why'd you bring her here?'

'Fanny? Not for the reason you think, I told you that! Here's Rupe.'

The door opened and the languid postman sauntered in. 'Off on your travels then,' he teased by way of greeting.

'For heaven's sake, did someone put an announcement in *The Times*? Everyone seems to know!'

'Actually, an open suitcase on a sofa tells its own story.' His eyes flicked sideways.

'Oh,' said Guy. 'Well, yes.'

Rupe helped himself to a drink. 'Before you go I think we should all have an off-the-record chat,' he said cheerily. 'Share a few things. Might be a help all round, especially with you disappearing for a bit.'

'I'll be back.'

'I daresay,' said Rupe in a tone of voice that left the matter open to doubt. 'But let's clear the air. You work for the Crown, I work for the government, Rodie here gives her efforts to the government but her heart belongs to the Crown. We're all supposed to be on the same side, so what's the harm in a little sharing out of information?'

'Experience has told me it's better to keep your trap shut. What do you want to know?'

Rodie limped out to the kitchen to fill the kettle.

'How was Madame Popowska?' laughed Rupe.

'You scallywag!' she hissed over her shoulder. 'I ain't going to do any more. I pulled a 'amstring thanks to you!'

'I gather it's sunnier climes you're off to,' said Rupe to Guy, ignoring this. 'I won't ask where because I had the memo from Tankerton. That's Crown business, nothing to do with the government, but what I'd like to do is sort out this Blackwater business before you go.'

'I thought everyone had agreed to forget it,' said Guy, nettled at his failure to solve the case. 'Certainly I was told to drop it by Tommy. But it doesn't appear to want to go away – it seems every conversation I have comes back to Blackwater. What's *your* interest?'

''E's just a nosy parker,' came Rodie's voice from the kitchen. 'Stickin' that nose into everyone's business. 'E loves it.' She was taking the ballet injury badly. 'Where's the aspirin?'

'Top shelf, left-hand side. Do tell me, Rupe, with so much going on elsewhere in this war, why the focus on Blackwater?'

'I might ask the same,' came the smooth reply. 'Your investigation's dead, but it won't lie down. So why don't we share?'

Charlotte completed one more circuit of the studio and came in to land on the balcony rail, muttering to herself.

'You know,' said Guy, 'you're a great friend and all that, but I don't feel I can entirely trust you. You've got Rodie spying on me . . .'

'What are you talking about?' snapped Rupert. 'Of course I haven't!'

'Oh yes 'e 'as,' came the voice from the kitchen. 'Only I ain't going to do it any more, Rupe. My first loyalty's to my *future husband.*' The words sounded as though they'd been spat out – aimed more at Guy than her boss.

'She told me,' said Guy. 'The spying. She said she can't go on like this, divided loyalties.'

'Dammit! It's her job! She's under orders!'

'Am I?' said Rodie, reappearing. 'Burglary's one thing, chum, but betrayal I don't do. Not to 'im, anyway.'

'Let's talk sensibly,' said Guy. 'After all, I may not be back from this trip for a while.' Or ever.

Rupe got out a small notebook. 'Tell me all you know about Blackwater, and what the Palace interest is.'

'Let me give you the most recent stuff first. He kept a diary. That would be of colossal interest to the Palace because of what it might say about life at Fort Belvedere during the time Blackwater was more or less a permanent guest there. There are so many secrets around the abdication that still need unravelling – simply because, according to Tommy, it must never happen again. If it does, it could mean curtains for the monarchy in Britain.

'Beyond that, the diary probably contains details of Blackwater's love affairs with all sorts of people, both within the royal household

186

but also further – much further – afield. That could be an unexploded bomb all of its own. But my guess is that's not what interests you.'

Rupert shook his head. 'These things may seem important to you but actually I'm much more concerned about the political element. I gather you're on a mission to see the Duke of Windsor.'

'I couldn't possibly say.'

'Very laudable but Tankerton has a looser mouth than you. Our concern is that through the Frenchman Bedaux, who lent Windsor his house to get married in, the Nazis have encircled the Duke and are using him. Pulling his strings. If I understand correctly, your job when you get to Nassau is more to assess whether the Duke is going to jump ship and head for permanent exile in America. Correct?'

'Pretty much,' said Guy, irritated that secrets he'd been protecting were apparently common gossip over at the Post Office – or wherever it was Rupert worked.

'Let's come back to that in a moment. From our perspective it'd be helpful if you could do a little digging for us.'

'Don't you have your own people out in the Bahamas, for goodness' sake? Trained operatives? It's going to be difficult enough filling the brief I've been given without working for your lot as well!'

Rupert snorted. 'They've all gone native and dance attendance on the Duke and Duchess. Either that or they stick their noses in the air because of what the Windsors did to our national prestige. One way or the other they're not doing a great job, to be frank. You'll be talking to the Windsors at some stage, I understand.'

'Maybe.'

'When you go, take two sun hats – one with "Palace" written inside, one with "Post Office". Wear them alternately. We desperately need stuff on the Bedaux angle, Guy. I'm sure you can manage to get somewhere with that. What else do you plan to do?'

'Well, I thought I might start out by asking the Windsors who killed Archy Blackwater,' came the sour response. 'I'm sure they must have an idea.'

'Ha ha. Not much chance of that, old friend.'

'No. But what amazes me is that *nobody* seems to care about this poor man. I mean, I know he wasn't much of a human being – rotten husband, gambler, all that – but people only seem interested in what secrets he had, not about the man himself. Does that seem right to you?'

'What d'you mean?'

'There seems to be no active plan to track down his killer.'

'Don't be so sure about that.'

'That's how it appears. But anyway, I think I may have the answer.' Guy described his conversation with Ronnie Morgan about Scabbard, and Morgan's belief that Scabbard's unpleasant prejudices might have led him to kill the peer.

'Not very likely,' said Rupe, turning away. 'How are the aches and pains, Rodie?'

She'd curled up in the big chair under the window and was sulking. 'You just get on with your man-talk,' she said bitterly. 'You don't care. Neither of you do.'

'You've got hold of the wrong end of the stick,' said Rupert, turning back to Guy. 'It's not some ancient King's Messenger with a bee in his bonnet, it's a bit more complicated than that.' He told Guy about the dead-letter boxes, the messages to the ballet company, the search for Simon Green.

'Oh,' said Guy, getting up and walking over to Rodie. 'So that's why you've been jumping through the hoop these past few days. You're going to burgle the ballet!'

'Don't be daft,' she said, and turned her head away.

'I just don't see it,' said Guy, shaking his head. 'I think only a man who knows Fort Belvedere inside out could lure Blackwater there and kill him.'

'But why? Why would an old geezer like that commit murder?'

'His *coloured socks*,' said Guy acidly. 'Why else?'

◆ ◆ ◆

The evening sun, lower in the sky, caught Guy's half-finished portrait of Rodie in a blaze of gold. She looked radiant, brave, full of energy. The real-life subject looked less vibrant as she limped around the studio bringing Guy's folded shirts over to the suitcase.

'Promise you'll stay safe and come 'ome soon.'

'Promise.'

'And no fancy tarts.'

'Not many. You stay safe as well. No climbing in through people's roofs while I'm gone.'

'Are you jokin', mate? I can barely crawl up the stairs.'

'No dancing tonight, then? No Billy Cotton at the Palais? Could you manage fish and chips over in Lisson Grove if I found a taxi? It's our last night!'

'Let's go to The Surprise. I can just about get there and back.'

'OK, but I must just use the telephone first.' Guy reached for his notebook and dialled a number while Rodie rearranged the chaos inside his suitcase.

There was a moment's pause and then, 'Is that Gwen? Guy Harford, you remember we . . . Ah, yes, good. Look, I have a question which I hope you can answer – did your former boss keep a diary?'

'He kept two,' replied the private secretary crisply. 'One for his engagements, I was in charge of that. The other was . . . private.'

'Can I ask, when did you last see it? The private diary?'

'Not for some years. He was living mostly in London, d'you see. He would have kept it with him.'

'Can you picture when you last saw it?'

'I've been working here for ten years, so three or four years after I arrived, I'd say.'

'So 1936 or -7?'

'Probably. After the abdication his life changed quite a lot and that's when he spent more and more time in London.'

'And,' said Guy, 'do you know what was in the diary?'

'Yes. But I'm not going to tell you. I work here for Lady Blackwater, that's all I'll say.'

'Meaning the contents were of a personal nature?'

'Mm.'

'Embarrassing?'

'Look, I think I've helped you as much as I—'

Guy sensed he was losing her. 'Let me just ask you this. If the contents were published, would they cause a stir?'

'Far worse than that,' snapped Gwen. 'Goodbye.'

'Just a moment! One last thing – when I first came up to Blackwater, had her ladyship been anywhere in the previous week?'

'She spent the weekend at Windsor with Princess Mary and Their Majesties.'

'You mean . . .' Guy sucked in his breath as he struggled to finish his question. 'Lady Blackwater was at Windsor when her husband died? Why on earth didn't she tell me that?'

The phone went dead.

Guy got up in anger. 'I wonder what the hell is going on!' he said. 'People being deliberately evasive if not telling out-and-out lies. The only thing is that deception never lasts long when it's murder – that's what they never realise. Come on,' he said briskly to Rodie, offering his arm. 'Let's go to the pub. Our last night.'

'Don't say that, you wossname. We got the rest of our lives together!'

Have we? he thought, as they made their slow progress up Tite Street towards The Surprise. That afternoon the news had come through that a civilian plane carrying actor Leslie Howard had been attacked and downed by a squadron of German fighters over the Bay of Biscay. All seventeen passengers on board had perished, and an urgent re-evaluation was in progress over whether this formerly safe route should be discontinued. Meantime, ridiculously, flights to Lisbon were to continue – including his.

As they squeezed past the sandbags surrounding the pub door-way the noise that greeted them sounded as if the record had got stuck: the celestial choir was still there, having one last stab at 'The White Cliffs of Dover'. It was just as ragged and tuneless as before.

'*Ter-morrer, jus' you wait an' see . . .*'

They were lucky enough to get the quiet table again and settled down with their drinks and a bag of Smith's crisps.

'Let me tell you what I'm not telling Rupe,' said Guy, tearing open the blue salt sachet. 'It's up to you what you pass on – my job at the Palace is supposed to be secret but if I can't tell you, who can I tell?'

'I told 'im I wouldn't spy on you no more,' she said, running her fingers over his hand.

'This is what I think. There were only a few months while Edward was king – January to December 1936. During that time the people closest to him included Archy Blackwater – he'd been the court jester at the Fort all those years when Edward was Prince of Wales. As the new King, he was suddenly surrounded by all the heavy apparatus of officialdom. As a way of protecting himself, those who'd been close to him became even closer – an inner guard.

'Archy Blackwater was one of them. But now Edward inherited the King's Messengers – and they, of course, included that man

Scabbard.' As he spoke his eyes swivelled round the room, certain they would discover the man with the bowler hat lurking in a corner somewhere.

'Scabbard, not to put too fine a point on it, is violently prejudiced against men whose interests don't extend to the opposite sex.'

'Pansies, yer mean.'

'If you want to put it that way. Anyway, I think it's probably likely he would have displayed that hatred and, not surprisingly, Archy Blackwater suggested to the King that Scabbard be sent away from the immediate royal circle. So he was whisked off to Holyrood, but Ronnie Morgan told me the other day that it did something to him – to Scabbard. That he came back a changed man, as though his honour had been impugned somehow. And then he started going off the rails.'

The chorus over by the bar had moved on to 'Who Do You Think You're Kidding, Mr Hitler?' but few of them seemed to know the words. It didn't stop them singing along, their words blurred by the fog of alcohol and smoke that had enveloped them.

'What Blackwater's secretary told me on the blower just now confirms what we thought – that he kept a diary which no doubt listed all his conquests. And that presumably included people within the royal household. If Scabbard knew about the diary, could he have killed Blackwater to get his hands on it?'

'And,' said Rodie, 'maybe 'is lordship kept it under the floorboards in 'is room at the Fort. That would explain the outline of dust on that envelope I found there.'

'Possibly. But that would mean that the diary would have to have ended in 1936 with the abdication – if you remember, the Fort was shut up by the new management. Nobody was allowed to go back. People's possessions were returned to them – they weren't allowed to go and collect them.'

''E could have nipped back at night when there was nobody there, picked it up and got away.'

'If it had been Blackwater, don't you think he would have taken those erotic poems as well? It's obvious he wrote them. Why would he take the diary and leave the poems? No, I think it had to be someone else who managed to get their hands on it.'

'Who? Scabbard?'

'Well, he certainly had easier access to the Fort than Blackwater did. As a royal employee he could simply cycle or drive up the Long Walk from the Castle – just like we did, Rodie – turn off, and get himself into the building.'

'But why? Why would he do that?'

'I've no idea. Let's have another drink and work on it.' He disappeared to the bar, sucked into the morass of heaving, sweaty bodies, now marching themselves all the way to Tipperary, bellowing his order to a barmaid of singular beauty but limited mathematical skills.

'Is this easing the pain?' he asked when he got back. 'I could still get us a taxi, go for those fish and chips.'

'I just want a nice night with you,' she said, smiling. 'We've got sausages in the meat safe, we could have those.'

'Whatever you'd like best.'

'I was thinking while you were getting the drinks – if Scabbard knew about the diary and what was in it, 'e could have fished it out so 'e could blackmail Blackwater.'

'If you'd met him, Rodie, you'd know that's impossible – a more upright citizen you've never met in your life. Blackmail? If you could see that bowler hat!'

'You said he'd got a screw loose, 'e'd gone a bit nutty.'

'Well, it's always possible, I suppose – just not very likely. Anyway, you watch out for him – he knows where we live. He's prone to violent outbursts and, Ronnie Morgan told me, he carries a swordstick. Really, the man ought to be arrested.'

''E works for 'Is Majesty, don't 'e? Nobody's going to arrest *him*.'

Nevertheless, both looked about cautiously as they emerged on to the street; in the half-light Scabbard could be hiding in a doorway, around a corner, the swordstick unsheathed and ready to do its bloody work. The summer heat lingered in the air, the streets smelt sweet, and for a moment Guy, bent upon departure to another world, could have given his heart to Chelsea. But that would be disloyal – his heart was already the possession of Tangier and its proud populace.

'Ouch!' Rodie cried, as she tripped on a paving stone on their walk back towards the river. 'That Rupe, what a bastard! There's no need for all this – I could have blagged my way through the job, wouldn't be the first time.'

'Tell me what this ballet business is all about,' he said.

She explained all over again about the coded letters being sent to an anonymous recipient at the Vic-Wells Ballet. How only one had been discovered in a routine search for dead-letter boxes, but that it made reference to other mail-collection points in the London suburbs, and detailed ballet phraseology with references to Ninette de Valois and Margot Fonteyn.

'The ballet words may be a code but also they make sense by themselves, so it's difficult to work out what the message means – that's what Rupe told me,' she said. 'What we do know is that there's a Nazi infiltrator in the company, and it's my job to find out who it is and what the hell they're doing there. In a ruddy ballet troupe, for heaven's sake!'

'So you're joining the company in the wardrobe department.'

'Tomorrow. And I'm being sent north to be part of the travelling company,' said Rodie. 'I've never been up north before – have you? What's it like?'

'Same but different. You've never been anywhere, have you?'

'Don't you come all lah-di-dah with me, just because you lived in Paris and dusty old Africa!'

Their inconsequential bickering carried them amiably home but when they arrived at the doorstep Rodie turned and grabbed Guy by the lapels.

'Kiss me,' she said, urgently. 'Then I've got to tell you something.'

'What's that?'

'It may be our last night, but, darlin', I'm sorry.'

'What?'

'No 'anky-panky. I aches too much.'

CHAPTER EIGHTEEN

At Heston aerodrome nobody mentioned the Leslie Howard flight, as if to do so would bring the Luftwaffe back, thirsting for more blood. There was the usual lengthy delay, the countermanding tannoy announcements, people getting up and gathering their things together only to sit down again, deflated, for another hour or two. Guy passed the time gazing glumly at a map on the wall showing the various ways to get across the Atlantic, but whichever route you took it was a hell of a journey, fraught with danger.

Where, he asked himself as he sat on a hard bench, was the most glamorous place to die? In the sea-green waters off Lisbon? In the richer tropical waters off Bathurst in West Africa? There were hundreds of miles of magnificent nothing between him and Nassau, plenty of places to get lost for ever – the longest flight he'd taken in his life and one in which he could do nothing but sit back and hope for the best.

At Foynes in the west of Ireland he changed planes and, as he waited for the massive seaplane out on the Shannon Estuary to be prepared, his thoughts went back to the previous year and another airport, another destination.

It had been a momentous return to Tangier, to find that life would continue after the war, that one day he could go back to his old existence. He thought about his minder on that trip, a bossy young Naval Intelligence officer called Dimont with a curious back-story and a razor-sharp brain. He wondered what had happened to her and whether she'd reunited with her fiancé, a cloak-and-dagger merchant, or whether he, like so many others, never came back.

He sat on in a depressed state, shutting his eyes to blot out his anxiety, and soon he fell asleep. He awoke to see by the reception desk a familiar profile, shrouded by a high collar and low-brimmed hat, but recognisable all the same.

Shaking his head in surprise, he got up and walked towards the woman. 'Fanny!' he called. 'Fanny Goldington! What an extraordinary coincidence! What on earth are you doing *here*, of all places?'

Without sparing him a glance the woman turned sharply away and spoke to an Air Force officer, who walked over to Guy. 'Can I help you, sir?' he asked, in a not particularly helpful tone.

'Excuse me,' said Guy, sidestepping him, 'just spotted a friend. Wanted to have a quick word, if you could just let me . . . Fanny!' he called again towards the disappearing back.

'Why are you using that name?' said the man, stepping closer to him. He seemed determined to be obstructive. 'That's Mrs Strudwick. I think you must have made a mistake.'

'Look,' said Guy, exasperated, 'I'm an artist, a painter – I've painted that lady's portrait. Recently. Unless she married someone else last week, she's still the Marchioness of Goldington. Fanny.'

'I'd pipe down and sit down if I were you,' said the man heavily. 'People get jumpy in an airport, especially in wartime. Pretty soon they can spread disquiet among the other passengers, and that we do *not* tolerate. Go back to your seat and wait to be called, there's a good chap, or I'll have to . . .' He didn't finish the sentence but nodded towards two bulky RAF Regiment men who looked ready for a fight.

So this is war, thought Guy, as he did what he was told. She's no more Mrs Strudwick than I am. Where's she going? What's she doing? After a few minutes he got up again and went over to the tea bar to order a sandwich.

'You'd better get that down you quick, feller, if you're for the north route. They're shutting the gate in a couple of minutes.'

'No,' said Guy, 'I'm going the other way.' Whatever the other way was – certainly he wasn't being herded on to Fanny Goldington's plane, but at least he knew now where she *wasn't* going. He took the sandwich back to his seat and looked again at the wall map.

His own journey would take him in a clockwise arc over the equator, via Bathurst to Brazil before heading up to Nassau. That, clearly, was the south route. The north route, he could see, went via Botwood in Newfoundland to Montreal and finally Washington DC. So we are both Atlantic-hopping, Fanny, but you're going to the US mainland – I wonder what you're doing there, and why you're travelling as Mrs Strudwick when every gossip columnist in the world knows who the hell you are, with your three husbands and your claws in the King of Albania.

He shrugged and tried to put the matter from his mind. There were many, many hours ahead to think of the task he'd been given, and how he was to approach the Windsors when he arrived. In his luggage he had a letter from Foxy to the Duchess, which would gain him access to her – but before that, he had to find out what exactly was going on in Nassau, and just what the Windsors were up to. How to achieve that, he had no idea.

The next couple of days were spent reading and sleeping in the vast Boeing seaplane. Despite the austerities of wartime, the aircraft was spacious and staffed by a courteous couple of stewards whose provisions were short on food but long on alcohol. Thus the stopovers in Lisbon and Bathurst, Belem and Trinidad came and went in a pleasant blur, and the fear of enemy aircraft evaporated as he sailed on between the blue of the sea and the azure empty wastes of sky.

At Nassau, thanks to instructions from Tankerton at the FO, he was whisked away without passport formalities and before long he found himself standing with his suitcase on a windswept airstrip in Whale Cay, a small island twenty minutes' flight away. The heat was blistering, the sunlight blinding.

Almost immediately a Willys Jeep drew up and a head poked around the windshield. 'Welcome to paradise,' said a singsong voice with a hockey-sticks accent.

'Guy Harford. Lovely to be here.'

'Hop in, I'm Hester.'

She was wind-blown, English, and a careless driver who held the steering wheel as if she wanted to shake it to death. 'Joe isn't here,' she said, crashing the gears. 'She's taking flying lessons. Ditched the last one off Grenadine beach the other day, but I think she's getting the hang of it now. I hear you live in Chelsea. We have an apartment in Mulberry Walk, is that near you?'

'Five minutes. Watch out, the—!' Hester swerved jerkily to avoid a snake in the road.

'We haven't been there since the start of the war. Joe told me to show you the island – doesn't take long.' She swerved down a dirt track through thick grassy dunes but soon they were on a recently constructed road which took them past a succession of white sand beaches. The shining turquoise sea seemed to rise to greet them.

'D'you fish? We have red snapper, grouper, parrot fish and angel fish inshore. If you like a bit of a challenge we've got blue-fin tuna, barracuda and the occasional shark further out.'

'I paint, I don't hunt.'

'That's not the spirit round here, old chum. We live off the sea!' She glanced at him and he could tell she was unimpressed. 'Joe used to race powerboats. She won every challenge cup going. Now she's taken up flying. She's like a boy who never wants to grow up. How long are you staying?' Her words flew at him like machine-gun bullets.

They turned into the sun and for a moment she seemed to lose control of the vehicle as she struggled to put on dark glasses. I've come all this way, thought Guy, just to end up a traffic accident statistic. I wonder if there's a hospital on this godforsaken island?

'Nine miles by four,' shouted Hester, as she revved the jeep into top gear. 'Hold on tight – we can do the whole lot in twenty minutes flat!'

'You know,' shouted back Guy, 'this is lovely, but could we do it some other time? I've been travelling for three days and what I'd love is a shower and a lie-down for half an hour.'

She slowed the jeep down. 'Yes, yes, of course,' she said, nodding. 'Just following orders. Joe's a stickler for doing things right. She'll ask if I've shown you the island and you'll say yes.'

'Yes. You have. And thank you, from what I've seen you're absolutely right – it's paradise.'

'I'll just drive you past the church – very important. It was built by Joe to commemorate her great love Ruth Baldwin – killed herself with a drug overdose back in Chelsea in '37, but hey-ho, now her spirit shines down from above on us all.'

'Are you . . .'

'Yes, I'm Ruth's replacement. Well, one of them. Oh look!' She pointed. 'That's the Dietrich beach. Named for Marlene – technically she owns it. She was another replacement.'

'Have there been many replacements?'

'With Joe, who's counting? Here we are – someone will get your bag. Come and have a cold drink before your shower.'

They'd pulled up outside a large white stone house surrounded by wide lawns which were dotted with palm and tamarind, oleander and mastic. Servants filed out, bowed, took Guy's case and ushered them indoors.

Hester stood in front of the mirror and rearranged her hair. As she put on lipstick she said, 'Don't be surprised by Joe. She's larger than life – and richer. She does what she wants and people let her be because she's a one-off. But she comes as a bit of surprise when you first meet her. I gather you're here about the Windsors.'

'Yes. Unofficially.'

'Yes, we got the message. And we understand. The person you should really talk to is Julian. He knows everything about the Windsors.'

'Julian?'

'Henshaw. He's our priest. Only, this being Whale Cay, he's a bit different from most men of the cloth.'

A gold-waistcoated footman brought a drinks tray and retired soundlessly. 'He was banished from Capri for dancing on a table in a nightie. Well, that's what he says, but I think he tried to make love to one of the altar boys after Mass. Though probably in his nightie, knowing Julian. He's a total sweetie.'

'And he knows about the Windsors because . . . ?'

'He'll tell you. If he likes you.'

Guy allowed himself a sigh of relief. To have come all this way, knowing nobody, in the hope that somehow he could work a miracle and gather the facts he'd been ordered to track down – it was a hopeless task, like so many he'd been thrown since he accidentally fell into royal service. But now, within a minute or two of arriving, he'd found someone who knew something.

Or claimed he did.

'This place is like an English village,' sighed Hester. 'Nothing but gossip. But you need to take care, Mr Harford.'

'Guy.'

'Guy, darling, light my cigarette.' Said without the vaguest hint of flirtation, it wasn't an invitation so much as a command. 'I'm going to put on a skirt. We dress for dinner.'

◆ ◆ ◆

He was woken hours later by a light tap on his shoulder. A tall black servant with a handsome grin said, 'Time for dinner, sah. Your clothes are laid out next door.'

As he struggled awake he looked through slatted blinds to a purple-streaked sky over a cobalt sea. The apricot smell of oleander came wafting through the window and the cicadas had already started up their nightly chit-chattery. He wandered into the adjoining dressing room to find his evening suit newly pressed and his white shirt freshly laundered. The room was large and simple, but the service could only be matched by The Ritz.

He came downstairs to be greeted by Hester, alluring in an off-the-shoulder grey silk dress and a cavalcade of diamonds encircling her neck.

'Good,' she said, 'you're on time. First impressions count with Joe.'

'That's a delicious smell.'

'My very own perfume,' she said proudly. 'Joe took me to Grasse and we chose the fragrances together. When you've inherited a large chunk of Standard Oil stock as a child the world's your oyster, really. Do what you like, buy what you like.' She looked at Guy steadily. 'She bought me.'

'Before that, I take it, she decided to buy the whole island.'

'Whale Cay – and Bird Cay, Cat Cay, half of Hoffman's Cay too. Ask her yourself – here she comes.'

In bustled a woman of only middling height but who seemed taller by virtue of the extravagant personality that preceded her. Dark, tough and compact, she was wearing a man's dinner jacket which Guy could see at a glance was cut by a Savile Row tailor, and no jewellery but for a man's signet ring on her left hand.

On her shoulder sat a large wooden doll.

'Meet Lord Tod Wadley!' cried Joe Carstairs. 'Isn't he looking handsome tonight?'

Apart from his immaculate attire – Lord Tod obviously used the same tailor as Joe Carstairs – he looked like any other doll to Guy, but he nodded his assent and thanked his hostess for inviting him to stay.

'Three days!' she boomed. 'House guests are like fish – they go off after three days, so don't get too comfortable! But I hear you're a painter – you can stay on longer if you promise to make a lovely portrait of Lord Tod. Others have attempted him but never quite got the likeness. You *do* do portraits, don't you?'

Not if I can help it, thought Guy, your doll's face is grotesque. But he replied, 'Of course, it will be a pleasure.' He hoped that finding paint and canvas on this sparsely inhabited island would get him out of that one.

'We'll have dinner on the terrace,' said Joe. 'Lord Tod sits at the head, and we gather round him. Just in case a word or two of wisdom should drop from his lips.' She threw back her head in a raucous laugh, revealing perfect teeth and a tiny pink tongue. 'Hester's put on her best dress for you, Mr Harford. Isn't she a peach?'

'Guy, please.'

'Or maybe she's cosying up to Lord Tod. You can never tell what goes on behind people's backs, ha ha!'

A liveried footman brought champagne but, glimpsing the label, Guy found it gratifying to see the vintage wasn't as special as Ronnie Morgan's. The whole set-up at Whale Cay was unnerving and surreal, a world within a world, and it was reassuring to think of old Ronnie with his own footman and vintage champagne back in the safer surroundings of St James's Palace. However odd Ronnie's set-up, it seemed to make complete sense when compared with this island queen, this human hurricane.

'We must know lots of people in common,' said Joe. 'I was in London so much before the war.'

'Possibly,' said Guy, 'but mostly I was in Tangier – I went there from Paris. Until I ended up in Buckingham Palace I'd barely set foot in London for ten years.'

'It's an odd combination, being an artist *and* a courtier. But it makes me like you more – you're unusual. We like the unusual, don't we, Hester?'

'You can say that again,' said Hester, fingering her diamonds. It wasn't difficult to see that she was bored with island life.

'So now tell me what you want with the Windsors,' ordered Joe, sitting down with a heavy bump. 'A rum couple, I can tell you. Frankly, he's an idiot – I mean, one minute the head of an empire, the next the king of nothing! What sort of a fool is that?'

'I imagine he sees his job as Governor of the Bahamas as a pivotal role in Anglo–American relations, given the proximity of these islands to the US mainland,' replied Guy cautiously. He didn't mean it but wanted to draw Joe out.

'There's nothing he can do here,' she replied, shaking her head. Lord Tod, seated next to her on the tapestry-covered couch, remained impassive, saving his word or two of wisdom until they reached the port, perhaps. 'The Bahamas are run by a bunch of wildcat business bullies – they call themselves the Bay Street Boys – who run the assembly and make the laws. They don't like his snooty ways and he thinks they're grubby, so he sits in Government House and twiddles his thumbs while they get on with the business of running this part of the world.'

Hester leant forward. 'When he arrived here in 1940 you took the Duke your plans to create a fighting task force and a separate farming task force, and he simply ignored them, Joe,' she prompted. 'Such shabby behaviour.'

'We try to remain friends.' Joe nodded. 'He and Wallis paid us a visit and I showed them round. But this governorship's all a fig leaf. She runs him and he runs nobody.'

'Part of the reason I'm here is because we think he's about to cut and run,' said Guy, putting down his champagne glass. 'You must have seen or heard about Vanderbilt's piece in the *New York Post*.'

'Talk to Julian about it. He'll join us after dinner.'

'Also, when he goes, what will he leave behind? Will it be a mess? I'm here to see what damage his governorship could do to our present king. I need to know about his Nazi connections and whether anyone's in a position to pull his strings.'

'I suppose,' said Joe, 'it must all look quite unnerving when you look at it from the other end of the telescope – from the London end. It must have seemed like a good idea to make the Windsors castaways on a desert island five thousand miles from home. Not picturing the damage he could do.'

'And under the thumb of that witch,' added Hester. 'I could see when they visited us here how he completely caved in to her.'

Hester may be beautiful but Joe pays not the slightest attention to her, thought Guy.

'We had a perfectly good governor who was kicked out to make way for the Windsors. Decent chap who went by the rules. Now we have this pair – she's all bitter and twisted at being stuck here—'

'They're just back from a nice holiday in Palm Beach,' interjected Hester. 'Staying with those frightful Donahues . . .'

'—and the Secretary to the Treasury in DC has been asking your people in Whitehall where he got his spending money from. They think he's money laundering – black market currency.'

'How d'you know that?'

Joe chuckled. 'Friends in high places, Guy. But the thing you need to look out for is the fact he's breaching the Trading with the

Enemy act. What you chaps would call treasonable activity. That's a jailable offence.'

'Can you give me more details on that?'

'In the morning, when my head's clearer.'

'Well,' said Guy, 'this is good of you, Joe. To help.'

'Listen, old chum,' she said, 'I'm half-English and half-American so I see things from both sides – how wonderful your royal family is, and how outdated it all seems. Perhaps that's part of its charm. So I want the royals to succeed, but I look down on royals who aren't up to scratch. Windsor is one of those, and anything I can do to help, I will.'

'Then help me find out to what extent he truly is a traitor,' said Guy sharply, 'wittingly or unwittingly. And whether he's going to become an American citizen.

'Because in wartime, for us Brits, that's as much an act of treason as sitting on Adolf Hitler's knee.'

CHAPTER NINETEEN

Joe waited till she'd lit her cigar to roll out her well-worn story about bumping into Greta Garbo in an optician's on Fifth Avenue. '"Hello, Miss Garbo," says I. "Hello, sir," says Garbo.' She broke into gales of laughter, though you could tell from the expression on Lord Tod's face he'd heard it a million times before.

'The Reverend Henshaw,' announced the butler, making way for a wiry, bespectacled man in a dusty suit and dog collar.

'Julian, I want you to meet Guy Harford, the famous artist. He's come here to paint Lord Tod, but he's very interested in the Windsors. I said you could tell him a thing or two.'

'Brandy, darling,' said the cleric with a sigh.

Two balloons later Henshaw was ready to talk.

'What exactly is your interest?' he asked, eyeing Guy like a man about to feast on a rare steak.

Guy frostily returned his gaze. 'I work for various people in London,' he said guardedly.

'A spy, then.'

'I wouldn't put it quite like that.' Guy wondered if the man knew anything at all or just made up stories after a night's carousing with his feathered friends in The Jungle Club in Nassau.

'*And you will know the truth, and the truth will set you free* – John, chapter eight, verse thirty-two.' Henshaw stared at Guy. 'What do you want, Mr Spy?'

He's drunk but no fool, thought Guy. 'What's your connection with the Windsors?'

Henshaw licked his lips. 'I have a special friend there. He's all ears, hears everything. Pillow talk, dear, costs lives – isn't that what the posters say in London?'

'OK, this is what I want to know,' said Guy, taking the plunge. 'Are there any whispers of the Windsors leaving the islands?'

'Shopping in Miami? They're at it all the time.'

'I mean permanently.'

'Ah, I see what you mean. In a word, quite possibly – well, that's two words. Better give me a top-up.'

'Mr Henshaw – Julian – this is important. What have you heard?'

'That some busybody in Washington is trying to push them out of Nassau, send them further afield. Trinidad, perhaps. Timbuctoo.'

'Not that they're going to cash in their chips here and head for the mainland where he'll take up American citizenship?'

'Oh, *that*,' said Henshaw. 'They're always going on about that. She's sick of it, being here – nothing she'd like better than to get the little man on to her home turf. Think of the kudos that would bring, bringing an ex-king back to Baltimore in her luggage – talk about a homecoming queen!'

'But have they actually done anything about it, have you heard? Are they packing their bags as we speak?'

Henshaw gave a lavish lick to the rim of his brandy balloon. 'Well, they've got some very iffy friends in Florida, including a man called Robert Young – Railroad Young, they call him. Owns the Chesapeake and Ohio Railway. He's rich enough and power-ful enough to bribe anybody in Washington, and he just adores hanging round with the Duke and Duchess. So, if our royal Governor decides to jump over the wall, he can do it quicker than I can say three Hail Marys.'

'What's this other business, about him being shunted further afield?'

'That comes from one of the equerries, Carey Fairfax. He's very special,' said Henshaw with a sideways smile. 'Some man in Washington, name of Lion or something like that, is gunning for him. They haven't told the Duke, he's jumpy enough as it is with everything else that's going on.'

'You say Fairfax is special. Is he a friend?'

'Or something.'

'Would he talk to me?'

'I doubt it. He's devoted to *them*, you see, so if you're hoping to screw information out of him you can toss that idea right away. An equerry's job is to lay down his life for those he serves, and Carey is the best there is.'

'I have a letter for the Duchess from an old friend. Would he at least see me so I can hand it over?'

Henshaw eyed him myopically through his glass. 'What's it say?' he drawled.

'I've no idea, but it's from a friend in London. I think she'd be happy to have it. It hasn't been through the censor, you see, unlike the Duchess's other mail, and I daresay it will give her a clearer picture of what's going on back home.'

I wonder if it does, thought Guy. Tommy warned me not to tell Foxy where I was going – but I thought a handwritten letter from her would strengthen my bona fides with the Duchess if we met face to face. Let's hope she hasn't dropped me in it.

'So, Mr Henshaw, Carey Fairfax?'

'I'll ask him.'

'That's kind of you,' said Guy. 'I'm planning on flying over to Nassau tomorrow. Could you telephone him and ask whether he'd agree to see me?'

'What am I supposed to say to him about who you are, what you do?'

'Just say I'm an old friend who happened to be passing through. I think he'll understand.'

'I don't like the look of you,' said Henshaw, suddenly clutching the tablecloth. 'I don't like the smell of you. You're a filthy dirty spy who's come here to make life difficult for the Duke and Duchess, you can see that a mile off. You . . . with your smarmy manner and fancy clothes!'

I'm not wearing coloured socks, thought Guy. What's brought this on?

'We get all sorts in Nassau, digging up the dirt. *As for a person who stirs up division,*' the cleric intoned, '*after warning him once and then twice, have nothing more to do with him. Titus three, ten.*'

'You've got hold of the wrong end of the stick,' said Guy. 'I'm the messenger, not an assassin.'

Henshaw grabbed the brandy decanter and sloshed more into his glass. '*A worthless person, a wicked man, goes about with crooked speech,*' he droned, wagging a finger in Guy's general direction. '*He winks with his eyes, signals with his feet, and with perverted heart devises evil, continually sowing discord.*'

'Um, that doesn't sound much like me.'

'*Therefore calamity will come upon him suddenly, and in a moment he will be broken beyond all healing.*'

'Are you sure you're all right?' said Guy, getting up.

'Proverbs six, verses twelve to nineteen,' mumbled Henshaw before putting his head gently on the table and proceeding to snore.

Guy wandered back into the drawing room where Joe and Hester were dancing to a scratchy record. 'All done?' asked Joe over Hester's shoulder. 'Was he helpful?'

'Yes and no. He has a particular friend who's the Duke's equerry.'

'Fairfax.'

'Yes. Do you know him?'

'Only by name.'

'Well, the reverend suddenly took against me, told me I was a troublemaker, started quoting the Bible and said he wouldn't help.'

Joe stopped dancing and pushed Hester away. 'You didn't handle that very well, Guy. I thought you were supposed to be a courtier. Diplomacy, good manners, the *comme il faut . . .* how did you manage to balls that up?'

Strangely the coarse phrase seemed entirely appropriate coming from this dinner-jacketed sea captain, but it stung all the same.

'He's drunk, Joe. But he's probably the only lead I've got in the short time I'm here. It all seemed to be going terribly well, then just as I—'

'Come on,' she said, grabbing his lapel and propelling him back to the terrace. She picked up an ice bucket and emptied the contents over the slumbering cleric's head.

'*Owwwwww!*'

'Philip Henshaw, of the parish of St Catherine of Whale Cay, I cast thee out!' bellowed Joe.

The priest sat up blinking.

'Thy vile and perverse ways bring discredit to this island,' she roared. 'From this moment I take from thee thy living, thy church, thy house, thy altar boy, and the colossal drinks bill you charged to my account which will be deducted from thy stipend before thee are kicked off this island. For ever.'

'I . . .' bleated Henshaw.

'And a day!'

'No, please, Joe! Please! What in the name of God's mercy have I done?'

Joe leant over him menacingly. 'Tomorrow morning when you've sobered up you'll call Carey Fairfax and say I have a special guest on Whale Cay who wishes to meet him. Make an arrangement for six o'clock at the British Colonial – that's when the royals have their pre-dinner nap – and tell him to be there or I'll have that car of his back!'

Crestfallen, Henshaw rose and walked over to the dining table on the terrace. 'Did anyone say grace before you broke bread?' he asked in a timid voice.

Before anyone could answer he shakily rose his right hand and intoned, 'Forgive me, Father, for I have sinned. Benedictus, benedicat, amen.'

A warm summer wind came off the shore towards the boat, stifling and lifeless. It was nearly evening but, even at the harbour's mouth, Guy could feel the heat still rising off the land.

High above him on a hill, a pink mansion looked superciliously down, shrouded and protected from the baking sun by tall palm trees, its occupants two of the most famous people in the world.

The launch took Guy smoothly into the dock and, after asking directions, he walked up towards Bay Street, past a statue of Queen Victoria – her face blank, unremitting – and into a bustling thoroughfare dotted with scarlet and coral-pink poinciana trees.

Guy carried with him the startling memory of his hostess, who'd joined him at breakfast, wearing an alarmingly convincing false moustache. It was impossible to tell whether she wore it as a joke or not.

Over eggs Benedict she told him things that, perhaps, Tommy Lascelles might have bothered to mention in his final briefing.

'Sir Charles Dundas was a good Governor, you know. A bit stuffy and not keen on Americans, but a decent sort. He intended to see out his days here, and was beside himself with anger when he was pushed out and sent off to Uganda. A most unbecoming end to a distinguished career, but he wasn't the only one who didn't want the Windsors here – I'm told Queen Elizabeth did everything in her power to have the appointment stopped.'

'That does come as a surprise,' said Guy. 'I know she wanted the Duke and Duchess sent as far away as possible – she's very protective of her husband – and you can't get much further away than Nassau.'

'Oh, the complaints came thick and fast – she objected to his governorship on moral grounds, on religious grounds, even that the Americans would hate having such a déclassé couple parked so close to their mainland. She tried everything, Guy, even suggesting they come out here on a trial basis to see if the people could tolerate them – reckoning they wouldn't, I suppose – but Winston decided it was for the best, and Her Majesty had to cave in.

'On top of that, dear boy, it was hell's own job to persuade the Duke to take the job on. Winston had to threaten him with a court martial if he didn't obey orders.'

'Court martial?'

'He's still a serving officer in the British Army. Thanks to the abdication he's reduced from Field Marshal to mere Major General, so all the easier to arrest as a result.'

Guy looked at her in genuine astonishment. 'How d'you know all this?'

'In case you hadn't noticed, I'm a very rich woman. All sorts of people like to come and stay here, and in return they invite me back. They talk, I listen.'

'Fascinating,' said Guy.

'And of course the Duchess's mail is intercepted. And she's been made aware of that – she sent a stupid telegram to someone after the appointment which the Palace warned Churchill about. Something about Wallis's anti-British activities, that she wanted to take revenge on Britain, and she was going to use her husband to exact that revenge. Their friends say they've been treated shabbily but you can see why – they're bloody difficult people.'

And now, with the evening sun on his back, Guy strolled up to the British Colonial Hotel to his appointment with the representative of these bloody difficult people. He asked at the desk for Captain Fairfax, and was shown to a table in the orangery where he found a stiff-backed young man with a jug of iced tea and two silver beakers before him.

'Fairfax? Guy Harford.'

He was wearing an immaculate linen suit, canvas shoes, regimental tie: the very picture of a royal equerry.

'Had a good trip over?' asked Fairfax. He was elegant, charming, but, Guy could see, tough. 'Away from the mad menagerie? I do love Joe, but the people she collects around her!'

'She says she hopes the Buick is still running well.'

A slight blush arose under the young man's golden tan. 'Yes, well,' he said. 'Joe needs a car when she comes to Nassau. I just keep it ticking over for her.'

'She likes to help her friends.'

'Yes.' He didn't want to talk about it.

'Look,' said Guy, 'this little chat may be a bit more complicated than Henshaw suggested. I'll come clean straight away and tell you, in case you didn't know, that I work for Tommy Lascelles at BP.'

It took a moment for this to sink in, but once it did the equerry got up in agitation. 'I can't talk to you,' he said, his voice rising. 'You're the enemy!'

'I think you'll find the enemy is out there' – Guy gestured towards the sea – 'in their U-boats. In their bomber planes. I am a friend, and I come with an olive branch.'

Fairfax looked undecided. 'Whatever passes for a cocktail round here, order two,' said Guy. 'This will all work better with a little lubrication.'

He took out of his pocket a long cream envelope with the single word 'Wallis' inscribed in an elegant hand. 'This is from Foxy Gwynne, now Lady Sefton – an old friend of the Duchess. I think she's keen to share a few things with her that the censor might object to.'

Fairfax nodded and took the envelope. 'So you know about that,' he said. 'Her letters being rummaged through.'

'I know quite a lot, working for Tommy.' Not everything though, he never told me about the court martial.

'When did you start working at the Palace?' said Fairfax. 'I don't know your name and, of course, out here we're a bit starved of news on staff changes.'

'A couple of years ago.'

'Which regiment?'

'No regiment. I'm an artist.'

'Good Lord. Ah well, I suppose it's wartime and . . .'

'. . . they'll take anybody. You're just about right there, Captain Fairfax.'

'Carey.' The first name slipped out reluctantly; he would have preferred to stay on last-name terms but innate good manners prevented him.

'Carey, this isn't a social call. I'm going to give you some information and in return ask for some. I'm on a flying visit and this is very important.'

Clearly the equerry was not ready for this. 'We don't deal with the Palace, you know that,' he said briskly, pushing his chair back.

'His Royal Highness is a government official, a civil servant – he talks to the British Ambassador in Washington, who's effectively his boss. All messages come and go through the embassy. What are you here for? A message from the King to his brother? I wouldn't if I were you – it won't go down well, surely you know that.'

The waiter brought their drinks and Guy lit a cigarette. 'Back at the Palace, people are worried about the Duke.'

'Are they now. They have a funny way of showing it.'

'I gather he's not altogether happy.'

'The understatement of the year. There he is, trying his best to do a good job in impossible circumstances and he's beset on all sides. The shameful business of the Duchess not being given her HRH, to which she's perfectly entitled! The endless stream of orders and directives coming out of the Washington Embassy, as if the Duke doesn't know how to put his trousers on! The constant backbiting by the Bay Street Boys, stopping him making any legislation to give the black population a better deal! Shall I go on?'

'I see your point, but—'

'And then there's the wretched press, all the time making nasty digs about how there's nothing he loves more than his pal Adolf! It makes you sick, and he can't answer back – *she* can't. She's doing a grand job with the Red Cross here – everybody says so – but they don't write that, they wait till the Windsors go to the mainland and then they count up how many pieces of luggage they brought with them.'

'I read it was one hundred and six last time round. That seems rather a lot to me. And that when they were last in New York the Duchess bought thirty-four hats.'

'You didn't see the ticker-tape welcome the city gave them! Stupendous! They're such a huge asset to our country.'

'If you think that,' said Guy, 'perhaps you can explain what's behind that columnist Vanderbilt in the *New York Post* saying the Duke is planning to quit his job and take up residence in America.'

'Rubbish. I—'

'And become an American citizen.'

'It's all nonsense.'

'You've just said how unhappy they are.'

'Not only that, the Duchess isn't a well woman – but do you see that? No, she just gets on with her work and not a word of complaint!'

'Vanderbilt comes from a distinguished family, he's well-connected. He wouldn't write something like that if he didn't believe it to be true.'

Fairfax drained his glass. 'I think I know who fed him that lie, and believe me, something very dreadful will happen to that person before too long.' The way he said it suggested violence, but Guy let it pass.

'So there's no truth in the rumour that the Windsors are about to quit?'

'I'd *know*. Let me assure you the Duke is talking to me about plans for next year, here in Nassau.'

'And no American citizenship?'

'Ah . . .' said Fairfax.

'Because if there was the slightest thought about that in his head, I have a message from Tommy which I'd be grateful if you'd pass on in words of your own choosing.'

The equerry's head jerked up.

'Tommy says that the US Treasury is asking where the dollars that they spend on their trips to the mainland come from. There's a belief that either the Duchess holds an account in the States in her name, or else the money is black-market currency. Tommy says—'

'Oh, Tommy this and Tommy that,' poo-pooed Fairfax. 'It's all Tommy-rot as far as HRH is concerned – they fell out long ago when he was Prince of Wales and he knows Lascelles has got it in for him.'

'Far from it,' countered Guy, 'he's trying to save his neck! What your duke doesn't realise is that he no longer has diplomatic immunity, and if the Internal Revenue Service, or the US Treasury, decide to arrest him he's on his own. Furthermore, if he were to take US citizenship, now they've got him in their sights, he could find himself paying very large sums of money in tax bills and attorneys. And you know how he hates to spend a single shilling.'

'Don't talk about him like that!' snapped Fairfax. 'But I'm not a fool. I'll pass on what you say.'

'Tommy's concern was that the Duke would cut and run, and ruin his reputation *and* that of the House of Windsor. He's got to stick it out.'

'I've told you,' said Fairfax, 'he's devoted to the job. He does not mix with Nazis. His dealings are above board and all he asks in return is recognition for his wife.'

'And of course, I will pass that on too. Now, there's something else I want to ask you about.'

'What's that?'

'Archy Blackwater.'

The man suddenly looked as though he was going to be sick.

CHAPTER TWENTY

Elena's hand was stretched out in the second arabesque position – perhaps the most triumphant gesture of her long climb back to stardom from those Vienna glory days, and summoning up the final act of tragic Odette as she is carried from life to an eternal swan lake. But there was no accompanying C major chord from Tchaikovsky to herald the final curtain – just the ugly roar of a motorbike as it sped away down the street and disappeared round a corner.

Elena's audience stepped forward from the pavement, but did not applaud. Instead there were shrieks of horror as they looked down at her broken body and the last fluttering of those long fingers. The blood ran from her head down the cobbled street, but more slowly now as her heart stopped pumping.

Soon a policeman was on the scene, and after that an ambulance. Later a police car arrived and its occupants jumped out, pleading for eyewitnesses to the accident. Nobody knew who she was, she wasn't local, but even in death she looked special – other, for there could be no denying the grace with which she'd said her farewell to the world.

It took time for the news of the dancer's death to seep back to the Victoria Theatre – indeed it was a reporter from the local paper who brought the sad tidings, as quite often they do, to what passed for Elena's family. The ballet company was at rest, preparing another week's touring across the north of England, taking a moment to lounge in the auditorium, write postcards and make casual conversation.

The company manager discovered her assistant wardrobe mistress perched in a small dressing room, her burglar's fingers as nimble with a needle and thread as they were with her lock-picking tools.

'Miss Carr!' said the woman agitatedly. 'Would you please come quickly to the box office? There's someone wants to talk to you.'

The uniformed policeman had followed hard on the reporter's heels and had a similar-sized notebook in his hand. 'Miss Carr?' he echoed.

A lifetime of running from the law told Rodie she should make a break for it, and she sized up the chances of getting through the swing doors and into the street before anyone could feel her collar – she'd done it before, could do it again, though that hamstring was still playing her up.

But something stopped her. This wasn't the sort of confrontation with a uniform she was used to. It was somehow strangely different. Around her, people stood in a distant circle, but there was no sense of the panic or urgency that usually went with such encounters – just an eerie silence.

The policeman had taken off his helmet and without it looked tough, handsome. 'You were a friend of Elena Hoffman?'

'Yes. Were? *Were?* What's happened?'

'Sorry, miss. She was knocked down by a motorbike in Albion Street an hour ago. I regret to inform you she died at the scene.' The words were trotted out at regulation pace.

'Are you sure . . . it's her?' gasped Rodie. 'Certain? I only saw her an hour ago!'

'Eyewitnesses say she left the theatre, wandered down the street to the chemist, came out again and prepared to cross the road when the accident occurred. Can you help us with contacting her family? I gather you were her friend.'

Rodie looked stunned. 'I . . . I only been 'ere just over a week,' she said. 'Blimey! I can't get over it! We . . . were goin' to have tea together . . .' She bit her cheek and turned away.

'They say,' said the constable, inclining his head, 'you two were close.'

'We were,' said Rodie, turning back. 'Well, very friendly. We sat in the bus together when we went off last week. Newcastle. Then Durham.'

'Her family?' said the copper hopefully. 'I have to pass the news on, you see.'

'I can save you the effort, mate,' said Rodie, stiffening. 'They're all dead. Gone. They were Jews in Vienna. The Nazis came and carted them off. You know what that means, dontcha?'

The young man nodded, looking down at his notebook. 'Anybody else we should let know?'

'The only one I can think of is Simon Green. He's one of our dancers. Only he left to go and join the company in London and seems to have disappeared.'

'Disappeared? Evading call-up, was he? Gone on the run?'

Rodie was staggered by this insensitivity – coppers! 'Not bloomin' likely! Elena said he knew it was coming and was ready for it. 'E was deferred, like, but 'e was ready to do his duty! His father's something posh in the army.'

'Got an address for him?'

'Me? Nah!' answered Rodie, thinking, What would my family say if I turned copper's nark? 'Ask the company manager, she'll know.'

'And where was Elena staying? I'll have to see her room.'

'Along with the rest of us in the Brinsley. She was in digs with a thievin' landlady but apparently the old bat didn't like all the comin' and goin' while we're on tour, so she came to join us in the Brinsley. She's room 210, an' before you ask, I'm in the annexe. Well,' she added, 'what they call an annexe but I'd call—'

'Thank you, Miss Carr. Can I have your home address, please? Just for the record.'

Oh no you don't, mate, she thought. 'Twenty-seven Whitehall Court, Balham, London,' she extemporised, then paused. 'What will they do with Elena's body?'

'We'll let the company manager know. There'll be a post-mortem and inquest, I expect, what with it being a hit and run.'

'*Oh!*' said Rodie, shocked. 'You didn't say hit and run!'

The constable looked interested. 'Does it make any difference?'

'Well, where I come from that's called murder, mate! Yes, it does make a difference – a ruddy great big difference!'

It was late in the evening before she could get hold of Rupe. 'Call me back. I can't keep shoving pennies into this coinbox. Burnley 4723.'

He was back straight away. 'What's happened? Are you OK? You weren't due to call until next week. You *must* stick to our arrangement!'

'Something's happened.' She described what she'd learnt of Elena's death. 'Bloke on a motorbike ran straight into her, like it was deliberate.'

'Is she of interest to us, this woman Elena?'

'You could say that. I tell you, Rupe, I got more from her in the back seat of that bus in a week than I'd have done if I'd lined up the whole company and threatened them with a Tommy gun. She didn't stop talking.'

'Really? Why's that? Did she suspect you? Could she tell you'd had no experience in the dance world? Was she feeding you disinformation?'

'Calm down, mate.' Rodie was standing in the phone box on the corner of the street. Usually on a lengthy call, after a couple of minutes someone would come along and rap on the glass, but tonight the street was empty. 'The reason she latched on to me was that she'd suddenly become a star and the other girls were jealous. She's pretty new to the company but after a couple of bit parts they suddenly realised she was hot stuff – or whatever they call it in the ballet world. The girls had more or less sent her to Coventry and she was feelin' low. They hated the fact she was so good. So I became her new best friend.'

'And?'

'She was Simon Green's girlfriend. Well, friend, more like, I don't think they ever . . . He looked after her when she first arrived, very nice and kind.'

'Where's she from?'

'Vienna.'

'One of us, or one of them? A Nazi?'

'Oh Rupe,' she said, exasperated. 'With a name like Hoffman? Why don't you just listen to what I've got to tell you? She fell in love with Simon but 'e was everybody's flavour – girls and boys – an' she knew it. 'E kept himself special though, didn't spread it around. Then 'e got this part in the ballet they're doing down in London and took off to join the company down there. Only 'e never arrived, she told me that – she rung the theatre to speak to him but he hadn't turned up.'

'Did she get from him – any hint at all – that he had Nazi sympathies? That his disappearance has to do with the fact he'd been picking up letters from Norway from this Marina Lee?'

'She was too in love to notice, mate.'

'So what d'you think is behind this death? Who was riding the motorbike? Was it him?'

'That was my first thought. But where's 'e been hiding for the past few days, and why would he suddenly want to kill Elena after being so nice?'

'Well, he killed Blackwater. Maybe he said something he shouldn't have, gave the game away.'

'That usually goes with piller talk,' said Rodie. 'They didn't have no piller talk, she'd have told me if they had.'

'Would she? You've never told Guy any secrets.'

'Look, mate, it's gettin' chilly out here in the phone box,' she replied evasively. 'Anything else?'

'Maybe she found one of those letters. From Norway. That could be it.'

'I 'ave no idea; we didn't get that far.'

'But it could have been him on the bike?'

'Maybe. 'Oo else would it be? If it *was* deliberate.'

There was a pause then Hardacre added, almost reluctantly, 'Look, this isn't your usual line of work and I must confess I'm worried about you. Be certain you keep your wits about you.'

The conversation drifted round in circles and though Rodie was grateful for the comfort of a familiar voice after the shock, she needed time to think. She put down the receiver and wandered back to the Brinsley Hotel, making her way through the grimy foyer to the tiny room she'd been allotted next to the kitchens.

Hunched up on the camp bed she tried to piece together what Elena told her as the tour bus had rattled over uneven roads towards the north-east coast. How she was in love with Simon because he'd been so kind in getting her into the company, the only one to encourage her and reawaken the self-confidence necessary if you are to succeed.

Curiously, Rodie had been accepted without question by the rest of the troupe – ballerinas need their torn tights stitched, their tutus washed, the ribbons for their hair organised and put out for them, and Rodie had learnt enough from her lessons with Madame Popowska to understand those needs and cater for them. That she looked like a dancer was enough for the incurious corps de ballet, too concerned about their next performance and who was in love with who to notice anything else.

The boys had come around sniffing – well, those with an interest in girls had – drawn to Rodie's beauty and poise. But most lost interest when they discovered she wasn't a resting dancer but merely another ballet wannabe. And so it had been easy to melt into the background after a couple of days, and soon she was in the back seat of the tour bus with Elena Hoffman.

They talked about boys and she was keen to pair Rodie off – pointing out the handsome Russians, Mikha and Pyotr, but confiding they were more absorbed in themselves, not romantically, but because of their shared background. But the boys had claimed seats up the front of the bus and had barely said more than hello.

The work was tough – four theatres in six nights, three performances a day – and mostly the team fell asleep the moment they got on the bus. But Elena, sensing something different in Rodie, had singled her out and seemed determined to draw her into her confidence: her poor upbringing off Vienna's Judenplatz, her parents determinedly scraping the money together to send her to ballet class, the growing threat of Nazism, and finally the Anschluss – the annexation of Austria by Nazi Germany in March 1938.

'Hitler came to call and didn't even bother to knock,' she said bitterly. 'And Austria just caved in – the Germans marched in and were greeted with Nazi salutes, Nazi flags and flowers – my fellow countrymen! At that time I was already dancing at the Staatsoper but I was warned I should leave immediately. It was difficult – I'd never been outside Austria – but I had to flee. My parents promised they'd follow, but though almost three quarters of Jews managed to get out of Austria before the arrests started, they hesitated and were rounded up and sent to Mauthausen. I haven't heard from them but, Rodie, you can tell – you just can. I *know* they're dead. My sisters too.'

Though horrified by what she learnt of Elena's long and dangerous journey to England, to London and to the Vic-Wells, Rodie was there to discover about Simon. It took time, but finally they got to it.

'I'm desperately, desperately worried about him,' said Elena. 'He's dedicated to his work – he would never miss an opportunity like this. To dance alongside Fonteyn . . . a dream come true!'

'Where could he have gone?' replied Rodie. 'Why would he disappear – unless 'e'd 'ad an accident? But then you would've heard by now, wouldn't you? Are you *sure* he didn't run away because he didn't want to join the army?'

'He told me about his father – he's a general, you know. Was very high up in the Norway campaign. Proud of him, but he wanted to prove there was something else to him apart from being a soldier. He knew his turn would come and he was ready for it. But he told me that when the war's over, he will have a career all of his own.'

By now Rodie was only half listening as the bus dragged its way through yet another northern suburb. Elena had established there was a connection between Simon and Norway, now it was time to see what else she knew.

'Did he ever mention the name Blackwater to you?'

'No, I don't think so,' said Elena after a pause.

'You sure?'

'Why are you asking these questions?' Elena was suddenly suspicious, on guard. 'Do you know something about him? Is that why you're asking about Simon? Because if you do, I think you should tell me!'

Rodie thought rapidly. 'Chum of mine knows a man called Blackwater,' she replied hastily. 'Said he had a special friend who seems to answer Simon's description. Back in London my friend used to go to a club called The Nut House and he was there one night with Blackwater and they met this chap,' she lied. 'Sounded just like Simon.'

'Well, I don't know the name. Where are we now, Rodie? Is it much further? I'm bursting.'

'Another ten minutes, darlin', can you hold on?'

Elena was looking tensely out of the window. 'Wait a minute,' she said. 'That name *does* ring a bell.'

'Which?'

'You said Blackwater, didn't you?'

'Yes.'

'It's the way you said it – I didn't get it then. But if you said it *bleckvttr*, then yes, I have heard it said.' She described to Rodie her night in Sheffield, the sherry drunk out of eggcups, the odd conversation with Mikha and Pyotr, which started with a few laughs but turned peculiar.

'They're nice boys, they really are – you should get to know them! But as I was sleeping they were chatting outside my room and I heard them through the open window. Most of it was in Russian but they mentioned Simon, which was not unusual – they danced with him. But the other word they repeated was . . . *bleck-vttr*, I'm pretty certain that's what it was. I thought it must be a drink, or a motorbike or something – they're always going on about bikes – or a girl. Probably a girl.'

'It's lovely bein' able to talk to you like this,' said Rodie. 'The others are nice but they're not interested in chattin' with wardrobe girls.'

'Oh – they only live for the dance, dearest girl. They only talk about what happened in class this morning, or food and love and the next performance. You're interesting, though, you're different. What did you do before you came to work for us?'

'Oh look,' said Rodie quickly, swallowing. 'Almost there! You rush on, I'll catch you up!'

The bus ground to a halt outside the theatre and Elena was the first off. Soon there was the usual company call onstage where instructions were issued for that night's performance and then the handing out of a roneoed sheet detailing their accommodation. A few dancers hopped down into the auditorium and made themselves at home in the stalls seats.

Rodie was there waiting. ''Ello, boys,' she said with a beaming smile. 'You look nice.'

Mick and Pete turned. If they hadn't noticed this black-eyed, Eton-cropped minx in the past week or so it must have been because they were too busy or tired or distracted. Now, standing in front of them in the stalls, she seemed a dazzling presence.

'I'm Rodie,' she said, hands on hips. 'I know 'oo you two reprobates are. Any time you need your tights darnin', just hop around to wardrobe and we'll do our best to *accommodate* you.' The message couldn't be more obvious.

'Rodie!' they cried. 'But you are beautiful! Where have you been all our lives?'

'Waitin' for you two monsters to come along. I been on the bus for a week – what does it take for a girl to get noticed?'

Their eyes shone and they energetically made space on the end of a row for her to sit down. Mick was slightly taller, but Pete was broader; both were muscly and eager.

'Rodie,' they said longingly. '*Rrrodieee!*'

She grinned at both and got them to tell their life stories. They didn't get very far before they started asking about what she did before the ballet.

'I was a dancer too,' she lied. 'Only I 'ad a bad fall when I was thirteen and did something to my hip. Never been the same since.'

'Do you long to dance still?' said Mikha, leaning forward, looking in her eyes.

'Can you still dance little bit?' said Pyotr. 'We can carry you!'

'We are strong!' they chorused, and burst into gales of laughter. 'Do you have boyfriend?'

Rodie looked at them mischievously. 'Always room for one more,' she said.

'But we are two!'

'Always room for *two* more,' said Rodie, waggling her fingers at them.

They all laughed, but it took time before she could manoeuvre the conversation around to Simon Green. Then, the atmosphere changed.

'How you asking about Simon when you have us two now?' demanded Mick.

'The both of us!' cried Pete, but she could see they were annoyed at the mention of his name.

'He's a friend of a friend. I was told to look out for him when I got up here from London,' she said. 'I didn't know anybody in the company and he was going to look out for me. But now I've got you two strong lads, who needs a Simon?'

She laughed and they joined in, but the mention of his name had clearly upset them – was it jealousy? They started to speak to each other in Russian. Just a couple of phrases, but enough to make Rodie realise she'd hit a nerve.

'You don't like him, I can see that, but I was told he was a lovely chap. Elena seemed to think so – she was talking to me on the bus about him.'

'He's snake,' said Mick.

'Dirty stinking snake,' said Pete. 'He make trouble for us with the company manager. He tell her we miss class, we elbow the other boys in the line so they lose their balance, we steal ration coupons and we seduce the girls.'

'I hope that's all true,' said Rodie, encouraging. 'I like my boys to be bad!'

'We much badder than that.'

'Now you intrigue me,' said Rodie with a seductive lilt to her voice. 'But did Simon really tell tales? I think you're just taradiddlin' me!'

Mick glanced round the stalls. His fellow dancers had their heads together in whispers or were asleep. Someone was playing a Chopin étude on one of the pianos in the orchestra pit, and a couple were trying out some steps on the stage. Nobody was paying much attention to them.

'He's spy,' said Mick.

'Really?' said Rodie. 'Are you serious? A ballet dancer is a spy?'

'He thinks we are communists who have come to this country to kill your king. How stupid is that!'

'Or that we blow up Big Ben,' added Pete, frowning at Mick, 'when we get the chance. He is telling authorities about this.'

'Really? Then why haven't they come and rounded you both up?'

'We run fast!' giggled Mick.

'We jump high, they can't catch us! We are . . . *Rooosian!*' The pair dissolved into more loud laughter.

I'm getting bored with this, thought Rodie. Tell me something I don't know. 'Was he jealous of you two? You're the best-looking boys in the company – I know,' she said, winking, 'I've 'ad a chance to look around!'

'A terrible flirt,' said Mick. 'Making up to Margot one minute, then it's Constant the next. Boys and girls, girls and boys – all same to Simon.'

'We only go for girls,' said Pyotr, and put his arm round Rodie. She wriggled comfortably.

'And Simon's friend, Blackwater – Elena was telling me all about '*im*. That would have been one of the boyfriends, was it then?'

It was like a tree crashing down in a gale.

The cosy atmosphere had gone, the boys' laughs silenced. Pete came round the other side of Rodie so that she was wedged between the two.

'*What*,' he asked, 'did she say?'

'Yes, what did Elena say?' said Mick. 'About Simon and this Bleckvttr?'

Rodie snorted, unafraid of their deliberate pincer movement – she'd had worse down the Elephant and Castle. 'I came up 'ere 'avin' been told what a saint this Simon was, now I discover 'e's a spy, an informant *and* a ruddy Casanova. You boys are havin' me on, aren'tcha?'

'Such an arrogant one,' said Mick with a sneer. 'Too snooty to mix with likes of us. Only wants to bed the rich and famous – Margot and Constant and Bleckvttr. And Bleckvttr so much older – poo!'

'Then killed him,' added Pete.

'What? Killed 'im? For heaven's sake, he's a dancer! What's he want going killin' people?' said Rodie, goading them on. 'Why?'

'For his secrets,' they chorused.

'What secrets?'

'You ask too many questions,' said Mick.

'We thought we liked you, but we don't,' snapped Pete. 'Get back to your wardrobe and stay in there out of harm's way, Miss Rodie. Or whatever your real name is.'

They shoved angrily past her and walked out. For a moment Rodie felt a shiver of fear overcome her.

CHAPTER TWENTY-ONE

It had taken the rest of the night and into the early hours to rid Captain Fairfax of his necktie. He dressed impeccably – as impeccably as the Duke himself – and did not relax easily. But after a few mint juleps he agreed to join Guy for dinner and, eventually, they found themselves in The Jungle Club.

Gradually the two men discovered they had more in common than they'd thought. Both worked for uncompromising bosses, both simultaneously endured and enjoyed the eccentricities of court life, and both felt separated from their home – Fairfax longed to be in London, just as Guy longed to be back in Tangier. Fairfax felt the exile from his regiment and fellow soldiers, but had been swept away in the avalanche that followed the abdication, and had felt it correct to resign his commission to stay with the ex-king.

Guy had no such loyalties – except now, perhaps, to Tommy Lascelles, who'd steered the royal family back into safer waters and was their backbone and strength. Never in his wildest dreams did Guy picture himself working inside Buckingham Palace, but he'd come to see the value of the job he was required by Tommy to do and admired the man, martinet though he be.

As the ice melted and Fairfax started to relax, the pair found they had acquaintances in common, both inside the Palace and without, and the ex-soldier's suspicions subsided as he began to see that they were, in fact, opposite sides of the same coin.

It was getting late, but it wasn't until the grass-skirted girls had completed their cabaret and the couples were back on the floor dancing the rhumba to 'The Peanut Vendor' that Guy cautiously returned to the matter of Archy Blackwater.

'You must have known him well back in the Belvedere days,' he ventured.

'Mm,' said Fairfax.

'Strictly on the QT, it was I who found his body.'

'What!' said Fairfax, sitting upright suddenly. The pink rings around his eyes seemed to disappear as he quickly sobered up.

'I took a . . . friend . . . up to the Fort when I was at Windsor – just thought I'd go and take a look around. Nobody ever mentions the place at court, it's as if it doesn't exist – and yet that's where history was made, far more than at Windsor or Balmoral. I was curious.

'When we got there we found a window open' – let's not mention Rodie's burgling skills – 'and in we went.'

'My God,' said Fairfax. 'You must tell me what sort of state the place is in today – I lived there, on and off, for years – but tell me about Blackwater first. You found him!'

'Not much to say. We went into the great octagonal room . . .'

'. . . where the Duke signed the abdication document – I was there, I saw him do it . . .'

'. . . and there in the middle of the floor was Archy Blackwater. I didn't know him in life and had no idea who this body was, but once we established he was dead we got out, and I went back to the Castle to alert the authorities.'

Fairfax wiped away a bead of sweat from his forehead and leant forward. 'We heard about his death only a day or two ago,' he said. 'News travels very slowly and the newspapers didn't have much to

233

say about it – nobody in Nassau gives a fig about British backwoods peers, alive or dead. What was it, a heart attack? And what the hell was he doing there, anyway?'

'Not a heart attack, no. Somebody punched him in the throat. Very hard. It was murder.'

'Bloody hell! They've kept that quiet! Who . . . who did it?'

'That's what we don't know, any more than why he was killed. But look, Carey, by all means tell your boss about this but, in return, I hope you can help. You knew Archy Blackwater after all, and I didn't.'

Fairfax nodded but the action turned into a shake of his head.

'You knew him well.'

Silence.

'I'm guessing, but maybe you knew him *very* well.'

The band had switched to a softer rhythm and the number of couples on the dance floor increased, swaying their hips and bending into the music, not ready to go home yet.

'Yes of course I did,' said Fairfax, looking straight ahead. 'If you want to know, he was one of the most remarkable people I ever met. He was caring, cultured, funny and a one-off – I've never met anybody like him. He was a huge support to HRH when he was king, and just fixed everything for him. You could rely on him for anything, everything – and he was such wonderful company.'

'He got Mrs Simpson – the Duchess – away when her situation became unbearable. Found her that bolthole in France,' Guy said, encouraging him to talk more.

'Well, no, that was the Rogers, old friends of the Duchess. But he introduced HRH to Charles Bedaux, who lent them his chateau for them to marry in '37.'

'And fixed up their trip to Nazi Germany afterwards.'

'Well, I—'

'Where the Duke met Hitler.'

'Oh!' spat Fairfax. 'All that's ancient history! Look what the Duke's doing now for his country – and would do a hell of a lot more, if he was allowed to!'

'Was Archy Blackwater a secret Nazi supporter?'

'*I have no idea!*' replied the equerry, half-rising from his chair. 'All I can tell you is what I know, which is that he was a lovely man, a gracious man, a generous man!'

'Did you ever meet Lady Blackwater?'

Fairfax's eyes narrowed. 'Why would I?' he said with a lift of his chin. 'She stayed in the country – *l'Abbesse de l'Abbaye*. Thick as thieves with the Princess Royal.'

'I went to see her. She had a rather different picture of her husband, but let that pass. Do you have any idea, any thoughts at all, about who might have killed him?'

'None at all,' said Fairfax, taking out a handkerchief and dabbing his eyes.

'Have you heard the name Simon Green in connection with Blackwater?'

'Who?'

'Son of General Greenleigh, Auchinleck's right-hand man.'

'I know Greenleigh, of course. Old-school soldier.'

Guy waved to the waiter. The night was lost to alcohol now, no reason not to have another. 'His son Simon is, perhaps surprisingly, a ballet dancer. He probably had an affair with Lord Blackwater. As far as we can tell he was one of the last people to see him alive.'

'You seem to know an awful lot.'

'And he probably killed him.'

'Oh.' Fairfax lifted the handkerchief once more.

'Perhaps to get his hands on a diary Blackwater kept. If you were that close to him, Carey, you must have known he was a compulsive diarist – a page every day, detailing the lives and loves of those around him.'

'Mm.'

'Did you know that he kept the diary under a floorboard in his room? You must have been in his room?'

'Look,' said Fairfax, half angry, half embarrassed. 'I'm employed by the ex-king in a position of trust. I'm here to protect him – both bodily and also his reputation. I understand clearly what you're asking me, but I can't answer your questions, it would be too dangerous.'

'Come on! The man's been murdered. Do you want his killer just to wander free?'

'There are greater considerations,' sighed Fairfax, shaking his head. 'Sorry, old chap, I see what you're trying to achieve but as far as I'm concerned, it's no can do. We have our reputations to think about.'

'I wasn't going to say this, Carey, but when I had breakfast with Joe Carstairs this morning, guess what? She was wearing a moustache.'

'Really.' He didn't want to hear it.

'Looking uncannily like yours, Carey. No explanation, no nothing – it was quite unnerving. Then afterwards as we walked down to the beach she complimented me on not asking the obvious question – why was she wearing a moustache? – and in return she was going to tell me a few things she didn't want the others to hear.'

'Really, I think it's time I—'

'About you, Carey.'

'Ah.'

'Things that would not preserve that reputation of yours – quite the opposite. Things that happened on Whale Cay. We had quite a long chat. There was a lot she wanted to tell me.'

'She's such a two-faced—'

'I gather the Duke got high-handed with her. She's a rich woman – richer than him, I should say – and doesn't take kindly to being told what to do. As far as she's concerned she's Empress of those islands she owns, and woe betide anybody who challenges her authority. Feel free, she said, to use what I tell you in any way that'll remind people that the Duke of Windsor and his raggle-taggle band of gypsies aren't quite as high and mighty as people think they are.'

'This is blackmail,' snapped the captain.

'Really?' Guy snapped back. 'I'd prefer to think of it as a sensible transaction – you tell me something, and in return I don't tell others something. Where's the harm in that?'

Fairfax groaned.

'The Americans have Charles Bedaux under lock and key. He's a traitor. They're hoping to get him to tell what he knows about the Nazis but so far, I gather, he's resisting. The Duke became very, very friendly with Bedaux – and it was Archy Blackwater who brought them together.'

Guy leant forward and spoke quietly. 'I have a memory like a sieve,' he said, 'and sometimes things just fall straight through it. Tell me what I need to know and I'll forget my walk down to the beach with a woman wearing your moustache.'

'I . . .'

'Tell me about Archy Blackwater's diaries. What they contain, who they name. No point in lying, Fairfax, I can tell you've read them. Did he write about the ex-king? The present king? The other members of the royal family?

'And why would he write it all down since he was, as you say yourself, such a devoted courtier to Edward VIII? Was it for self-protection in case he was ever arrested? For blackmail?'

Fairfax was shaking his head and swigging back his cocktail.

'Come on, man! Time to speak out!'

In the early morning light, on the deck of the steam launch taking him back to Whale Cay, Guy used the artist's sketchpad that was his constant companion to make notes. Whether it was because of homesickness, the shock loss of a man he'd loved, the terrible realisation that his life was going nowhere and he was growing old in the service of a crotchety, selfish man, Guy wasn't sure, but finally Fairfax had started to open up.

It was after Guy told him about his conversation with Gwendolyn, the Abbey secretary. She'd described to him how Archy Blackwater's life had fallen apart on his return from France in 1937.

'He felt betrayed by the Duke,' she'd said. 'He'd done everything for him, and for her – risked his reputation, and lost his friends who swapped sides quicker than you can say "knife" once the new king came in. He was completely loyal to Windsor while the rats deserted the sinking ship. But he soon discovered that with HRH, loyalty was a one-way street.'

She explained how, in his desire to please his master, Blackwater devised the Windsors' visit to Nazi Germany, advising his friend Bedaux how best to bring the two sides – the Windsors and the Nazi high command – harmoniously together. The Duke had wanted to show his new wife what it was like to be royal, but also knew he'd said goodbye to the cheering, adoring hordes the moment he put the ring on Wallis's finger.

'I don't know anything about all that,' said Fairfax. 'I was returned to my regiment the moment they pushed off. I didn't see either of them again until war broke out and he asked me to come back as his equerry again. I went because I was too old to fight and wanted to do something worthwhile.'

Guy repeated Gwendolyn's description of how Blackwater, learning that the Windsors were having second thoughts, put pressure on Bedaux to hasten the German visit. 'The Duke himself wasn't that pro-Nazi – no proof that he was, though he was definitely pro-German; there's a difference, you know. But he was getting cold feet – he'd suddenly woken to the fact this trip wouldn't go down well back home, that he could lose a lot of the support of people who'd stayed loyal even after the abdication. Cosying up to the Nazis was worse than abdicating.

'But by now, *she* wanted it. And he, very much under her thumb, desperately wanted to impress with a repeat of those big rapturous welcomes he used to get only a couple of years before. So Blackwater urged Bedaux to aggrandise the visit to the utmost degree, and to get things fixed up before the Duke changed his mind.'

'The German trip was very much of Blackwater's making, an attempt to secure a position as Windsor's permanent right-hand man in exile. The Duke could impress his wife that he still was a world figure and – perhaps more importantly – how she'd joined him now as a glittering centrepiece on the world stage. She was no longer a woman whose windows were being smashed and gutter names called after her. She could don a tiara with the best of them.

'Archy said, and the Duke believed it, that they could set up an alternative court, one to which people would flock because they preferred David Windsor to the stuffy old institution of monarchy. And the next thing would be a triumphant tour of America,' went on Guy.

'But then the whole thing collapsed. The moment the Duke and Duchess left Germany the Nazis murdered two trade union leaders and within a couple of days the union movement in America threatened big trouble if the Duke landed on American soil and went on a Bedaux-sponsored tour. It was a terrible, shocking slap in the face for both Windsors, and ended the Duke's relationship with Bedaux.

'As a consequence, he dumped Archy Blackwater overnight. Archy came home to find his name was worse than mud in the royal court and despite years and *years*,' he emphasised these words to Fairfax, 'of unblemished service to the crown, he was suddenly a social outcast.

'In addition he was no longer welcome at Blackwater Abbey – Lady B made it clear she'd taken over running the place – and he suddenly was in a deep black hole.'

Fairfax was polishing his nose with his handkerchief, his face pale under his Caribbean tan.

'You understand what I'm saying,' said Guy. 'The Duke betrays all his friends in the end. It's only a matter of time. How do you get on with the Duchess?'

'We have a good working relationship,' said Fairfax evenly.

'Meaning she's not keen on you.'

'I didn't say that.'

'I hardly need remind you of something you know far better than I – that he listens to her every word. You're safe for as long as this posting continues, but then what? Do you want to end up like Archy Blackwater with no friends, no family and nothing to do with the rest of your life?'

Carey Fairfax got up and reached for a glass of water. 'Come out into the garden,' he said. 'I hadn't expected the evening to end this way.'

They made their way through the ballroom past the last lingering couples and out into the black heat of the night. Far away could be heard the swash of water as the ocean hit the sea-wall, and they made their way down to a bench underneath the bowing palm trees.

'If you want to know,' said Fairfax, sitting down, 'I've been thinking about ending it all. All that you said back there is true. The Duchess despises me for some reason. As a result, the relationship I had with the Duke – one I cherish from the days when he was that dazzling Prince of Wales – has become virtually non-existent. She seeks to destroy everything that pre-dates her, so Lord Brownlow, Fruity Metcalfe, Archy Blackwater – all devoted to him, all cast aside. Ruthlessly.'

'Because of their devotion.'

'Yes. Perhaps if they'd shown it less . . . Well, now I belong with them. What a small and elite little club we are.' He laughed bitterly. 'And all we did was try to do our best for him.'

'I'm glad you see it for what it is,' said Guy sympathetically. 'It'll make the break that much easier to bear when the time comes. Now, are you going to help me?'

In the fronds of palmetto above their heads there were faint stirrings but the first members of the dawn chorus were not properly awake just yet.

'What I told you about Simon Green wasn't true,' Fairfax began. 'I know all about him. Just before I was seconded to join the Duke out here back in 1940, Archy and I went to a ballet given at Cadogan Hall and we met Green – well, he's Greenleigh, really – afterwards.

'By that stage Archy and I were . . . just friends. No longer . . . well . . . you know. But I looked out for him – he was so easily entranced by beauty and youth and, of course, those two things often come wrapped up in a dangerous little package labelled blackmail. He is – was – a member of the House of Lords and he was highly regarded. He should have been more careful than he was.

'Anyway, he took to Simon in a big way and for a time they were inseparable. There was a big age gap but that's not so unusual. I was happy for Archy because, until he met Simon, life was running away from him. He was gambling, gambling – nobody could stop him. But Simon did.

'The trouble with Simon is that he wants to be loved by all. If he goes on the way he does, he'll become a ballet dancer famed for his looks and his promiscuity.'

'Did Simon know Archy kept a diary?'

'Quite possibly. Archy showed it to me one day when we were all at the Fort. He was extremely proud of it. And so he should be – it's a unique chronicle of what you might call the rich and famous, certainly all the people that *matter*. Beautifully written but shockingly indiscreet.'

'Did it include references to the royal family?'

'What do you think! Because of his family background – after all, the Blackwaters were around long before William the Conqueror came to call – he secretly looked on them as parvenus, johnny-come-latelies. To be looked up to, certainly, because of the position they hold in the land. But not to be deified, as some seem determined to do.'

'I gather you wouldn't include yourself in that group.'

'We Fairfaxes go back just as far as the Blackwaters do.'

'So the diaries are dynamite if anyone got their hands on them. What would Simon want with them?'

'Simon? Why d'you ask?'

'Because it must have been him with Archy Blackwater at Fort Belvedere. We know that whoever was with him that last time killed Archy and stole the diary. Why would Simon do that?'

'He wouldn't. He's a golden boy all right, believes he walks on water, maybe, but there's nothing violent about him.'

'We think he did it. He's due to open in a new ballet at Sadler's Wells next week but he hasn't been seen since I discovered Archy Blackwater's body. He's gone missing, Fairfax – and he needs to be found quickly. He's a killer!'

'Oh God,' murmured the equerry, standing up and staring out towards the sea's dawn.

CHAPTER TWENTY-TWO

They told Rodie to take care of Elena's possessions because there wasn't anybody else. A small suitcase and a larger one, two handbags and the usual array of make-up and underclothes and dresses and tops and shoes were all there was. Rodie was ordered by the company manager to move into her room. 'Her replacement can have the annexe,' she was told. 'She's coming up from London on the night train. You get in there and clear up.'

The following day was a rest day before the long road trip into Wales, and the company call would not be until five o'clock. After breakfast she came back to Elena's room and started shifting the debris of human existence which loses its purpose the moment its owner dies.

The thing I noticed most about her was her hands, Rodie thought – the most beautiful she thought she had ever seen. Why would Simon want to do this? Why, when he was on the brink of stardom? Why, when so recently he'd found time to comfort Elena when nobody else even looked her way?

Mechanically she folded up the clothes and placed them in the larger suitcase. She was sliding the dance tights and their daytime equivalent into the elasticated panel in the suitcase lid when her hand felt a hard object tucked inside. Pulling it out she discovered a small engagement diary dated 1942.

Rodie went to sit on the bed, turning the pages slowly. Written in a neat hand inside were last year's engagements, but superimposed on top were this year's – she'd made the diary last two years. The early days of the previous year bore witness to the fact that Elena, no matter how talented, had no work as a dancer. Day after day the entry said merely 'Class' but gradually the name 'Simon' began to appear, replaced by 'S' as their meetings became more frequent. But apart from a brief note recording her entry into the Vic-Wells Ballet, there was little extra information. Occasionally there were unexplained numbers and other initials, but no clue as to whom they belonged. It was a memory-jogger for the person whose memory could no longer be jogged.

Rodie inspected the cheap leatherette cover but it offered nothing more. She went back to the suitcase, took out the clothes she'd carefully folded in, and felt around the lining in case something else had been hidden there. She turned it upside down, inspected the locks, and summoned all her powers of concentration to deduce what message lay in this now-defunct object.

It had no effect.

She turned to the smaller suitcase in which she'd placed Elena's combs and brushes and make-up. 'Come on,' she said, half-aloud. 'I know you're in there somewhere! Come on, darlin', tell me something! Give me a clue!'

It didn't.

'Tell me why Simon turned murderer, why he stole the diary, why he's gone missing. Tell me where the hell he's hiding!'

The suitcase remained mute, inanimate, obdurate.

She picked up the diary again and went through it page by page, looking for clues she might have missed, but all it could offer was a bald statement of the pitifully few events in Elena Hoffman's life.

In desperation Rodie threw Elena's possessions on to the bed and started to go through them again. They offered nothing more so she turned on her burgling skills and searched the room – wardrobe, dressing table, bed, mattress. If there was a single clue to be had, the burglar in her was sure to find it.

She did not.

In despair she sat down and was opening the diary once more when the door burst open.

'*Give me that!*' shouted Mick. 'What you doing in here? This Yelena's room!'

'You must have heard, Mick, she's dead! And don't shout like that. Put me right off me breakfast you did.'

But the dancer was in no mood to joke around. 'Get back to your own room! We look after Yelena's things! We are her friends! What's that in your hand?' he said, grabbing.

'Don't you turn nasty on me, mate, or I'll have you sorted out in no time,' Rodie replied, jumping on the bed to give her a height advantage. She'd experienced worse – a lot worse – in childhood, and though frightened by the Russian's unexpected aggression, she wasn't going to let it show – she had a few tricks up her sleeve should he come any closer.

'Wass this all about then, Mick?' she said, her voice high and rasping. 'One minute you're all lovey-dovey, you an' you fellow Russky, now you look like you want to kill me. What's your problem?'

Subsiding, Mick backed away to the door. 'Come down, silly girl,' he replied. 'You look ridiculous up there.'

'Open the door and I will.'

'No open door till we talk. We talk, Rodie, then everything will be fine.'

Everything wasn't fine. Mick started on a lengthy explanation about how Elena always said that if anything should happen to her then he and Pete should take care of her things, and she would do the same for either one of them. 'She was our dearest friend,' he said, applying a doleful expression and recalling their times together on the road. But as he spoke his eyes flicked round the room continually, as if looking for something.

'What are you going to do with her things?' he said. 'Honest, Rodie, you should leave this to us.'

'I'm here now – the company manager told me to tidy things up. There's a new girl coming up from London for next week's tour and the bus is at seven thirty tomorrow morning, so don't be late, ducky. By the way, where's your twin brother?'

'Pyotr? He likes the country air. He's gone for a ride. Now let me help you, Rodie.'

'No, mate, you push off and I'll see you later. Got a job on me hands here.'

'I help! Let me show you!' He grabbed at the clothing on the bed, feverishly wrenching the items apart.

There was a knock on the door. 'Need any help?' said the company manager through it.

'Nah, Mick's just leaving,' she called back. 'He's been *of considerable assistance*.' She said this at full volume in a fake upper-class accent, making a rude gesture to the dancer at the same moment.

Seething with barely concealed frustration, Mick yanked open the door and went out.

'And don't come back!' she shouted after him.

Later, locking the door and pocketing the key, she slipped out of a back exit and wandered down St James's Street. Churchgoers, in what passed for Sunday best in this third year of privation, strolled slowly towards the park, their devotions done and their Sunday roast – or whatever they could muster to the table – still an hour away. The town was silent, no traffic.

The Victoria Theatre, massive and important, made up in grandeur what it lacked in polish these days, its sooty exterior in need of a clean along with most of Burnley's buildings. Rodie slipped down a side entrance to the stage door where she found a pair of cleaning ladies, their hair wrapped up in scarves, making their way out.

'Mornin', ladies,' she said. 'Just hoppin' up to collect something. I'm wardrobe.'

'The things they leave behind,' said one witheringly. 'You wouldn't credit it! I ask you, how those girls are goin' to explain themselves to their mothers come laundry day!'

Rodie laughed and plunged into the backstage gloom, skipping up the iron staircase to the dressing rooms and the wardrobe room beyond. As she made her way along the narrow corridor a voice whispered, 'Elena! In here!'

She froze. Elena had been dead less than twenty-four hours, but everyone in the company knew it. Nobody else in this town knew her name or, if they'd seen it in the printed programme, would hardly remember it among the long list of other credits. Who was calling her now?

'Elena! Here!'

The corridor was in near darkness, lit only from a dirty skylight high above which let in a meagre streak of sunshine.

'Come *on*!' said the voice urgently. 'I've been waiting over an hour! You did say eleven, didn't you?'

And then he emerged into the corridor, his face transformed the moment he set eyes on Rodie into a mask of shock.

'Who . . . are you?' he stammered.

''Oo are *you*, mate!' she snapped back. 'An' don't come any closer, I've got a knife!'

He took no notice of this and walked towards her, his blond hair shining like a halo as he stepped into the shaft of sunlight. He was tall, muscular, and – Rodie couldn't help notice, despite her anxiety – exceptionally good-looking.

'Go away,' he said, quite menacingly. 'I don't know who you are but you shouldn't be here.'

'You got it the wrong way round, mate,' said Rodie, crouching slightly and making a show of feeling in her jacket pocket for the non-existent switchblade; she was on the balls of her feet and ready to run. 'It's you 'oo shouldn't be 'ere – Vic-Wells only! No pretty boys comin' round tryin' to get a peek at the girls. Or the boys! It's their day off anyway.'

'Just tell me,' he said, and though he was clad in a dirty leather jacket and greasy trousers, there was an authority in his voice, 'who you are.'

'If ya wanna know, I'm the assistant wardrobe mistress, and I've come up here to collect a few things. Why are you askin' after Elena?'

'You're Shirley's replacement?'

'Yes. 'Ow do you know *her* name?'

'Because I belong to the company too,' he said. 'Are you here alone?'

'What's it look like? And don't come any closer! Where I come from we learn 'ow to slice up a man like a rasher of bacon, so keep your distance!'

He spread his hands wide. 'I'm not going to hurt you,' he protested. 'I've come here to see Elena. We had an arrangement.' He took a step back as if to reassure her but he was looking at her oddly, not entirely believing her story.

''Oo are you anyway?' she said. 'And the name's is Rodie Carr – if it's any of your business.'

He flashed her a smile but it was cold, vacant, unpleasant. 'Pleased to meet you, Miss Carr. I'm Simon Green.'

She sucked in her breath, fighting for air. He just stood there, unrepentant, at ease now he could see she was unarmed. In her shock at the sound of a murderer's name her hand had slipped out of the jacket pocket; there was no knife.

'It's OK,' he said, 'I'm not going to harm you. Why don't we go into the dressing room and you can help me with some questions.'

'No thanks,' she said, thinking fast. 'Just going to pick up something before a couple of friends come 'ere to collect me. They'll be along in a minute.'

'Don't worry,' he said. 'Come on in. I just came to see Elena.'

The man must be mad, she thought. He killed Lord Blackwater. Now, though Elena's dead, he's acting as if he's about to take her out to lunch.

'Stay away,' she said. 'Don't come near me! You know ruddy well Elena's dead – what are you playin' at? What's your game?'

He moved slightly in the pool of light and in that moment she could see from his body language there was no threat. 'Say that again,' he said slowly.

'She's dead. You know that. You're the bastard 'oo killed 'er!'

'What? *What?* What are you saying?' One hand clutched at his hair and he seemed to stagger slightly.

'Look,' she said, 'I'm goin' to walk past you, down the stairs and out into the street. Don't touch me and I promise not to call the cops.' And if you believe that, mate . . .

'Don't go anywhere,' he replied, his features tightening. 'Don't do anything. Just tell me what's happened.'

'You know, all right – you run 'er over with your motorbike! You bastard!'

'I don't have a motorbike.'

'No use lyin' to me. An' then what about your boyfriend, Lord Blackwater? I suppose you didn't kill him either!'

'No, I did not.'

'Well, you tell all that to the rozzers. I'm sure they'll believe you.'

Simon looked at her blankly. 'I don't know who you are,' he said, 'but you're no wardrobe mistress. You know far too much for that.'

'I know nuffin', mate.'

'Then tell me what you *think* you know about Elena's death and I'll see if I can trust you enough to give you some information.'

Realising she wouldn't be able to get past him to escape down the stairs, Rodie decided the only thing was to humour him, in the hope that some theatre worker would come along soon. She strained her ears to hear any movement downstairs but there was none.

She told him what she knew about Elena's murder – but why was he asking? Was there some sadistic streak in him that wanted to hear the effect her death had had on the company? Or was he hoping to get something of significance out of Rodie without her realising?

As she finished he took a step forward. 'You have to believe me,' he said. 'I didn't kill her. But what the devil are you doing here? You're no wardrobe mistress – are you with the police?'

'I'll give you three guesses,' she retorted, her tone harsh and uncompromising.

'Look,' he said, 'whoever you are, let me tell you something. This time two weeks ago I was a dancer just about to solo in a new ballet – it was my big break. Then something happened. A dear friend, Archy Blackwater, was murdered. You mentioned his name just now, that's what made me realise you probably work for CID or military intelligence.'

'Wrong on both counts, mate. Two guesses down, one to go.'

'We'll get to that eventually,' he said. He really was strikingly handsome with perfect teeth, a healthy tan, and a firm jawline. 'I know who killed Archy, and I know who killed Elena. It's the same person or persons and they are extremely – *extremely* – dangerous.'

'If you know so much, you'd better tell me,' said Rodie, playing for time. Surely someone would come along in a minute?

'MI6,' said Simon. 'I know something about these things. You're probably aware my father is a—'

'General. Yes I do know.'

'Right, well, now I do know who you are – or I think I do – I'll tell you a few things because they're probably circulating in that secret world of yours already. If you know anything about my story, you should be asking, "Why would Simon Green suddenly disappear, just when he's got a starring role in a West End ballet? This was his big chance . . ." and so on.'

'That's simple,' replied Rodie. 'You killed someone important and went on the run. Then for some reason you came back up here and killed Elena – why? Because she knew something that could tie you to Blackwater's death? Probably she did learn something about you – you was as thick as thieves, they tell me.'

'You don't really believe that guff, so listen and I'll tell you,' he said crisply. 'One of the Russian boys, I don't know which, killed Archy Blackwater. In a way it's my fault – he came to one of the London ballets I was in before we came up here. He and I had been . . . close . . . and he wanted to see me dance again. At the party afterwards Mikha and Pyotr, you must have met them by now, were there and I introduced them to Archy.

'Behind my back, Pyotr had a fling with Archy – I don't think anything earth-shattering, just one of those things, but those boys own a motorbike and Pyotr took Archy on joyrides around London. It gave him a thrill – he's been so used to a more sedate way of life, but with a crash helmet and goggles on even his best friends couldn't recognise him.

'I think what must have happened was Pyotr decided to give him a ride out of London and they ended up at Windsor. No doubt Archy told Pyotr about the glory days when he was close to the Prince of Wales and they'd all hang out at the weekends at Fort Belvedere, and so Pyotr took him over there.'

He turned and leant against the wall. Rodie reckoned she could have got past him to reach the stairs but what he was saying seemed at least partially convincing. She waited.

'Here we get to the point of it all. Archy was a compulsive diary-writer, noting down everything he heard and saw during those years – he was a brilliant observer of life, brilliant. I only met him after war broke out, but he showed me the diary he was writing then – astonishingly frank, X-rated material about all the people whose names you see in the newspapers today. It was dazzlingly funny, hugely indiscreet, and would have got him into a hell of a lot of trouble if it was ever discovered – I told him that.

'What I do know is that he longed to get his hands on the previous diary, which got left behind when King Edward did a flit in December '37. The moment the King had gone, the Fort was locked, shuttered and everyone associated with it told to stay away; the new King didn't want it used as a gathering point for an alternative court, and he shut it right down. They said it was going to be turned into government offices, though that never happened. But what it meant was that Archy couldn't get his hands on the diary. They sent his clothes and things back to him all right, but the diary was hidden away . . .'

'Under the floorboards,' said Rodie.

'Ah! Now I'm certain who I'm talking to!' said Simon with a grim smile. 'You've obviously done your homework. But I bet you don't know what a *balancé* is? There, you see, not so good on the ballet side, are we?'

She hadn't a clue what he was talking about. 'The diary,' Rodie prompted.

'Under the floorboards in his room, as you say. Carpet over the top. Pretty conventional hiding place but there weren't many alternatives open to him.'

'There was a poem about you in there as well. A long one.'

For a second Simon looked as though he might burst into tears. 'Really? About me? I didn't know . . .'

'A kind of love letter. Anyway, go on.'

'I would love to have seen that. I can't believe he's dead even now. And Elena too.'

Beneath her, Rodie could hear people moving around on the stage floor – a reassuring sound, but she was no longer in a hurry to escape. She could always shout for help.

'Elena told me it was Pyotr who handed over the diary to her. And it's he who rides the motorbike, not Mikha. It was Pyotr who killed Archy, no question – they went to the Fort together, he came back alone – and Archy was dead. QED. But why, I have no idea. Did they have a fight? *Why?*'

'OK,' said Rodie slowly. 'Let's go and sit in the dressing room.'

She led the way and sat with her back against the big make-up mirror, looking for all the world like a ballerina in the reflected light, even if she didn't know the terminology. She explained how it was she who discovered Archy Blackwater's body, and how later she went back to the Fort and discovered the hiding place in Blackwater's room, how it was empty now except for the poems to Simon.

'What a remarkable person you are,' said Simon, gathering only gradually what it was she'd done. 'A state-sanctioned burglar – what an extraordinary thing!'

'Just another bleedin' civil servant, mate. With a pension at the end of the day. Where's the diary now?'

'I'll come to that. Pyotr can't read English, and he wanted to know what was in it. He left it with Elena and she gave it to me as I was leaving for London – something to read on the train. I think she had no idea what she was reading – she could understand the words but not their significance, but I took one look and of course I knew. But I couldn't tell her – she had no idea about my relationship with Archy or the political dynamite she held in her hands. And for me,

253

at that moment, I had no idea Archy was dead. It just seemed very strange that these two Russians had got their hands on the one thing Archy longed to have back in his possession – but I thought perhaps a royal servant must have found it and it had ended up in their hands by some means.

'So I told her I'd take care of things and I would speak to Pyotr and Mikha about it – there was no reason for her to get mixed up in all of this. But it was at just the moment when I was due to catch the train for London, so I left her a note – she'd gone off to Oldham – saying there was nothing of interest in the diary but I'd hang on to it for safekeeping. I was in a hurry to catch the train but they could have it back when we all met up again.'

'That put her in a difficult position, surely? You'd pinched something they thought was valuable?'

'I didn't realise that then. My mind was full of the new ballet and getting back to London, but also I knew something had to be done about the diary. It was only when I got to King's Cross station and I saw the newspaper billboards that I learnt that Archy was dead and, of course, putting two and two together I realised that something must have happened between him and Pyotr – even though the papers said he'd had a heart attack in his car.'

'You left her a bit in the lurch, mate, din'tcha?'

'I had no idea they'd want to do anything to her. I'd warned her about them when she first joined the company. They were rough. They came out of Soviet Russia where life is cheap. Plus, they'd decided I was a spy for some reason – we had a chat one evening and I said something they objected to, and they accused me. I suppose where they come from, everyone's a spy.'

'And why d'you think they killed Elena?'

'I can't say. But if she was knocked down by a motorbike, it can only have been one of those two who did it – it's too much of a coincidence.'

'OK,' said Rodie, 'I'm beginning to believe ya, though thousands wouldn't. But where have you been these past few days? Everyone's been lookin' for you – you just disappeared, walked away from your big break on the West End stage.'

Simon paused. 'I went to see my father and took him the diary to look at. He said the contents were appalling, and that by rights he should burn it on the spot. But instead he went to see someone at Buckingham Palace—'

'Not by the name of Lascelles, by any chance?'

'Good God,' said Simon, 'and to think I thought you were just a burglar. You do seem to know a lot! Anyway, yes, my father handed it over, and the Palace can do whatever it likes with it. I doubt Archy's son would want to have that waiting for him when he gets back from prison camp.'

'But where did you go? People have been looking for you all over the place. You do realise, don't you, that you're the main suspect in both these killings?'

'That doesn't worry me. I can prove where I was on both occasions. In answer to your question, I was handed over to Army Intelligence by my father and sent down to Brookwood, where they spent the next couple of days quizzing me about Archy and his diaries – and about his relationship with Charles Bedaux.'

'Those seem to be questions everybody wants to ask you,' said Rodie. 'I have an old friend who'd like to join the queue.'

'Feel free,' said Simon. 'I have all the time in the world. The ballet's been postponed – Constant Lambert hates the music and is rewriting, so my big chance will have to wait. Probably till the end of the war – I'm due to join up in a few weeks.'

Rodie looked at his handsome face and wondered if he would come home and become a star, or whether his moment had come and gone; if his father would say, 'Told you so' . . . Or whether he would even come home at all.

'I was just going to see if Elena had left anything here that would solve what's been going on,' she said. 'What are you going to do?'

'I'll go and see the company manager, see if anything can be done for Elena before the funeral. I feel responsible – dreadfully responsible.'

And so you should, she thought, but didn't say. Simon got up and wandered out down the stairs heading for the hotel while Rodie went into the wardrobe department. A moment or two later there was a thudding noise, followed by a sickening crash.

And then two voices in turn called from the foot of the stairs.

'Rodie . . . Oh, *Rrrrroooodieee . . .*'

'We've come to get you, *dorogaya milaya . . .*'

'Come out, wherever you are. We have surprise for you . . .'

The wardrobe room was at the end of the corridor. There was no escape.

CHAPTER
TWENTY-THREE

The cocktail party was in full swing by the time Guy got there. Earnest, bespectacled fellows were outnumbered two to one by entrancingly dressed women who, while appearing to be hanging on their every word, were actually scanning the room for handsome young officers.

'Guy Harford,' he said to the man at the door. 'The Ambassador . . .'

'We have your name,' said the flunkey, eyeing his socks dubiously, 'on the list. His Excellency is detained, but I will take you to the First Secretary.'

Guy was led across the ballroom and introduced to a short and scholarly man by the name of Oliphant. 'Welcome to Washington,' he said. 'You don't have to drink the bourbon, we have plenty of Scotch.'

'Just water, thank you.'

'HE is busy but sends his felicitations and hopes you'll be comfortable. Good trip up from Nassau?'

'Surprisingly easy,' said Guy.

'We expect your full written report in the morning, but I'll just ask you how things are going down there.'

'He's staying.'

'That's what we wanted to hear. I can't tell you the earache that man gives us. Neat trick of the Palace to turn him into a civil servant so we have to listen to his constant gripes instead of them. It's like having a pain that won't go away. What's the detail, in a nutshell?'

'Are we speaking confidentially?' asked Guy. 'I'm a Palace servant, I don't work for you lot.'

'Well, yes, you do, Mr Harford, you're on the FO payroll. I've seen your file, so give it to me straight. And, yes, it's confidential.'

'I didn't see the Duke but I had a long chat with Fairfax, one of the aides de camp – you know his name. For various reasons' – let's not mention blackmail, he thought – 'he was remarkably frank. In brief, the Duke's champing at the bit, wanting to get away. He's done a more than competent job as Governor but feels constrained by the council, by the directives being sent from the embassy here, and by an antagonistic press.'

'He brings that upon himself. Now he's no longer King he's accident-prone, lacking in judgement, guided by that dreadful woman into making mistake after mistake – then he blames everyone but himself. You should see the telegrams!'

'Well, he's staying put.'

'And the business about becoming a US citizen?'

'No answer on that. I think he holds it in reserve as an implied threat – treat me any worse and I'm off. But I had the opportunity to point out the tax implications of such a decision and I think Fairfax will have made that very clear to him, so on balance I don't think he'll jump. Not now, anyway.'

'That Vanderbilt article caused a hell of a stink. We had Mr Churchill on the blower, screaming like a banshee.'

'Well, it all seems to have calmed down. As for the Nazi-sympathiser business, talking to Fairfax it's pretty clear it's been overblown. Everyone's spooked by the idea of his cuddling up to Hitler, but it wasn't like that – he just wanted to show the Duchess what it was like to be a princess. State visit and all that.'

'It'll never happen again.'

'Don't be so sure. He was talking about Brazil.'

'A state visit to Brazil?' laughed Oliphant. 'Let him make a fool of himself if he wants to, he'll certainly get no support from us!' The cocktails were circulating but Guy had a report to write and shook his head at the waiter.

'And that's about it,' he said. 'The worry for us at the Palace is what he's going to do when the war's over. The King won't have him back in Britain, you know.'

'Let that take care of itself. Now, who can I introduce you to? You may as well circulate and have a spot of fun before you catch your airplane.'

'No thanks, I think I'll just go and . . .' began Guy, but as he spoke his elbow was jogged by a woman who'd stepped back from the group behind, and the water from his glass splashed over his suit.

'Sorry,' he said, not meaning it.

'My fault,' said the woman, turning. 'Good Lord, it's . . .'

Guy looked her up and down. 'Do you go by the name of Mrs Strudwick this evening,' he said tartly, 'or are we flying the flag as Lady Goldington?'

'Just say Fanny.'

'You taught my parrot to say that. I can't unteach her and I can tell you, it's a bloody nuisance.'

The woman burst into laughter. She was wearing a low-cut dress and more diamonds than the entire Crown Jewels. She glittered like the Blackpool illuminations.

'May I ask what you're doing here in Washington?' said Guy. When drinking together in the Chelsea Arts Club he'd been rather taken by her, but now he wasn't so sure; he could see an evil glint in her eye.

'No,' she snapped back.

'Then this conversation is going to be pretty short.'

'Tell *me* what brings *you* here.' She moved forward, apparently to let a waiter pass by, and he could smell her rich, heavy perfume.

'You'd hardly know there was a war going on,' he parried. 'A few extra uniforms, but no shortages that I can see. Food, drink – a bit different from back home.'

'Come off it!' she snapped. 'You've been to see David Windsor and that ghastly witch of his.'

'I wonder where that idea came from.'

'Your friend Oliphant.'

'I've only just met him. He can't possibly know,' Guy muttered evasively.

'Darling, your brave mission is the talk of the diplomatic circuit. "Stay in post, Your Royal Highness, or we'll have you shot for desertion."'

'That's funny,' said Guy. He really didn't like her now. 'Way off target, Lady Goldington, and didn't you know that careless talk costs lives?'

'Silly boy!' she said dismissively. 'You have no idea what goes on here in Washington. Everybody knows everybody's business – we're all in this together. We share our little trade secrets around.' She gave him a cynical smile. 'Oh! You thought I was just an old gold-digger – after rich men and their titles!'

'To be honest I didn't think anything,' he replied. 'I thought you were worth painting, though. But neither of us really had our heart set on getting a portrait out of our meetings, did we? What the hell were you after when you came round to the studio?'

'Just wanted to look you over,' she said, raising her eyebrows. 'See what sort of a set-up you've got there. You have Rupert Hardacre as a semi-permanent resident, and that little light-fingered trollop. Hardacre's a bit of a loose cannon, works for a sub-branch of our business – not always to be trusted.'

'And you *are* to be trusted, Lady Goldington?'

'Ha! I know a thing or two that might have saved you a hell of a lot of effort.'

'What d'you mean?' said Guy stiffly. He hated her patronising tone.

'Your little jaunt down to Nassau. Total waste of time, Guy!'

'I wouldn't say that.'

'If only you'd come clean while we were in London I could have filled you in.'

Guy scratched his chin. The woman was infuriating, with her supercilious smile and her beautiful shoulders. 'You seem to know more about my business than I do,' he said.

'That's the game here in DC. Don't go to bed until you've heard the last morsel of gossip. And be up before the lark so you don't miss a whisper at breakfast. Come over here,' she said, leading him by the shirt cuff to a sofa away from the cocktail crowd. 'And listen, instead of being stuck-up proud about your little jaunt across the water.'

Biting his lip, Guy did as he was bidden. The woman was completely aware of her magnetism and took it for granted he would follow to where she sat.

'A case of the left hand not knowing what the right hand's doing,' she went on, crossing her legs and beckoning a waiter. 'Two Scotch,' she ordered briskly. 'And cigarettes.

'Now, if the little bird who whispered in my ear got it right, you were sent by the Palace to check on the Duke and Duchess. To see if they were going to run away.'

'I—'

'Don't talk, listen. The reason you went was because of Cornelius Vanderbilt's article in the *New York Post* saying David Windsor was about to resign and take US citizenship. The Palace didn't consult anybody about sending you – they were desperately scared if he did a bunk what the effect would be on world opinion of the King and Queen, and their ability to run the House of Windsor.'

'I—'

'Or whether it was a case of the tail wagging the dog – David doing what the hell he liked and, in so doing, making his brother look like a complete lame duck. They're terrified of comparisons between glamorous David and dull-as-ditchwater Bertie.'

'Couldn't be further from the truth. We have the right man on the throne at the right time. Imagine what a mess we'd be in if the Duke of Windsor were still King today – what chaos there'd be!'

'Think what you like, darling – that's what it looks like from Fifth Avenue!'

'What's the point you're trying to make, Lady Goldington?'

'Fanny. The Palace didn't bother to check with Washington before sending you off. If they had, you could have been saved the journey. Here at the embassy we have the not wholly loveable figure of David Bowes-Lyon, kid brother to Her Majesty, whose big job was setting up something called the Political Warfare Executive. He's a colossal asset, in that he carries an aura of royalty about him and they can always wheel him out when they want to impress someone. But he's a bloody nuisance, poking his nose in here and there, and nobody of course has the power to stop him doing that.

'Someone had the bright idea of promoting DBL, as he's known, to get him away from here, so he was offered the governorship of Bermuda. Nice place, have you ever been?' She didn't wait for an answer. 'Lots of uniform-wearing and plumed helmets and cocktail parties like this one, not much else though – he would have been perfect. But Mrs BL dug her toes in and said over her dead body, etc.'

'What's this got to do with me?' said Guy, irritated that he was so infuriated by her superior air he'd started drinking the whisky when he'd promised himself the night off.

'So what DBL did was to set in motion a transfer order which meant that the Windsors would get their dearest wish, to get the hell out of Nassau . . .'

'That was kind.'

'. . . and end up in Bermuda instead.'

'But that would be a demotion, surely?'

'Exactly. David Windsor was furious and kicked up such a stink that the idea was dropped. In return DBL was seeing red because that refusal meant he could still end up in Bermuda, so he hopped up to New York – he's always going there anyway – and guess who he had a drink with?'

'Go on.'

'Your man Vanderbilt. How else d'you think an American, however well-connected, could get hold of top-drawer royal gossip like that? Vanderbilt buys DBL a drink. DBL says, "A little bird tells me the Windsors are jumping ship and the little man's going to betray his country by applying for American citizenship. In fact, he already has."'

'Are you sure about this?'

'I get up, darling, while the birds are still slumbering and listen to the dawn chorus – you should try it.'

'Thanks for the advice.'

'So what is Vanderbilt going to do in the face of being given this juicy piece of black propaganda by the brother-in-law of the King of England? Of *course* he believes it, of *course* he's going to print it!'

'I find this almost impossible to believe.'

'Listen, you ape – the Queen hates David Windsor, you know that, surely?'

'Well, maybe it's—'

'She and DBL were the babies of the family, late arrivals up at Glamis Castle, so there's a special closeness between them, and DBL has always been particularly protective of the Queen. And because she harbours such a hatred for David Windsor, so does he – *now* do you get it?'

'He wants the Windsors humiliated in any way they can be. So if he can't shuffle them off to Bermuda, then let the jackals of Fleet Street rip him to shreds by labelling him a traitor for jumping ship.

'Except they didn't. The Vanderbilt story was suppressed – not a single British newspaper printed it.'

'Agreed – but you see his motivation. Anyway, all I'm saying, Guy, is if instead of sketching my shoulders and telling me how perfect they were you'd opened up your heart and told me about your secret mission, I could have saved you all that effort.

'Your huge mission to save David Windsor from himself was based on a single piece of malicious gossip, no more – what a hoot!'

◆ ◆ ◆

'What time's your plane?' said Oliphant, shuffling the report in front of him.

'Not till this evening.' Guy had rings under his eyes from lack of sleep – first writing up his notes, then lying awake asking himself just how much of a fool he'd been to picture himself as a hero, flying across the Atlantic, ordering the ex-king about.

'Hm,' said Oliphant equivocally. 'I'm not quite sure what to say about . . . this.' His hand made a vague gesture towards the file. 'On the one hand it might be said you achieved what you set out to do – alert HRH to the need, both for himself and the country he serves, to stay in post in Nassau until he's told to stand down.

'You warned him of the tax consequences of becoming a US citizen, which it's evident he had not considered up to that point – or he wouldn't have gone as far with his plans as he did. You uncovered the extent to which he was a Nazi sympathiser, and your evidence offers us some relief there, because there'll be scores to settle after the war.

'But I dunno,' he said, shaking his head. 'The way you go about doing things, Harford, you break all the rules! It's all so darned *irregular*, blackmailin' people and all that. Takin' letters to the Duchess when you were told not to – did you give her a curtsey while you were at it? God knows what they'll say back in Whitehall, let alone the Palace.'

Maybe Vanderbilt's story *was* a complete fabrication, thought Guy – with Fanny Goldington there was no way of knowing whether she just wanted to stick the knife into him, or DBL, or had some other ulterior motive. She was a dangerous customer.

'Mr Oliphant,' he said, 'just before I go, may we have a word about Lady Goldington?'

'Mrs Strudwick,' corrected the diplomat with a wintry smile. 'I didn't know you knew her, but you seemed to be getting along like a house on fire last night.'

'Well, yes and no. What exactly is her capacity?'

'She's an FO butterfly. She flits here and there, sucking nectar from the most unlikely sources, and very good at it she is.'

'Back in London most people see her as a ruthless social climber, crawling over one titled husband to get to the next.'

'Well!' Oliphant beamed. 'No better disguise, then!'

'You mean she married all those men just to advance her work for the intelligence services?'

'Oh, not at all. It takes all sorts, you know, to make up a team in these dark days of war. I think one of our talent scouts saw this woman striding around the boudoirs of Mayfair, making a nuisance of herself, infuriating every titled wife in Debrett's by getting her paws on their husband – and thought, what better as a cover? So she was reeled in and trained up, and she's turned out to be a bloody marvel.'

Guy scratched his jaw. 'I have a professional interest in her.'

'I heard you were painting her portrait, yes.'

'I didn't mean that. I meant in my capacity at the Palace. His Majesty's a bit worried about King Zog.'

'How so?'

'Zog doesn't play the game. Who knows how many crowned heads and ex-kings and queens we've got hanging around the place, staying at the Palace and at Windsor and who knows where. They all know that this is temporary and one day they'll be back on their thrones, but while they're here they accept King George as sovereign and fall in with his wishes.

'But Zog's a different matter. He came sailing in with a load of thugs for bodyguards and, as far as one can tell, the bulk of the Albanian exchequer in gold bars in his back pocket. He set up home in The Ritz – which did *not* go down well with His Majesty, far too flashy – and helped himself to ladies of easy virtue here, there and everywhere. There's a certain standard expected of kings when they're in London as His Majesty's guests, and Zog doesn't live up to it. What's more, he doesn't care. If it was left to His Majesty, he'd be on a boat back to Albania tomorrow.'

'What do you expect,' replied Oliphant, amused, 'from a man who plonked the crown on his own head? He's got no form, as they say on the racetrack – there was no monarchy in Albania before he decided it would be nice to have a king and that king would be him. He's a phoney.'

'So what about him and Fanny Goldington – er, Mrs Strudwick?'

266

'*What* a ball of fire!' said Oliphant admiringly. 'Especially when it comes to the sack! She may be getting a bit long in the tooth, but she certainly knew what to do with old Zog – probably gave him a good spanking, I shouldn't wonder – and he fell for her hook, line and sinker!'

'The purpose being?'

'It's simple. He used to be Mussolini's chum, but then Italy decided to invade Albania in '39 and Zog had to scarper. We needed to find out to what extent this was a put-up job – whether Musso warned him in advance so he could clear out the cash register, and whether in fact he still had contacts with the Italians.

'We reckon the Italians will be knocked out of the war in the autumn and we needed to know what Zog's plans were. He's played his cards close to his chest but when the war's over we'll need to count up which countries are on our side and which aren't. Zog is a man who likes to play both ends against the middle, but I can tell you, our Mrs Strudwick has come up trumps!'

'You know his future plans?'

'We even know his inside leg measurement, old boy. Have some more coffee!'

CHAPTER
TWENTY-FOUR

They thundered up the steps like elephants, not ballet dancers, shouting her name and banging on the walls as they advanced. From their throats came the bloodcurdling sounds of predators nearing the kill.

Wild, uncontrolled – something had released them from the world of absorbed self-discipline that goes with being a dancer, and their cries grew louder and louder as they reached the top of the stairs. Rodie retreated, quietly shutting the wardrobe-room door and shoving a chair under the handle.

'Rodie, *oh Rrrrrrrrroooooodieeee!*' they yelled. 'Come to us, our little *dorogaya milaya . . .*'

She could hear them wrenching open dressing-room doors down the corridor, kicking chairs, and sweeping make-up items to the floor.

They know their cover's blown, she thought, otherwise why behave in this outraged, mad way? Did they kill Simon as he came down the stairs – was that it? Or did he manage to escape – after all, he was just as light on his feet as they. Crouched behind the locked door, there was no way of knowing.

The noise from the two raging animals grew louder as they worked their way up the corridor and immediately Rodie realised she was trapped – the only exit from the room was the locked door, or a window set high in the wall.

Quickly she pushed a wardrobe trunk against the wall and jumped up, scraping at the window with her bare hands in a desperate attempt to force it open. 'Come on, mate,' she said to herself, 'you've been in worse than this. Concentrate. Think of this as a blag. It's just another job. Get that window open and you're free.'

Calmed by this thought, even though they were virtually at the wardrobe-room door now, she eventually managed to prise open the casement window. When shut it was barely possible to see out of it, so dirty were the windowpanes; now it was open, the view revealed a blank wall with a sheer drop to the street, maybe forty feet below. There was no way out.

'Rodie!' one of them bellowed. 'We don't hurt you, *dorogoy malysh*. Where are you? Come out now!'

There was a sudden crash as they first tried to push open the flimsy door, then within seconds they had put their combined weight to it and fallen into the room as it came off its hinges.

'Window!' shouted Mikha, jumping on to the packing case with an ease of movement borne of many years' daily dance class – Madame Volkova would have been proud! But the same sight greeted him that had confronted Rodie: a sheer and fatal drop to the street below.

He jumped down again and prowled up and down the long room, crammed with row upon row of costumes, slashing wildly at them with his fist while Pyotr yanked open the door of the props cupboard and elbowed his way into the small room stuffed with every stage artefact known to the dance world, from fans and ribbons and hats and gloves to sashes and sticks and swords.

Rodie, crouched on top of an old wooden storage rack and hidden from view by a chorus-line collection of feather boas, held her breath and waited. The Russian kicked his way angrily around the store and walked out, but as she tried to reposition herself to see what the men were doing, the structure started to creak alarmingly and she began to feel it give way.

'Let's go,' said one to the other and they stalked out of the doorway, continuing their conversation in Russian.

Rodie stayed still and waited. They were light of foot and it was difficult to hear how far they'd retreated down the corridor, but as she leant forward to listen, the rack lurched and gave way, throwing her to the floor. The crash had the men running back. As she got to her feet, Rodie grabbed the nearest thing she could to defend herself.

'Ah, *Rrrrrrrrrroooooodieeee*,' they cried, wild-eyed. 'There you are! We are looking for you!'

'Keep back!' she warned, waving the object she'd grabbed from the floor. It turned out to be a sword from the fight scene in *Romeo and Juliet* – a flimsy prop and unlikely to inflict any grave injury, but at least something to keep them at bay.

'Ha ha! If you going to kill us, hold it right way round,' jeered Pyotr, roaring with laughter as she hastily reversed the sword, grabbing hold of the hilt with her other hand. 'You are dangerous, Rodie, too dangerous. We cannot let you go free when you threaten with lethal weapon.'

'Call the cops, then!' she snapped, crouched and ready to make a break for it. 'Where's Simon? What've you done with him?'

'Simon sleeping now,' said Mikha with a vicious smile. 'Very quietly. So now we ask you – where is book he gave you?'

'What book?'

'*You know what book*,' came the Russian's heavy response. 'Bleckvttr book!'

'He didn't give me no book an' I don't know what you're talkin' about,' said Rodie. 'Never seen him before in my life till today. I dunno 'oo 'e is or what 'e's doin' here. But what I do know is you two are in it up to your necks.'

'What is this up to necks?' said Pyotr liltingly. Now they were playing with her, knowing her only escape was a fatal plunge to the pavement below. They were in no rush.

'I found Blackwater's body! Out at that old fort! You bastards killed 'im – now why did you do go and do that?'

The two men looked at each other and nodded. 'We tell you,' they said, 'then you have nice long sleep like Simon. You are tired, no?'

'Keep back!' she said, slicing the prop sword from side to side in front of her, but all they did was laugh.

'You are sexy girl,' Pyotr said. 'You should be nice to us. Then we don't put you to sleep maybe.'

'Back!' she shouted. 'I don't know where you come from, but down my way there's words for the likes of you. *And* a price to pay if you try any funny business!'

'We come from St Petersburg,' said Mikha. 'Only now Petrograd. We go to Moscow, then Oslo. We follow the only true ballerina, Marina Lee. She love us and we adore her.'

'We would die for her,' echoed Pyotr.

'She loves you too,' replied Rodie. 'She must do or she wouldn't keep writing you love letters.'

'What letters?' they said, uncomprehending.

'Those dead letter boxes all over London. That's why you rented the motorbike from that nice garridge in Tottenham. So you can ride about all day an' night picking up her billy-doos wherever she drops 'em.'

The pair looked startled. Whatever they thought Rodie might be, it could hardly have amounted to more than an attractive sideshow. What was she doing with this high-grade information, and was she really serious when she said she'd discovered Blackwater's body?

'What's your game?' snarled Pyotr, advancing towards her. 'You are spy? Like Simon?'

'Simon isn't a spy,' she said, shaking her head. 'And neither am I. Tell me why you killed Blackwater.'

They looked at each other. 'We are here on mission. One greater than dance, though many would say there is no greater mission than dance. We are here to kill your King. And Queen.'

'Don't talk rubbish!' snorted Rodie. 'You haven't a hope in hell. Are you mad?'

Mikha laughed a hollow laugh. 'Yes, we mad. After what we have seen in Russia, the stupid White Russians, the filthy fucking Bolsheviks, everyone killing everyone. One thing worse than communism, it's royalty – ask anyone in Russia, they tell you. The czars, they let us starve, they kill us; then do not bother to bury us.

'Marina is so clever. She alone gave Norway to the Germans in 1940 when you British thought you knew how to defend that stupid country. You stupid, she is heroine. And the Germans reward her and ask her what else she can do to help. And she say, what you want?'

Pyotr broke in, 'She say, "I have Mick and Pete, they my slaves, I send them anywhere. What do you want?" And the Nazis say, "Kill that useless King and Queen and we will put Duke of Windsor back on throne. Then everyone happy."'

'You must be jokin', mate! Anyway, how were you going to do it? The two most protected people in the land? How the hell would two dozy blokes like you pull that off?'

'Easy.' Mikha grinned. 'Marina knows through, what you call it, grapevine? She knows through grapevine how much King and Queen love ballet, how they want a royal ballet company. How they will come to Sadler's Wells to watch us dance. We join the Vic-Wells company – we are good dancers, Rodie! – and we wait for the moment.'

'You're going to shoot them as they sit there? Like President Lincoln?'

'Shoot? Who said shoot? You not much of a spy, *Rrrroooodieee*!'

'Watcha going to do then? Walk up to 'em and shake 'em by the throat?'

'We have ballet, they come, honoured guests. Interval, we go in our costume to the royal box, say hello, nobody suspect. We leave bomb in box – only small bomb, nobody notice!' said Pyotr.

'Then boom – we are back onstage, nobody *suspect*!' added Mikha.

'Then zoom-zoom, we disappear. To Potters Bar.'

'That's the stupidest thing I ever heard,' said Rodie, dropping the sword. 'You blokes are complete idiots if you think you'd get anywhere near the royal box. There are people there ready to lay down their lives for the King and Queen.'

'They are fools then,' sneered Pyotr. 'Give up your life for royal, it's crazy!'

'We don't all think like you, mate. And I'd say if you really want to kill them you'd better come up with a better plan. Unless you want to get torn to pieces in the attempt.'

'Why you know so much?' bellowed Mikha. 'What are you? Quisling? Mata Hari? Or wardrobe-spy woman! Discovering dead body in the room with many walls!'

'So it *was* you!' she riposted. 'You did it! Which one of you killed him?'

'Him!' the pair chorused, pointing at each other and dissolving into gales of laughter.

'Why did you do it? He's not the King, ya know!'

'But he wears Coronation crown! He show us picture when we go to his flat!' said Mikha.

'He drink champagne like all bourgeois, but he is like the czars, spit on proletariat. Walk on them. He want to show us where he slept when he was friends with the King – your other king – so we take him to ancient fort. On our motorbike.'

'Which one of you?'

'Him!' they chorused, laughing again.

'Why? Why kill him, though?'

'When we get there we break in,' said Pyotr. 'He show us his room, then he lifts carpet and take up the boards and he digs out his book. "This is precious," he says, "is gold dust, is crown jewels." And we go downstairs and he wants to boast about book and how important he was when your old King Windsor was on throne.'

'So we say, show us this famous book, tell us what it says, let us look inside – and he say, no, too precious for ignorant brute like you, stay away.' Mikha this time.

'And he get excited and we calm him down with slap or two. Then suddenly he fall over dead.' Pyotr again – from the way they told it, it was impossible to judge who was responsible for Blackwater's death.

'Bit more than a slap,' said Rodie. 'You punched him in the throat. Hard.'

'Where we come from, we call that slap.'

'So we ride away and take stupid book with us. We ask Yelena what it says, and she, stupid girl, give it to Simon.'

'Who run away like yellow coward.'

'But she tell him first what in Bleckvttr book.'

'But she no tell us, and we need to tell Marina in Oslo.'

'So she can tell her lover Adolf!' They both started laughing hysterically.

'So bye-bye poor Yelena, she very unhappy girl anyway. She happier now.'

They're mad, thought Rodie. They're both certifiable. 'You honestly think you're going to kill the King?' she asked.

'We have to, we are Marina's slaves. Our duty. But you make it sound . . . complicated.'

'You want to die when you're doing it, or do you want to get away?'

'We live to dance,' said Pyotr. 'We only promise to do this to make Marina happy. She promise to get us away when we have done it.'

'How?'

'We don't know, we told go to Potters Bar and wait.'

Rodie laughed. 'And you believe that? You really believe she's got someone waiting patiently in some place you've never heard of to whisk you away to safety? Where did you think you were going to go? Do you know how difficult it is to get out of this country?'

The pair looked at each other, then at her. There was a long pause.

'Kill her now,' said Mikha, showing his teeth.

CHAPTER
TWENTY-FIVE

The airplane journey back from Washington had been unnerving – there was little turbulence and only one enemy aircraft scare, but what plunged Guy into the deepest despair was the knowledge his mission would be marked down as a failure. The high politics of the royal family and its relatives were way above his head, and if the Queen's brother wanted to start spreading rumours about the Duke of Windsor, who was he to get involved?

The only morsel he could bring home for Tommy Lascelles was David Bowes-Lyon's determination to influence matters that had nothing to do to him. That, he felt sure, Tommy would want to know – and the fact of quite how much unofficial gossip, coloured by his own prejudices, Bowes-Lyon was pouring into Her Majesty's ear, which could lead to the King forming crucial judgements based on false information. It seemed a hollow victory, though, when others were losing their lives daily and with the conflict still in full flood.

The official car that brought him from the airport had dropped him on the Chelsea Embankment and before making for home he walked over to the parapet and watched the light thicken as the sun dropped behind the chimneys of Lots Road Power Station.

Behind him, loving couples strolled arm in arm in the warm night air, but the sense of isolation that had gripped him throughout his return journey refused to lift. He was alone, just as he had been in Tangier when the FO men bundled him on to a plane to rescue him from a diplomatic incident. As a painter he was enjoying a measure of success maybe, but as a servant of the Crown things always seemed to turn to dust.

A tugboat manfully hauled its lighters upstream, heading who knew where, and for once the world seemed calm and ordered. Gone was the veiled hysteria of Nassau politics and the diplomatic backstabbing on Capitol Hill. Instead the great grey Thames rolled onwards, oblivious and untouched by the affairs of man.

He let himself into the studio and called Rodie's name, but the reply he got came from Rupert. 'A little bird told me you'd be back,' he said, 'so I brought Johnny Walker Black Label – Kilmarnock's finest. We need to chat.'

'Rodie? I brought her a present.'

'Away on a job,' said Rupert with a distant note in his voice. 'Tell you about that in a minute. How was your journey?'

'OK. I guess you want to know what I managed to pick up while I was beachcombing.'

'If you don't mind.'

Guy gave a crisp summary of the points of most interest to Rupert – that after the furore surrounding the so-called state visit to Germany, and the murder of the trades union leaders by the Nazi high command, the Duke of Windsor panicked and dropped the Nazi Charles Bedaux like a stone. Psychologically he'd moved to a new place, and for a time he thought he would quit public life altogether. Whatever secrets remained about Bedaux's pre-war relationship with the Duke were most likely to be found in the pages of Archy Blackwater's diary, wherever that may be.

The Duke's other close Nazi associate, Axel Wenner-Gren, had quit the Bahamas for Mexico and – almost despite Captain Fairfax's protestations of the ex-king's loyalty to Britain – it became clear to Guy that the ex-king was less interested in German promises of restoring him to the throne than in finding a lucrative occupation once the war was over. 'He's not a man to look back,' said Guy. 'Or more accurately, she's not one to look back, so he doesn't. And as a matter of fact, despite the general down on him, he's interested in doing as good a job as he can in Nassau – as long as he gets the holidays to keep her happy.'

The conversation was brief but seemed to satisfy Rupert who was edgy, on his feet, eager to be gone. 'Not staying for another glass?' said Guy, finally relaxing.

'Business to attend to,' said Rupert, gathering up his hat and making for the door. As he reached it, he turned to face Guy. 'Look,' he said, 'I've been debating over and over whether I should tell you this, but I think I must. I'm going up to Lancashire now, and maybe you should come too.'

'Lancashire? I've only just—'

'It's Rodie,' Rupert said tersely.

'Oh. Trouble?'

'Afraid so. Are you coming? The car will take us to the station.'

The night train seemed to take for ever, stopping here and there for no apparent reason, sliding through stations at a snail's pace and then halting half a mile down the line.

Long ago both men had given up trying to fathom the logic of wartime public transport and weathered the tiring, frustrating journey as best they could – Rupert with a novel, Guy with a crossword that refused to reveal its secrets to him. Both men's faces were stretched with tension but neither voiced their secret fears to the other.

On the ride to King's Cross Rupert had outlined the disjointed telephone conversation with Rodie from her call box outside the theatre, how it had broken their arranged routine for communication – which in itself signalled that something had gone badly wrong. It wasn't so much the death of the Austrian dancer, more the heavy tinge of doubt in Rodie's voice as she assured him that everything was going fine. But when their scheduled call earlier that evening had failed to come through, Rupert realised there must be an emergency. Rodie was out on her own up in Burnley with no back-up – against his own rules, but in situations like this you had to improvise.

Now he was beginning to bitterly regret having sent her solo into an unknown situation, far from London and far from the chances of help being on hand. There was a killer on the loose – Blackwater and the dancer Elena Hoffman's murders stood testament to that – but where was he, and why didn't Rodie answer the phone?

'I tried and tried for an hour,' he'd told Guy. 'If there's one thing about Rodie, she follows orders to the letter. If she wasn't in that phone box between six and seven, something had to be wrong.'

Now Guy was lost in his own thoughts. All the time he'd known her he'd deliberately sidestepped examining his feelings for Rodie – he didn't know whether this was a wartime fling, like so many others, or whether it was something that could last into peacetime. He was so different from her, or, put the other way round, she had almost nothing in common with his world – no reference points, no comprehension of the beauty of art. And yet in those long hours over the Atlantic he'd come to realise that she had qualities that transcended mere book-learning and aesthetic appreciation. She had the joie de vivre he lacked, and she'd injected some of her joyous, devil-may-care nature into his veins. His life, he realised, had been altered not so much by his sudden ejection from the comfort zone of an artist's routine in Tangier, but by this push-me-pull-you relationship.

She'd come up to him in a pub, never having set eyes on him before, and within an hour she was telling him she loved him, was going to marry him. Next morning when he went into his office he discovered she'd burgled her way into Buckingham Palace just to leave a rose on his desk. She wasn't normal.

But then, was he? He'd run away from school, studied art in Paris, fallen in love with Foxy Gwynne, hidden his hurt when she abandoned him. He accepted an aunt's offer of a house on the mountain in Tangier – and there he'd stayed, painting and brooding. Have I been hiding all this time, he asked himself as the night skies cleared over the Atlantic and dawn embraced his seaplane. Have I been in hiding?

The Burnley train jangled over a set of points and the two men looked up and exchanged glances. There was nothing to be said – the compartment was crowded with servicemen, most asleep, but their heavy bodies a bulwark against conversation. Guy returned to his crossword, but the puzzle remained untouched as his thoughts strayed back to Rodie.

She had a poise he'd never seen in women of his own class – an out-and-out confidence that, combined with quite startling looks, gave her a magnetism he'd rarely encountered anywhere else. No wonder he wanted to paint her, struggle to capture the creature within; and no wonder his portrait of her had created newspaper headlines when it was unveiled at the Gardner Gallery last year. Its reception had been a turning point in his artistic career.

And now, what was happening to her? What sort of danger was she facing? Rupert had outlined the bare facts, describing Rodie's mission and its likely success, but in his dry, matter-of-fact tones Guy could detect a genuine anxiety. That heightened his own fears which this long, heavy, blacked-out voyage through the night did nothing to quell.

There were no taxis at the station – it was either too late or too early – and, getting directions for the Victoria Theatre from a somnolent porter, they marched off in step, their heels ringing on the pavement.

'Not quite sure what you're going to do when we get there,' said Guy.

'Oh I have a plan,' replied Rupert, but Guy wondered whether he had.

'Shouldn't we first go to the hotel where they're billeted?'

'Think about that for a moment,' snapped Rupert, his voice tense with anxiety. 'D'you think we'd find Rodie tucked up nice and comfortable in bed? Not having answered the phone for a whole hour – against *orders*? She can be a handful, I grant you, but she does what she's supposed to when she's supposed to. She's a reliable operative.'

Guy had to smile – the idea that this cat burglar from the Elephant and Castle, born into a family of scoundrels and whose best friend was the most gifted pickpocket in Mayfair, could be described by a senior government official as a reliable operative had its comic side, even though as they walked up Burnley's main street a sense of dread was beginning to grip him by the throat.

They finally arrived outside the heavy-set building with its serried ranks of ornate windows just as dawn broke. Not surprisingly, the doors were firmly shut, offering no suggestion as to how to gain entry. There was no bell, but even if there were, who'd be there to answer it at this time of day?

'We'll try the side,' said Rupert, as if this was a bright and original idea. Guy began to lose faith in his friend's powers of detection.

They walked on till they reached an alley and turned into it to find a sign saying, 'Stage Door. Autograph-hunters Queue in an

Orderly Fashion. No Screaming Allowed.' The alley was deserted, but further away a motorbike lay on its side, the front wheel sticking up and the spreading stain from the emptied petrol tank still wet on the cobbles.

'Door's open,' called Guy to Rupert, who'd gone on to inspect the bike. 'Come on, Rupe!'

'Just a moment, there's a—'

'Come *on*! Have you forgotten why we're here?' Guy yanked open the door and plunged into the theatre's back lobby with its doorkeeper's cubby-hole and a large blackboard chalked up with rehearsal times.

'Are you coming, Rupe? For heaven's sake, we've got to find her!' Guy's voice cracked. The deathly silence in the lobby seemed an omen; he dreaded what he would find beyond the green baize door in front of him.

But just as he moved forward to open it, the door swung inwards and a diminutive figure stepped out.

'Mornin', gents,' said Rodie, dusting her hands together and flashing a triumphant smile. 'What kept cha?'

'Potters Bar.'

'What?'

'I said, Potters *Bar*.' She'd switched on the big mirror lights in the principal dressing room and was helping herself liberally to the greasepaint laid out in readiness for the next performance. The result was alarming.

'It just made me laugh,' said Rodie, pulling her face into grimaces as she piled on more and more eyeliner. 'When they said Potters *Bar*. I mean, you would, wouldn't cha?'

'Go back a bit,' said Guy. 'I'm not sure I follow.'

'They were goin' to kill me. And honest, I think they would've. It was that, or me out the window – and we were four storeys up, mate, no chance. So I started the old chinwag, the palaver, and they're dim, darling, no wits – what you might call *headstrong*. I said, you ever been to Potters Bar, they said no, I said do you honestly think after you've bombed the King and Queen and gawd knows 'oo else to death, there's going to be a man standin' on a street corner waitin' for you to turn up so he can get you away?'

Guy laughed.

'I said to them, I said, be reasonable, boys, 'ow's 'e going to know when you're going to turn up? Did your blessed Marina give you an address? A map how to get there? A name? A telephone number?

'They said they'd be told before the bomb went off, but I pointed out they needed a concrete plan *now* in case things turned upside down sooner. I piled on the old yabba-dabba, like you do in the pub when a feller wants to take you outside – kept 'em sweet! And soon I could see they realised they were up the creek without a paddle. I said, "That woman don't care for you. She hopes you're going to blow yourselves up or get arrested. Then they'll hang you, an' that's the best you can hope for." They had no idea how they were goin' to escape.'

'So what happened?'

'So then they threatened to kill me, an' I said, "Go ahead, mate – then where will you be? No diary to give to Marina, and no way of getting out of the country."

'I said, "I've got a cousin down Elephant and Castle. 'E don't care about anything 'cept money – if you've got money he'll get you away." They said, "You come with us then," and I said, "OK."

'I knew I could give 'em the slip, so off we went. Only when we got downstairs their bike had been pushed over, and they started shoutin' that someone had taken the spark plug. All the petrol's drained out and the thing's about as useful as a chocolate teapot.'

'How did that happen?' asked Rupert from the back of the room.

'Simon. They beat 'im up pretty bad, but while they were busy with me, 'e pulled 'imself together and got out of the building. Pushed the bike over, got into the pannier and found the doings to get the spark plug out. That was when the police turned up and arrested 'im – only Simon was in such a state they believed 'im when 'e said they'd beaten him up.'

'So how did you get away?'

'We come out just when the cops had gone to get back-up. Mick and Pete started shouting about their bike, rantin' on and on, and they were walking up to the high street to find Simon when they was nabbed. There was a bit of a dust-up, I can tell yer.'

'So where's Simon?'

''Orspital. The boys are in the clink and I'm just about ready for my bed. Coming, Guy?'

'Wait, wait, wait!' ordered Rupert. 'Haven't they arrested Simon?'

'What for? Stealin' a spark plug?'

'Murder, you idiot. He killed a peer of the realm, or have you forgotten that?'

Guy sat back and enjoyed the lengthy lecture delivered to a senior intelligence officer by a woman who, only months before, had been a lowly burglar with few prospects beyond a lengthy spell behind bars. Now she was explaining, as if to a child, how Simon Greenleigh could never have been considered a murder suspect and how, if Rupe used his common sense, he would have guessed that.

'So this Pete killed Blackwater?'

'Punched 'im up the throat. I think it was accidental but the old boy was getting panicky about 'im getting 'is paws on 'is precious diary. A bit of a struggle and, bam, the poor chap's dead.'

'And the dancer, Elena?'

'That was deliberate. They panicked because she'd read the diary – they actually *gave* it to 'er, the chumps! So she knew it was written by Blackwater, and had read in the newspapers of Blackwater's death. It all added up, and she accused them of killing him. She had to go.'

'And the diary?'

'She'd given it to Simon, Simon gave it to his dad, the general, who whisked it round to the Palace quick smart.'

'Well, we'll never see that again,' said Rupert. 'A shame. I'm sure it could tell us some interesting things about a lot of very important people. Useful background for people in my line of business. Isn't there something you can do about that, Guy?'

'It'll be a pile of ashes now,' came the reply. 'Sorry, Rupe.'

Later, in her cramped hotel bed, Guy and Rodie went over their escapades since they'd last met. It was mid-afternoon but they hadn't stopped talking yet.

'I like this ballet dancin', darlin' – bit different from the old Hammersmith Palais. You'll have to take me to a show.'

'I was hoping we could go and see Billy Cotton.'

'Trouble with you, mate, you got no *kulchur*.'

'Well, I'll have plenty of time for culture soon. I ballsed up this job. They'll probably let me go at the Palace as soon as they can find someone else.'

'The way you told it to me, you made that stupid Duke think twice about quitting. He won't become a US citizen, plus you've nobbled the King's creepy brother-in-law. Not bad for a few days' work. Plus that tan of yours doesn't half make you look 'andsome, darlin'!'

'I won't be looking quite so *'andsome* when I'm in the dole queue.'

'I'll still love ya. When are you goin' to propose?'

THE END

But . . .

AFTERWORD

Buckingham Palace
17 July 1943

His Majesty the King is pleased to confer upon Guy Petrarch Harford the order of Commander of the Royal Victorian Order in recognition of his valiant and unique contribution to the war effort.

Mr Harford is promoted to Assistant Private Secretary to His Majesty.

'*Petrarch?*' she yodelled, hooting with laughter. 'Wass that when it's at 'ome?'

'Oh shut up,' he said crossly. 'And move over, you've got all the bedclothes.'

AUTHOR'S NOTE

In the third year of the Duke of Windsor's governorship of the Bahamas, the *New York Post* carried a short paragraph within the regular column of Cornelius Vanderbilt IV, the celebrated author, journalist and publisher, and scion of America's leading society family.

Vanderbilt wrote that he'd learnt from 'an unimpeachable source' that the Duke had tendered his resignation as Governor and was attempting to become an American citizen. The article suggested the reason behind this alarming decision to quit was that the Duchess could take no more of the heat and provinciality of the island archipelago, and was ready to jump ship – with or without him.

If true, it meant that the Duke was preparing to desert his post – a court-martial offence in times of war. Just as important, taking US citizenship would be a betrayal of his mighty heritage as king and emperor, a tawdry repudiation of a thousand years of monarchy in Britain. America, his decision would signal, is a better place for royals to live than their own country.

Was Vanderbilt's story true? Who was his 'unimpeachable source'? And why was the story never followed up by the British press?

In a long career in publishing, Vanderbilt worked as a reporter for the *New York Times* before launching a string of newspapers in Los Angeles, San Francisco, Miami and elsewhere. He was a documentary film-maker, and in World War II worked in counter-intelligence.

Such a track record is not that of a hack who, short of a paragraph, dreams something up in desperation. Vanderbilt had got the story from somewhere – but where?

His cousin Alice 'Kiki' Preston had, notoriously, been the mistress of the Duke of Kent and kept in touch with him after war broke out. It was to Alice's Kenyan house that the Duchess of Kent's sister Princess Olga, and her husband Prince Paul of Yugoslavia, were banished during hostilities. After the Duke's death in 1942, Kiki kept in touch with the Duchess.

Vanderbilt's cousin by marriage, Josephine 'Foxy' Gwynne, was one of the Duchess of Windsor's closest friends. In 1941 she married the seventh Earl of Sefton, an intimate of the royal family.

Either one of these women could have been Vanderbilt's source. But the most likely candidate, as offered fictionally in these pages, is David Bowes-Lyon, the younger brother of Queen Elizabeth. A powerful figure in the wartime transatlantic alliance, he was expected to be rewarded for his service with a plum diplomatic appointment.

One possibility was the Bahamas. And, whether the Duke's defection was imminent or not, it's likely he gave the story to Vanderbilt in order to get the Windsors out of Nassau. Coming as it did from the brother of the Queen, who was Vanderbilt to question it?

But why didn't the British press jump on the story – and why subsequently has it never been investigated by Windsor historians?

In 1912, in the run-up to World War 1, the British government introduced the D-Notice, a gagging system to ensure that journalists would not endanger national security. Editors were told, effectively, what they could and could not publish in the national interest.

The alarm bells were ringing all over Buckingham Palace and Whitehall when word came through of Vanderbilt's scoop. That the ex-king could desert his post and abandon his nationality in the midst of war would be colossally damaging to national morale, if it ever got out.

And so not a word or hint of Vanderbilt's scoop ever appeared in British newspapers or in the many biographies of the Windsors that followed – the story had been killed stone dead.

Until now.

ABOUT THE AUTHOR

TP Fielden is the fiction-writing name of the acclaimed royal biographer and commentator Christopher Wilson, who has penned biographies of Prince Charles, Camilla, Diana and other members of the British royal family.

For twenty years a leading Fleet Street journalist with columns in *The Times*, *Sunday Telegraph*, *Daily Express* and *Today*, he is now a bestselling biographer and (as TP Fielden) novelist.

Most recently the creator of the English Riviera Murders featuring 1950s supersleuth Miss Dimont, he remains an internationally in-demand writer on royal matters, with regular appearances in TV documentaries and reports across the globe.

His biography of Camilla, Duchess of Cornwall, is the acknowledged source material for all other books and TV films on the subject, and his ground-breaking research on the life and family of Catherine, Duchess of Cambridge, is also a primary source for biographers and filmmakers.

His biography *A Greater Love: Charles and Camilla* was turned into a top-rated TV documentary screened in the USA, UK and twenty-six other countries around the globe, and he has co-produced several major TV documentaries on the British royals. He lectures widely on the subject.

He is the co-founder of the Oxford University journalism awards, and for this work he was honoured by St Edmund Hall, the university's oldest college, with membership of its Senior Common Room.

He is married to an American writer and lives on Dartmoor, England.